AUTHORITY

ORITY

JEFF VANDERMEER

FOURTH ESTATE • *London*

Fourth Estate
An imprint of HarperCollins*Publishers*
77–85 Fulham Palace Road
London W6 8JB
4thestate.co.uk

First published in Great Britain by Fourth Estate 2014
First published in the United States by Farrar, Straus and Giroux 2014

1 3 5 7 9 10 8 6 4 2

A catalogue record for this book is
available from the British Library

HB ISBN 978-0-00-755346-4
TPB ISBN 978-0-00-755352-5

Page design by Abby Kagan

Printed and bound in Great Britain by
Clays Ltd, St Ives plc

MIX
Paper from
responsible sources

FSC www.fsc.org   **FSC™ C007454**

For Ann

INCANTATIONS

000

In Control's dreams it is early morning, the sky deep blue with just a twinge of light. He is staring from a cliff down into an abyss, a bay, a cove. It always changes. He can see for miles into the still water. He can see ocean behemoths gliding there, like submarines or bell-shaped orchids or the wide hulls of ships, silent, ever moving, the size of them conveying such a sense of power that he can feel the havoc of their passage even from so far above. He stares for hours at the shapes, the movements, listening to the whispers echoing up to him . . . and then he falls. Slowly, too slowly, he falls soundless into the dark water, without splash or ripple. And keeps falling.

Sometimes this happens while he is awake, as if he hasn't been paying enough attention, and then he silently recites his own name until the real world returns to him.

First day. The beginning of his last chance.

"These are the survivors?"

Control stood beside the assistant director of the Southern Reach, behind smudged one-way glass, staring at the three individuals sitting in the interrogation room. Returnees from the twelfth expedition into Area X.

The assistant director, a tall, thin black woman in her forties, said nothing back, which didn't surprise Control. She hadn't wasted an extra word on him since he'd arrived that morning after taking Monday to get settled. She hadn't spared him an extra look, either, except when he'd told her and the rest of the staff to call him "Control," not "John" or "Rodriguez." She had paused a beat, then replied, "In that case, call me Patience, not Grace," much to the stifled amusement of those present. The deflection away from her real name to one that also meant something else interested him. "That's okay," he'd said, "I can just call you Grace," certain this would not please her. She parried by continually referring to him as the "acting" director. Which was true: There lay between her stewardship and his ascension a gap, a valley of time and forms to be filled out, procedures to be followed, the rooting out and hiring of staff. Until then, the issue of authority might be murky.

But Control preferred to think of her as neither patience nor grace. He preferred to think of her as an abstraction if not an obstruction. She had made him sit through an old orientation video about Area X, must have known it would be basic and out of date. She had already made clear that theirs would be a relationship based on animosity. From her side, at least.

"Where were they found?" he asked her now, when what he wanted to ask was why they hadn't been kept separate from one another. Because you lack the discipline, because your department has been going to the rats for a long time now? The rats are down there in the basement now, gnawing away.

"Read the files," she said, making it clear he should have read them already.

Then she walked out of the room.

Leaving Control alone to contemplate the files on the table in front him—and the three women behind the glass. Of course he had read the files, but he had hoped to duck past the assistant director's high guard, perhaps get her own thoughts. He'd read parts of her file, too, but still didn't have a sense of her except in terms of her reactions to him.

His first full day was only four hours old and he already felt contaminated by the dingy, bizarre building with its worn green carpet and the antiquated opinions of the other personnel he had met. A sense of diminishment suffused everything, even the sunlight that halfheartedly pushed through the high, rectangular windows. He was wearing his usual black blazer and dress slacks, a white shirt with a light blue tie, black shoes he'd shined that morning. Now he wondered why he'd bothered. He disliked having such thoughts because he wasn't above it all—he was *in* it—but they were hard to suppress.

Control took his time staring at the women, although their appearance told him little. They had all been given the same generic uniforms, vaguely army-issue but also vaguely janitorial. Their heads had all been shaved, as if they had suffered from some infestation, like lice, rather than something more inexplicable. Their faces all retained the same expression, or could be said not to retain any expression. Don't think of them by their names, he'd told himself on the plane. Let them carry only the weight of their functions at first. Then fill in the rest. But Control had never been good at remaining aloof. He liked to burrow in, try to find a level where the details illuminated without overwhelming him.

The surveyor had been found at her house, sitting in a chair on the back patio.

The anthropologist had been found by her husband, knocking on the back door of his medical practice.

The biologist had been found in an overgrown lot several blocks from her house, staring at a crumbling brick wall.

Just like the members of the prior expedition, none of them had any recollection of how they had made their way back across the invisible border, out of Area X. None of them knew how they had evaded the blockades and fences and other impediments the military had thrown up around the border. None of them knew what had happened to the fourth member of their expedition—the psychologist, who had, in fact, also been the director of the Southern Reach and overridden all objections to lead them, incognito.

None of them seemed to have much recollection of anything at all.

In the cafeteria that morning for breakfast, Control had looked out through the wall-to-wall paneled window into the courtyard with its profusion of stone tables, and then at the people shuffling through the line—too few, it seemed, for such a large building—and asked Grace, "Why isn't everyone more excited to have the expedition back?"

She had given him a long-suffering look, as if he were a particularly slow student in a remedial class. "Why do you think, Control?" She'd already managed to attach an ironic weight to his name, so he felt as if he were the sinker on one of his grandpa's fly rods, destined for the silt near the bottom of dozens of lakes. "We went through all this with the last expedition. They endured nine months of questions, and yet we never found out anything. And the whole time they were dying. How would that make you feel?" Long months of disorientation, and then their deaths from a particularly malign form of cancer.

He'd nodded slowly in response. Of course, she was right. His father had died of cancer. He hadn't thought of how that might have affected the staff. To him, it was still an abstraction, just words in a report, read on the plane down.

Here, in the cafeteria, the carpet turned dark green, against which a stylized arrow pattern stood out in a light green, all of the arrows pointing toward the courtyard.

"Why isn't there more light in here?" he asked. "Where does all the light go?"

But Grace was done answering his questions for the moment.

When one of the three—the biologist—turned her head a fraction, looking into the glass as if she could see him, Control evaded that stare with a kind of late-blooming embarrassment. Scrutiny such as his was impersonal, professional, but it probably didn't feel that way, even though they knew they were being watched.

He hadn't been told he would spend his first day questioning disoriented returnees from Area X, and yet Central must have known when he'd been offered the position. The expedition members had been picked up almost six weeks ago, been subjected to a month of tests at a processing station up north before being sent to the Southern Reach. Just as he'd been sent to Central first to endure two weeks of briefings, including gaps, whole days that slid into oblivion without much of anything happening, as if they'd always meant to time it this way. Then everything had sped up, and he had been given the impression of urgency.

These were among the details that had caused a kind of futile exasperation to wash over him ever since his arrival. The Voice, his primary contact in the upper echelons, had implied in an initial briefing that this was an easy assignment, given his past history. The Southern Reach had become a backward, backwater agency, guarding a dormant secret that no one seemed to care much about anymore, given the focus on terrorism and ecological collapse. The Voice had, in its gruff way, typified his mission "to start" as being brought in to "acclimate, assess, analyze, and then dig in deep," which wasn't his usual brief these days.

During an admittedly up-and-down career, Control had started as an operative in the field: surveillance on domestic terror cells. Then he'd been bumped up to data synthesis and organizational analysis—two dozen or more cases banal in their similarities and about which he was forbidden to talk. Cases invisible to the public: the secret history of nothing.

But more and more he had become the fixer, mostly because he seemed better at identifying other people's specific problems than at managing his own general ones. At thirty-eight, that was what he had become known for, if he was known for anything. It meant you didn't have to be there for the duration, even though by now that's exactly what he wanted: to see something through. Problem was, no one really liked a fixer—"Hey, let me show you what you're doing wrong"—especially if they thought the fixer needed fixing from way back.

It always started well, even though it didn't always end well.

The Voice had also neglected to mention that Area X lay beyond a border that still, after more than thirty years, no one seemed to understand. No, he'd only picked up on that when reviewing the files and in the needless replication from the orientation video.

Nor had he known that the assistant director would hate him so much for replacing the missing director. Although he should have guessed; according to the scraps of information in her file, she had grown up lower-middle class, had gone to public school at first, had had to work harder than most to get to her current position. While Control came with whispers about being part of a kind of invisible dynasty, which naturally bred resentment. There was no denying that fact, even if, up close, the dynasty was more like a devolving franchise.

"They're ready. Come with me."

Grace, conjured up again, commanding him from the doorway.

There were, he knew, several different ways to break down a colleague's opposition, or their will. He would probably have to try all of them.

Control picked up two of the three files from the table and, gaze now locked in on the biologist, tore them down the middle, feeling the torque in his palms, and let them fall into the wastebasket.

A kind of choking sound came from behind him.

Now he turned—right into the full force of the assistant director's wordless anger. But he could see a wariness in her eyes, too. Good.

"Why are you still keeping paper files, Grace?" he asked, taking a step forward.

"The director insisted. You did that for a reason?"

He ignored her. "Grace, why are none of you comfortable using the words *alien* or *extraterrestrial* to talk about Area X?" He wasn't comfortable with them, either. Sometimes, since he'd been briefed on the truth, he'd felt a great, empty chasm opening up inside of him, filled with his own screams and yelps of disbelief. But he'd never tell. He had a face for playing poker; he'd been told this by lovers and by relatives, even by strangers. About six feet tall. Impassive. The compact, muscular build of an athlete; he could run for miles and not feel it. He took pride in a good diet and enough exercise, although he did like whiskey.

She stood her ground. "No one's sure. Never prejudge the evidence."

"Even after all this time? I only need to interview one of them."

"What?" she asked.

Torque in hands transformed into torque in conversation.

"I don't need the other files because I only need to question one of them."

"You need all three." As if she still didn't quite understand.

He swiveled to pick up the remaining file. "No. Just the biologist."

"That is a mistake."

"Seven hundred and fifty-three isn't a mistake," he said. "Seven hundred and twenty-two isn't a mistake, either."

Her eyes narrowed. "Something is wrong with you."

"Keep the biologist in there," he said, ignoring her but adopting her syntax. *I know something you don't.* "Send the others back to their quarters."

Grace stared at him as if he were some kind of rodent and she couldn't decide whether to be disgusted or pitying. After a moment, though, she nodded stiffly and left.

He relaxed, let out his breath. Although she had to accept his orders, she still controlled the staff for the next week or two, could check him in a thousand ways until he was fully embedded.

Was it alchemy or a true magic? Was he wrong? And did it matter, since if he was wrong, each was exactly like the others anyway?

Yes, it mattered.

This was his last chance.

His mother had told him so before he'd come here.

Control's mother often seemed to him like a flash of light across a distant night sky. Here and gone, gone and here, and always remembered; perhaps wondered what it had been—what had caused the light. But you couldn't truly *know* it.

An only child, Jackie Severance had followed her father into the service and excelled; now she operated at levels far above anything her father, Jack Severance, had achieved, and he had been a much-decorated agent. Jack had brought her up sharp, organized, ready to lead. For all Control knew, Grandpa had made Jackie do tire obstacle courses as a child, stab flour sacks with bayonets. There weren't a whole lot of family albums from which to verify. Whatever the process, he had also bred into her a kind of casual cruelty, an expectation of high performance, and a calculated quality that could manifest as seeming indifference to the fate of others.

As a distant flash of light, Control admired her fiercely, had, indeed, followed her, if at a much lower altitude . . . but as a parent, even when she was around, she was unreliable about picking him up from school on time or remembering his lunches or helping with homework—rarely consistent on much of anything important in the mundane world on this side of the divide. Although she had always encouraged him in his headlong flight into and through the service.

Grandpa Jack, on the other hand, had never seemed fond of the idea, had one day looked at him and said, "I don't think he has the temperament." That assessment had been devastating to a boy of sixteen, already set on that course, but then it made him more determined, more focused, more tilted skyward toward the light. Later he thought that might have been why Grandpa had said it. Grandpa had a kind of unpredictable wildfire side, while his mother was an icy blue flame.

When he was eight or nine, they'd gone up to the summer cottage by the lake for the first time—"our own private spy club," his mother had called it. Just him, his mother, and Grandpa. There was an old TV in the corner, opposite the tattered couch. Grandpa would make him move the antenna to get better reception. "Just a little to the left, Control," he'd say. "Just a little more." His mother in the other room, going over some declassified files she'd brought from the office. And so he'd gotten his nickname, not knowing Grandpa had stolen it from spy jargon. As that kid, he'd held that nickname close as something cool, something his grandpa had given him out of love. But he was still astute enough not to tell anyone outside of family, even his girlfriends, for many years. He'd let them think that it was a sports nickname from high school, where he'd been a backup quarterback. "A little to the right now, Control." Throw that ball like a star. The main thing he'd liked was knowing where the receivers would be and hitting them. Even if always better during practice, he had found a pure satisfaction in that kind of precision, the geometry and anticipation.

When he grew up, he took "Control" for his own. He could feel the sting of condescension in the word by then, but would never ask Grandpa if he'd meant it that way, or some other way. Wondered if the fact he'd spent as much time reading in the cottage by the lake as fishing had somehow turned his grandfather against him.

So, yes, he'd taken the name, remade it, and let it stick. But this was the first time he'd told his coworkers to call him

"Control" and he couldn't say why, really. It had just come to him, as if he could somehow gain a true fresh start.

A little to the left, Control, and maybe you'll pick up that flash of light.

⟋

Why an empty lot? This he'd wondered ever since seeing the surveillance tape earlier that morning. Why had the biologist returned to an empty lot rather than her house? The other two had returned to something personal, to a place that held an emotional attachment. But the biologist had stood for hours and hours in an overgrown lot, oblivious to anything around her. From watching so many suspects on videotape, Control had become adroit at picking up on even the most mundane mannerism or nervous tic that meant a signal was being passed on . . . but there was nothing like that on the tape.

Her presence there had registered with the Southern Reach via a report filed by the local police, who'd picked her up as a vagrant: a delayed reaction, driven by active searching once the Southern Reach had picked up the other two.

Then there was the issue of terseness versus terseness.

753. 722.

A slim lead, but Control already sensed that this assignment hinged on the details, on detective work. Nothing would come easy. He'd have no luck, no shit-for-brains amateur bomb maker armed with fertilizer and some cut-rate version of an ideology who went to pieces within twenty minutes of being put in the interrogation room.

During the preliminary interviews before it was determined who went on the twelfth expedition, the biologist had, according to the transcripts in her file, managed to divulge only 753 words. Control had counted them. That included the word *breakfast* as a complete answer to one question. Control admired that response.

He had counted and recounted the words during that drawn-out period of waiting while they set up his computer, issued him a security card, presented to him passwords and key codes, and went through all of the other rituals with which he had become overly familiar during his passage through various agencies and departments.

He'd insisted on the former director's office despite Grace's attempts to cordon him off in a glorified broom closet well away from the heart of everything. He'd also insisted they leave everything as is in the office, even personal items. She clearly disliked the idea of him rummaging through the director's things.

"You are a little off," Grace had said when the others had left. "You are not all there."

He'd just nodded because there was no use denying it was a little strange. But if he was here to assess and restore, he needed a better idea of how badly it had all slipped— and as some sociopath at another station had once said, "The fish rots from the head." Fish rotted all over, cell corruption being nonhierarchical and not caste-driven, but point taken.

Control had immediately taken a seat behind the battering ram of a desk, among the clutter of piles and piles of folders, the ramble of handwritten notes and Post-its . . . in the swivel chair that gave him such a great panoramic view of the bookcases against the walls, interspersed with bulletin boards overlaid with the sediment of various bits of paper pinned and re-pinned until they looked more like oddly delicate yet haphazard art installations. The room smelled stale, with a slight aftertaste of long-ago cigarettes.

Just the size and weight of the director's computer monitor spoke to its obsolescence, as did the fact that it had died decades ago, thick dust layered atop it. It had been halfheartedly shoved to the side, two shroud-shadows on the calendar blotter beneath describing both its original location and the location of the laptop that had apparently supplanted it— although no one could now find that laptop. He made a mental note to ask if they had searched her home.

The calendar dated back to the late nineties; was that when the director had started to lose the thread? He had a sudden vision of her in Area X with the twelfth expedition, just wandering through the wilderness with no real destination: a tall, husky, forty-year-old woman who looked older. Silent, conflicted, torn. So devoured by her responsibility that she'd allowed herself to believe she owed it to the people she sent into the field to join them. Why had no one stopped her? Had no one cared about her? Had she made a convincing case? The Voice hadn't said. The maddeningly incomplete files on her told Control nothing.

Everything in what he saw showed that she had cared, and yet that she had cared not at all about the functioning of the agency.

Nudging his knee on the left, under the desk: the hard drive for the monitor. He wondered if that had stopped working back in the nineties, too. Control had the feeling he did not want to see the rooms the hardware techs worked in, the miserable languishing corpses of the computers of past decades, the chaotic unintentional museum of plastic and wires and circuit boards. Or perhaps the fish did rot from the head, and only the director had decomposed.

So, sans computer, his own laptop not yet deemed secure enough, Control had done a little light reading of the transcripts from the induction interviews with the members of the twelfth expedition. The former director, in her role as psychologist, had conducted them.

The other recruits had been uncappable, unstoppable geysers in Control's opinion: Great chortling, hurtling, cliché-spouting babblers. People who by comparison could not hold their tongues . . . 4,623 words . . . 7,154 words . . . and the all-time champion, the linguist who had backed out at the last second, coming in at 12,743 words of replies, including a heroically prolonged childhood memory "about as entertaining as a kidney stone exploding through your dick," as someone had scrawled in the margin. Which left just the biologist and her terse 753 words. That kind of self-control had made him look not just at the words but at the pauses between them. For example: "I enjoyed all of my jobs in the field." Yet she had been fired from most of them. She thought she had said nothing, but every word—even *breakfast*—created an opening. Breakfast had not gone well for the biologist as a child.

The ghost was right there, in the transcripts since her return, moving through the text. Things that showed themselves in the empty spaces, making Control unwilling to say her words aloud for fear that somehow he did not really understand the undercurrents and hidden references. A detached description of a thistle . . . A mention of a lighthouse. A sentence or two describing the quality of the light on the marshes in Area X. None of it should have gotten to him, yet he felt her there, somehow, looking over his shoulder in a way not evoked by the interviews with the other expedition members.

The biologist claimed to remember as little as the others.

Control knew that for a lie—or it would become a lie if he drew her out. Did he want to draw her out? Was she cautious because something had happened in Area X or because she was just built that way? A shadow had passed over the director's desk then. He'd been here before, or somewhere close, making these kinds of decisions before, and it had almost broken him, or broken through him. But he had no choice.

About seven hundred words after she came back. Just like the other two. But unlike them, that was roughly comparable to her terseness before she had left. And there were the odd specifics that the others lacked. Whereas the anthropologist might say "The wilderness was empty and pristine," the biologist said, "There were bright pink thistles everywhere, even when the fresh water shifted to saline . . . The light at dusk was a low blaze, a brightness."

That, combined with the strangeness of the empty lot, made Control believe that the biologist might actually remember more than the others. That she might be more present than the others but was hiding it for some reason. He'd never had this particular situation before, but he remembered a colleague's questioning of a terrorist who had suffered a head wound and spent the interrogation sessions in the hospital delaying and delaying in hopes his memory would return. It had. But only the facts, not the righteous impulse that had engendered his action, and then he'd been lost, easy prey for the questioners.

Control hadn't shared his theory with the assistant director because if he was wrong she'd use it to shore up her negative opinion of him—but also to keep her off-balance for as long as possible. "Never do something for just one reason," his grandpa had told him more than once, and that, at least, Control had taken to heart.

The biologist's hair had been long and dark brown, almost black, before they'd shaved it off. She had dark, thick eyebrows, green eyes, a slight, slightly off-center nose (broken once, falling on rocks), and high cheekbones that spoke to the strong Asian heritage on one side of her family. Her chapped lips were surprisingly full for such a thin frown. He mistrusted the eyes, the percentages on that, had checked to confirm they hadn't been another color before the expedition.

Even sitting down at the table, she somehow projected a sense of being physically strong, with a ridge of thick muscle where her neck met her shoulders. So far, all the tests run had come back negative for cancer or other abnormalities. He couldn't remember what it said in her file, but Control thought she was probably almost as tall as him. She had been held in the eastern wing of the building for two weeks now, with nothing to do but eat and exercise.

Before going on the expedition, the biologist had received intense survival and weapons training at a Central facility devoted to that purpose. She would have been briefed with whatever half-truths the Southern Reach's command and control deemed useful, based on criteria Control still found arcane, even murky. She would have been subjected to conditioning to make her more receptive to hypnotic suggestion.

———

The psychologist/director would have been given any number of hypnotic cues to use—words that, in certain combinations, would induce certain effects. Passing thought as the door shut behind Control: Had the director had anything to do with muddying their memories, while they were still in Area X?

Control slid into a chair across from the biologist, aware that Grace, at the very least, watched them through the one-way glass. Experts had questioned the biologist, but Control was also a kind of expert, and he needed to have the direct contact. There was something in the texture of a face-to-face interview that transcripts and videotape lacked.

The floor beneath his shoes was grimy, almost sticky. The fluorescent lights above flickered at irregular intervals, and the table and chairs seemed like something out of a high-school cafeteria. He could smell the sour metallic tang of a low-quality cleaning agent, almost like rotting honey. The room did not inspire confidence in the Southern Reach. A room meant as a debriefing space—or meant to seem like a debriefing space—should be more comfortable than one meant always and forever for interrogation, for a presumption of possible resistance.

Now that Control sat across from the biologist, she had the kind of presence that made him reluctant to stare into her eyes. But he always felt nervous right before he questioned someone, always felt as if that bright flash of light across the sky had frozen in its progress and come down to stand at his shoulder, mother in the flesh, observing him. The truth of it was, his mother did check up on him sometimes. She could get hold of the footage. So it wasn't paranoia or just a feeling. It was part of his possible reality.

Sometimes it helped to play up his nervousness, to make the person across from him relax. So he cleared his throat, took a hesitant sip of water from the glass he'd brought in with him, fiddled with the file on her he'd placed on the table between them, along with a remote control for the TV to his left. To preserve the conditions under which she'd been found, to basically ensure she didn't gain memories artificially, the assistant director had ordered that she not be given any of the information from her personnel file. Control found this cruel but agreed with Grace. He wanted the file between them to seem like a possible reward during some later session, even if he didn't yet know if he would give it to her.

Control introduced himself by his real name, informed her that their "interview" was being recorded, and asked her to state her name for the record.

"Call me Ghost Bird," she said. Was there a twinge of defiance in her flat voice?

He looked up at her, and instantly was at sea, looked away again. Was she using hypnotic suggestion on him somehow? It was his first thought, quickly dismissed.

"Ghost Bird?"

"Or nothing at all."

He nodded, knew when to let something go, would research the term later. Vaguely remembered something in the file. Perhaps.

"Ghost Bird," he said, testing it out. The words tasted chalky, unnatural in his mouth. "You remember nothing about the expedition?"

"I told the others. It was a pristine wilderness." He thought he detected a note of irony in her tone, but couldn't be sure.

"How well did you get to know the linguist—during training?" he asked.

"Not well. She was very vocal. She wouldn't shut up. She was . . ." The biologist trailed off as Control stifled elation. A question she hadn't expected. Not at all.

"She was what?" he prompted. The prior interrogator had used the standard technique: develop rapport, present the facts, grow the relationship from there. With nothing really to show for it.

"I don't remember."

"I think you do remember." And if you remember that, then . . .

"No."

He made a show of opening the file and consulting the existing transcripts, letting the edge of the paper-clipped pages that gave her most vital statistics come clear.

"Okay, then. Tell me about the thistles."

"The thistles?" Her expressive eyebrows told him what she thought of the question.

"Yes. You were quite specific about the thistles. Why?" It still perplexed him, the amount of detail there about thistles, in an interview from the prior week, when she'd arrived at the Southern Reach. It made him think again of hypnotic cues. It made him think of words being used as a protective thicket.

The biologist shrugged. "I don't know."

He read from the transcript: "'The thistles there have a lavender bloom and grow in the transitional space between the forest and the swamp. You cannot avoid them. They attract a variety of insects and the buzzing and the brightness that surrounds them suffuses Area X with a sense of industry, almost like a human city.' And it goes on, although I won't."

She shrugged again.

Control didn't intend to hover, this first time, but instead to glide over the terrain, to map out the extent of the territory he wanted to cover with her. So he moved on.

"What do you remember about your husband?"

"How is that relevant?"

"Relevant to what?" Pouncing.

No response, so he prompted her again: "What do you remember about your husband?"

"That I had one. Some memories before I went over, like I had about the linguist." Clever, to tie that in, to try to make it seem part and parcel. A vagueness, not a sharpness.

"Did you know that he came back, like you?" he asked. "That he was disoriented, like you?"

"I'm not disoriented," she snapped, leaning forward, and Control leaned back. He wasn't afraid, but for a moment he'd thought he should be. Brain scans had been normal. All measures had been taken to check for anything remotely like an invasive species. Or "an intruder" as Grace put it, still unable to say anything to him remotely like the word *alien*. If anything, Ghost Bird was healthier now than before she'd left; the toxins present in most people today existed in her and the others at much lower levels than normal.

"I didn't mean to offend," he said. And yet she *was* disoriented, Control knew. No matter what she remembered or didn't remember, the biologist he'd come to know from the pre-expedition transcripts would not have so quickly shown irritation. Why had he gotten to her?

He picked up the remote control from beside the file, clicked twice. The flat-screen TV on the wall to their left fizzled to life, showing the pixelated, fuzzy image of the biologist standing in the empty lot, almost as still as the pavement or the bricks in the building in front of her. The whole scene was awash in the sickly green of surveillance-camera noir.

"Why that empty lot? Why did we find you there?"

A look of indifference and no answer. He let the video continue to play. The repetition in the background sometimes got to the interviewee. But usually video footage showed a suspect putting down a bag or shoving something into a trash bin.

"First day in Area X," Control said. "Hiking to base camp. What happened?"

"Nothing much."

Control had no children, but he imagined that this was more or less what he'd get from a teenager asked about her day at school. Perhaps he would circle back for a moment.

"But you remember the thistles very, very well," he said.

"I don't know why you keep talking about thistles."

"Because what you said about them suggests you remember some of your observations from the expedition."

A pause, and Control knew the biologist was staring at him. He wanted to return fire, but something warned him against it. Something made him feel that the dream of falling into the depths might take him.

"Why am I a prisoner here?" she asked, and he felt it was safe to meet her gaze again, as if some moment of danger had come and gone.

"You aren't. This is part of your debriefing."

PRAISE FOR THE SOUTHERN REACH TRILOGY

'A tense and chilling psychological thriller about an unravelling expedition and the strangeness within us. A little Kubrick, a lot of Lovecraft, [*Annihilation*] builds with an unbearable tension and claustrophobic dread that lingers long afterwards'
LAUREN BEUKES, author of *The Shining Girls*

'A lasting monument to the uncanny ... you find yourself afraid to turn the page'
SIMON INGS, *Guardian*

'VanderMeer's story is thrilling ... But its deepest terror lies in its exploration of the vacancies of the human heart, and the terror that can grow from the ways in which we are untrue to each other, and to ourselves'
JARED BLAND, *Globe and Mail*

'*Annihilation* owes much to the explorations of psycho-geographical landscapes in early J. G. Ballard and also to the work of the old masters of weird fiction ... a tale with a deliciously creepy atmosphere of dread'
JAMES LOVEGROVE, *Financial Times*

'Immersive, insightful and often deeply bloody creepy, this is a startlingly good novel ... the Southern Reach series will be a major work'
WILL SALMON, *SFX Magazine*

'A clear triumph for VanderMeer ... a compelling, elegant and existential story of far broader appeal ... A novel whose world is built seamlessly and whose symbols are rich and dark'
LYDIA MILLET, *LA Times*

'A teeming science fiction that draws on Conrad and Lovecraft alike ... The writing itself has a clarity that makes the abundancy of the setting more powerful'
PAUL KINCAID, *Sunday Telegraph*

"But I can't leave."

"Not yet," he admitted. "But you will." If only to another facility; it might be another two or three years, if all went well, before they allowed any of the returnees back out in the world. Their legal status was in that gray area often arbitrarily defined by the threat to national security.

"I find that unlikely," she said.

He decided to try again. "If not thistles, what would be relevant?" he asked. "What should I ask you?"

"Isn't that your job?"

"What is my job?" Although he knew perfectly well what she meant.

"You're in charge of the Southern Reach."

"Do you know what the Southern Reach is?"

"Yesss." Like a hiss.

"What about the second day at base camp? When did things begin to get strange?" Had they? He had to assume they had.

"I don't remember."

Control leaned forward. "I can put you under hypnosis. I have the right to. I can do that."

"Hypnosis doesn't work on me," she said, disgust at his threat clear from her tone.

"How do you know?" A moment of disorientation. Had she given up something she didn't want to give up, or had she remembered something lost to her before? Did she know the difference?

"I just know."

"For clarity on that, we could recondition you and then put you under hypnosis." All of this a bluff, in that it was more complicated logistically. To do so, Control would have to send her to Central, and she'd disappear into that maw forever. He might get to see the reports, but he'd never have direct contact again. Nor did he particularly *want* to recondition her.

"Do that and I'll—" She managed to stop herself on the cusp of what sounded like the beginning of the word *kill*.

Control decided to ignore that. He'd been on the other end of enough threats to know which to take seriously.

"What made you resistant to hypnosis?" he asked.

"Are *you* resistant to hypnosis?" Defiant.

"Why were you at the empty lot? The other two were found looking for their loved ones."

No reply.

Maybe enough had been said for now. Maybe this was enough.

Control turned off the television, picked up his file, nodded at her, and walked to the door.

Once there, the door open and letting in what seemed like more shadows than it should, he turned, aware of the assistant director staring at him from down the hall as he looked back at the biologist.

He asked, as he had always planned to, the postscript to an opening act: "What's the last thing you remember doing in Area X?"

The answer, unexpected, surged up toward him like a kind of attack as the light met the darkness: "Drowning. I was drowning."

002: ADJUSTMENTS

Just close your eyes and you will remember me," Control's father had told him three years ago, in a place not far from where he was now, the dying trying to comfort the living. But when he closed his eyes, everything disappeared except the dream of falling and the accumulated scars from past assignments. Why had the biologist said that? Why had she said she was drowning? It had thrown him, but it had also given him an odd sense of secret sharing between them. As if she had gotten into his head and seen his dream, and now they were bound together. He resented that, did not want to be connected to the people he had to question. He had to glide above. He had to choose when he swooped down, not be brought to earth by the will of another.

When Control opened his eyes, he was standing in the back of the U-shaped building that served as the Southern Reach's headquarters. The curve lay in the front, a road and parking lot preceding it. Built in a style now decades old, the layered, stacked concrete was a monument or a midden—he couldn't decide which. The ridges and clefts were baffling; the way the roof leered slightly over the rest made it seem less functional than like performance art or abstract sculpture on a grand and yet numbing scale. Making things worse, the area coveted by the open arms of the U had been made into a courtyard, looking out on a lake ringed by thick old-growth forest. The edges of the lake were singed black, as if at one time set ablaze, and a wretched gnarl of cypress knees waded through the dark, brackish water. The light that suffused the lake had a claustrophobic gray quality, separate and distinct from the blue sky above.

This, too, had at one time been new, perhaps back during the Cretaceous period, and the building had probably stood here then in some form, reverse engineered so far into the past that you could still look out the windows and see dragonflies as big as vultures.

The U that hugged them close inspired no great confidence; it felt less a symbol of luck than of the incomplete. Incomplete thoughts. Incomplete conclusions. Incomplete reports. The doors at the ends of the U, through which many passed as a shortcut to the other side, confirmed a failure of the imagination. And all the while, the abysmal swamp did whatever swamps did, as perfect in its way as the Southern Reach was imperfect.

Everything was so still that when a woodpecker swooped across that scene it was as violent as the sonic boom of an F-16.

To the left of the U and the lake—just visible from where he stood—a road threaded its way through the trees, toward the invisible border, beyond which lay Area X. Just thirty-five miles of paved road and then another fifteen unpaved beyond that, with ten checkpoints in all, and shoot-to-kill orders if you weren't meant to be there, and fences and barbed wire and trenches and pits and more swamp, possibly even government-trained colonies of apex predators and genetically modified poison berries and hammers to hit yourself on the head with . . . but in some ways, ever since Control had been briefed, he had wondered: To what point? Because that's what you did in such situations? Keep people out? He'd studied the reports. If you reached the border in an "unauthorized way" and crossed over anywhere but the door, you would never be seen again. How many people had done just that, without being spotted? How would the Southern Reach ever know? Once or twice, an investigative journalist had gotten close enough to photograph the outside of the Southern Reach's border facilities, but even then it had just confirmed in the public imagination the official story of environmental catastrophe, one that wouldn't be cleaned up for a century.

There came a tread around the stone tables in the concrete courtyard across which little white tiles competed with squares of clotted earth into which unlikely tulips had been shoved at irregular intervals . . . he knew that tread, with its special extra little dragging sound. The assistant director had been a field officer once; something had happened on assignment, and she'd hurt her leg. Inside the building, she could disguise it, but not on the treacherous grouted tiles. It wasn't an advantage for him to know this, because it made him want to empathize with her. "Whenever you say 'in the field,' I have this image of all of you spooks running through the wheat," his father had said to his mother, once.

Grace was joining him at his request, to assist him in staring out at the swamp while they talked about Area X. Because he'd thought a change of setting—leaving the confines of the concrete coffin—might help soften her animosity. Before he'd realized just how truly hellish and prehistoric the landscape was, and thus now pre-hysterical as well. Look out upon this mosquito orgy, and warm to me, Grace.

"You interviewed just the biologist. I still do not know why." She said this before he could extend even a tendril of an opening gambit . . . and all of his resolve to play the diplomat, to somehow become her colleague, not her enemy—even if by misdirection or a metaphorical jab in the kidneys—dissolved into the humid air.

He explained his thought processes. She seemed impressed, although he couldn't really read her yet.

"Did she ever seem, during training, like she was hiding something?" he asked.

"Deflection. You think she is hiding something."

"I don't know yet, actually. I could be wrong."

"We have more expert interrogators than you."

"Probably true."

"We should send her to Central."

The thought made him shudder.

"No," he said, a little too emphatically, then worried in the next split second that the assistant director might guess that he cared about the biologist's fate.

"I have already sent the anthropologist and the surveyor away."

Now he could smell the decay of all that plant matter slowly rotting beneath the surface of the swamp, could sense the awkward turtles and stunted fish pushing their way through matted layers. He didn't trust himself to turn to face her. Didn't trust himself to say anything, stood there suspended by his surprise.

Cheerfully, she continued: "You said they weren't of any use, so I sent them to Central."

"By whose authority?"

"Your authority. You clearly indicated to me that this was what you wanted. If you meant something else, my apologies."

A tiny seismic shift occurred inside of Control, an imperceptible shudder.

They were gone. He couldn't have them back. He had to put it out of his mind, would feed himself the lie that Grace had done him a favor, simplified his job. Just how much pull did she have at Central, anyway?

"I can always read the transcripts if I change my mind," he said, attempting an agreeable tone. They'd still be questioned, and he'd given her the opening by saying he didn't want to interview them.

She was scanning his face intently, looking for some sign that she'd come close to hitting the target.

He tried to smile, doused his anger with the thought that if the assistant director had meant him real harm, she would have found a way to spirit the biologist away, too. This was just a warning. Now, though, he was going to have to take something away from Grace as well. Not to get even but so she wouldn't be tempted to take yet more from him. He couldn't afford to lose the biologist, too. Not yet.

Into the awkward silence, Grace asked, "Why are you just standing out here in the heat like an idiot?" Breezily, as if nothing had happened at all. "We should go inside. It's time for lunch, and you can meet some of the admin."

Control was already growing accustomed to her disrespect of him, and he hated that, wanted an opportunity to reverse the trend. As he followed her in, the swamp at his back had a weight, a presence. Another kind of enemy. He'd had enough of such views, growing up nearby as a teenager after his parents' divorce, and, again, while his father slowly died. He'd hoped to never see a swamp again.

"Just close your eyes and you will remember me."

I do, Dad. I do remember you, but you're fading. There's too much interference, and all of *this* is becoming much too real.

Control's father's side of the family came originally from Central America, Hispanic and Indian; he had his father's hands and black hair, his mother's slight nose and height, a skin color somewhere in between. His paternal grandfather had died before Control was old enough to know him, but he had heard the epic stories. The man had sold clothespins door-to-door as a kid, in certain neighborhoods, and been a boxer in his twenties, not good enough to be a contender but good enough to be a paid opponent and take a beating. Afterward, he'd been a construction worker, and then a driving instructor, before an early death from a heart attack at sixty-five. His wife, who worked in a bakery, passed on just a year later. His eldest child, Control's father, had grown up to be an artist in a family mostly composed of carpenters and mechanics, and used his heritage to create abstract sculptures. He had humanized the abstractions by painting over them in the bright palette favored by the Mayans and by affixing to them bits of tile and glass—bridging some gap between professional and outsider art. That was his life, and Control never knew a time that his father was not that person and only that person.

The story of how Control's father and mother fell in love was also the happy story of how his father had risen, for a time, as a favorite in high-end art galleries. They had met at a reception for his work and, as they told it, had been enamored with each other right from the first glance, although later Control found that difficult to believe. At the time, she was based in New York and had what amounted to a desk job, although she was rising fast. His father moved up north to be with her, and they had Control and then only a year or two later she was reassigned, from a desk job to active duty in the field, and that was the start of the end of it all, the story that anchored Control as a kid soon revealed as just a brief moment set against a landscape of unhappiness. Not unique: the kind of depressingly familiar painting you'd find in a seaside antique store but never buy.

The silence was punctuated by arguments, a silence created not just by the secrets she carried with her but by those she could not divulge, and, Control realized as an adult, by her inner reserve, which after a time could not be bridged. Her absences tore at his father, and by the time Control was ten, that was the subtext and sometimes the transcript of their dispute: She was killing his art and that wasn't fair, even though the art scene had moved on and what his father did was expensive and required patrons or grants to sustain.

But still his father would sit there with his schematics, his plans for new work, spread out around him like evidence when she came back between field assignments. She bore the recrimination, Control remembered, with calm and a chilly, aloof compassion. She was the unstoppable force that came blowing in—not there, there—with presents bought at the last minute in far-off airports and an innocent-sounding cover story about what she'd been up to, or a less innocent story that Control realized years later, when faced with a similar dilemma, had been coming to them from a time

33

delay. Something declassified she could now share but that had happened to her long ago. The stories, and the aloofness, agitated his father, but the compassion infuriated him. He could not read it as anything other than condescending. How can you tell if a streak of light across the sky is sincere?

When they divorced, Control went south to live with his dad, who became embedded in a community that felt comfortable because it included some of his relatives and fed his artistic ambitions even as his bank account starved. Control could remember the shock when he realized how much noise and motion and color could be found in someone's house, once they'd moved. How suddenly he was part of a larger family.

Yet during those hot summers in that small town not very far from the Southern Reach, as a thirteen-year-old with a rusty bike and a few loyal friends, Control kept thinking about his mother, out in the field, in some far-off city or country: that distant streak of light that sometimes came down out of the night sky and materialized on their doorstep as a human being. Exactly in the same way as when they'd been together as a family.

One day, he believed, she would take him with her, and he would become the streak of light, have secrets no one else could ever know.

Some rumors about Area X were elaborate and in their complexity seemed to Control like schools of the most deadly and yet voluminous jellyfish at the aquarium. As you watched them, in their undulating progress, they seemed both real and unreal framed against the stark blue of the water. *Invasion site. Secret government experiments.* How could such an organism actually exist? The simple ones that echoed the official story—variations on a human-made ecological disaster area—were by contrast so commonplace these days that they hardly registered or elicited curiosity. The petting-zoo versions that ate out of your hand.

But the truth did have a simple quality to it: About thirty-two years ago, along a remote southern stretch known by some as as the "forgotten coast," an Event had occurred that began to transform the landscape and simultaneously caused an invisible border or wall to appear. A kind of ghost or "permeable pre-border manifestation" as the files put it—light as fog, almost invisible except for a flickering quality—had quickly emanated out in all directions from an unknown epicenter and then suddenly stopped at its current impenetrable limits.

Since then, the Southern Reach had been established and sought to investigate what had occurred, with little success and much sacrifice of lives via the expeditions—sent in through the sole point of egress. Yet that loss of life was trifling compared to the possibility of some break in containment across a border that the scientists were still studying and trying to understand. The riddle of why equipment, when recovered, had been rendered nonfunctional, some of it decomposing at an incredibly fast rate. The teasing, inconsistent way in which some expeditions came back entirely unharmed that seemed almost more inexplicable.

"It started earlier than the border coming down," the assistant director told him after lunch in his new-old office.

She was all business now, and Control chose to accept her at face value, to continue to put away, for now, his anger at her preemptive strike in banishing the anthropologist and the surveyor.

Grace rolled out the map of Area X on a corner of his desk: the coastline, the lighthouse, the base camp, the trails, the lakes and rivers, the island many miles north that marked the farthest reach of the . . . Incursion? Invasion? Infestation? What word worked? The worst part of the map was the black dot hand-labeled by the director as "the tunnel" but known to most as "the topographical anomaly." Worst part because not every expedition whose members had survived to report back had encountered it, even when they'd mapped the same area.

Grace tossed files on top of the map. It still struck Control, with a kind of nostalgia rarely granted to his generation, how anachronistic it was to deal in paper. But the concern about sending modern technology across the border had infected the former director. She had forbidden certain forms of communication, required that all e-mails be printed out and the original, electronic versions regularly archived and purged, and had arcane and confusing protocols for using the Internet and other forms of electronic communication. Would he put an end to that? He didn't know yet, had a kind of sympathy for the policy, impractical though it might be. He used the Internet solely for research and admin. He believed a kind of a fragmentation had crept into people's minds in the modern era.

"It started earlier . . ."

"How much earlier?"

"Intel indicates that there may have been odd . . . activity occurring along that coast for at least a century before the border came down." Before Area X had formed. A "pristine wilderness." He'd never heard the word *pristine* used so many times before today.

Idly, he wondered what *they* called it—whoever or whatever had created that pristine bubble that had killed so many people. Maybe they called it a holiday retreat. Maybe they called it a beachhead. Maybe "they" were so incomprehensible he'd never understand what they called it, or why. He'd asked the Voice if he needed access to the files on other major unexplained occurrences, and the Voice had made "No" sound like a granite cliff, with only flailing blue sky beyond it.

Control had already seen at least some of the flotsam and jetsam now threatening to buckle the desk in the file summary. He knew that quite a bit of the information peeking out at him from the beige folders came from lighthouse journals and police records—and that the inexplicable in it had to be teased out from the edges, pushed forward into the light like the last bit of toothpaste in the dehydrated tube curled up on the edge of the bathroom sink. The kind of "strange doings" alluded to by hard-living bearded fishermen in old horror movies as they stared through haunted eyes at the unforgiving sea. Unsolved disappearances. Lights in the night. Stories of odd salvagers, and false beacons, and the hundred legends that accrete around a lonely coastline and a remote lighthouse.

There had even been an informal group—the Séance & Science Brigade—dedicated to applying "empirical reality to paranormal phenomenon." Members of the S&S Brigade had written several self-published books that had collected dust on the counters of local businesses. It was the S&SB that had in effect named Area X, identifying that coast as "of particular interest" and calling it "Active Site X"—a name prominent on their bizarre science-inspired tarot cards. The Southern Reach had discounted S&SB early on as "not a catalyst or a player or an instigator" in whatever had caused Area X—just a bunch of (un)lucky "amateurs" caught up in something beyond the grasp of their imaginations. Except, almost every effective terrorist Control had encountered was an "amateur."

"We live in a universe driven by chance," his father had said once, "but the bullshit artists all want causality." Bullshit artist in this context meant his mother, but the statement had wide applications.

So was all or any of it random coincidence—or part of some vast, pre–Area X conspiracy? You could spend years wading through the data, trying to find the answer—and it looked to Control as if that's exactly what the former director had been doing.

"And you think this is credible evidence?" Control still didn't know how far into the mountain of bullshit the assistant director had fallen. Too far, given her natural animosity, and he wouldn't be inclined to pull her out of it.

"Not all of it," she conceded, a thin smile erasing the default frown. "But tracking back from the events we know have occurred since the border came down, you begin to see patterns."

Control believed her. He would have believed Grace had she said visions appeared in the swirls of her strawberry gelato on hot summer days or in the fracturing of the ice in another of her favorites, rum-and-diet with a lime (her personnel file was full of maddeningly irrelevant details). It was in the nature of being an analyst. But what patterns had colonized the former director's mind? And how much of that had infiltrated the assistant director? On some level, Control hoped that the mess the director had left behind was deliberate, to hide some more rational progression.

"But how is that different from any other godforsaken stretch of coast half off the grid?" There were still dozens of them all across the country. Places that were poison to real-estate agents, with little infrastructure and a long history of distrust of the government.

The assistant director stared at him in a way that made him feel uncomfortably like a middle-school student again, sent up for insolence.

"I know what you're thinking," she said. "Have we been compromised by our own data? The answer is: Of course. That is what happens over time. But if there is something in the files that is useful, you might see it because you have fresh eyes. So I can archive all of this now if you like. Or we can use you the way we need to use you: not because you know anything but because you know so little."

A kind of resentful pride rose up in Control that wasn't useful, that came from having a parent who *did* seem to know everything.

"I didn't mean that I—"

Mercifully, she cut him off. Unmercifully, her tone channeled contempt. "We have been here a long time . . . Control. A very long time. Living with this. Unable to do very much about this." A surprising amount of pain had entered her voice. "You don't go home at night with it in your stomach, in your bones. In a few weeks, when you have seen everything, you will have been living with it for a long time, too. You will be just like us—only more so, because it is getting worse. Fewer and fewer journals recovered, and more zombies, as if they have been mind-wiped. And no one in charge has time for us."

It could have been a moment to commiserate over the vagaries and injustices perpetrated by Central, Control realized later, but he just sat there staring at her. He found her fatalism a hindrance, especially suffused, as he misdiagnosed it at first, with such a grim satisfaction. A claustrophobic combination that no one needed, that helped no one. It was also inaccurate in its progressions.

The first expedition alone had, according to the files, experienced such horrors, almost beyond imagining, that it was a wonder that they had sent anyone after that. But they'd had no choice, understood they were in it for "the long haul" as, he knew from transcripts, the former director had liked to say. They hadn't even let the later expeditions know the true fate of the first expedition, had created a fiction of encountering an undisturbed wilderness and then built other lies on top of that one. This had probably been done as much to ease the Southern Reach's own trauma as to protect the morale of the subsequent expeditions.

"In thirty minutes, you have an appointment to tour the science division," she said, getting up and looming over him, leaning with her hands on his desk. "I think I will let you find the place yourself." That would give him just enough time to check his office for surveillance devices beforehand.

"Thanks," he said. "You can leave now."

So she left.

But it didn't help. Before he'd arrived, Control had imagined himself flying free above the Southern Reach, swooping down from some remote perch to manage things. That wasn't going to happen. Already his wings were burning up and he felt more like some ponderous moaning creature trapped in the mire.

As he became more familiar with it, the former director's office revealed no new or special features to Control's practiced eye. Except that his computer, finally installed on the desk, looked almost science-fictional next to all the rest of it.

The door lay to the far left of the long, rectangular room, so that you wandered into its length toward the mahogany desk set against the far wall. No one could have snuck up on the director or read over her shoulder. Each wall had been covered in bookcases or filing cabinets, with stacks of papers and some books forming a second width in front of this initial layering. At the highest levels, or in some ridiculous cases, balanced on the stacks, those bulletin boards with ripped pieces of paper and scribbled diagrams pinned to them. He felt as if he had been placed inside someone's disorganized mind. Near her desk, on the left, he uncovered an array of preserved natural ephemera. Dusty and decaying bits of pinecone trailed across the shelves. A vague hint of a rotting smell, but he couldn't track down the origin.

Opposite the entrance lay another door, situated in a gap between bookcases, but this had been blocked by more piles of file folders and cardboard boxes and he'd been told it opened onto the wall—detritus of an inelegant remodeling.

Opposite the desk, on the far wall about twenty-five feet away, was a kind of break in the mess to make room for two rows of pictures, all in the kinds of frames cheaply bought at discount stores. From bottom left, clockwise around to the right: a square etching of the lighthouse from the 1880s; a black-and-white photograph of two men and a girl framed by the lighthouse; a long, somewhat amateurish watercolor panorama showing miles of reeds broken only by a few isolated islands of dark trees; and a color photograph of the lighthouse beacon in all its glory. No real hints of the personal, no pictures of the director with her Native American mother, her white father—or with anyone who might matter in her life.

Of all the intel Control had to work through in the coming days, he least looked forward to what he might uncover in what was now his own office; he thought he might leave it until last. Everything in the office seemed to indicate a director who had gone feral. One of the drawers in the desk was locked, and he couldn't find the key. But he did note an earthy quality to the locked drawer that hinted at something having rotted inside a long time ago. Which mystery didn't even include the mess drooping off the sides of the desk.

Ever-helpful, unhelpful spy Grandpa used to reflexively say, whether it was washing the dishes or preparing for a fishing trip, "Never skip a step. Skip a step, you'll find five more new ones waiting ahead of you."

The search for surveillance equipment, for bugs, then, was more time-consuming than he'd thought it would be, and he buzzed the science division to let them know he'd be late. There was a kind of visceral grunt in response before the line went dead, and he had no idea who had been on the other end. A person? A trained pig?

Ultimately, after a hellish search, Control to his surprise found twenty-two bugs in his office. He doubted many of them had actually been reporting back, and even if they had, if anyone had been watching or listening to what they conveyed. For the fact was, the director's office had contained an unnatural history museum of bugs—different kinds from different eras, progressively smaller and harder to unearth. The behemoths of this sort were bulging, belching metal goiters when set next to the sleek ethereal pinheads of the modern era.

The discovery of each new bug contributed to a cheerful, upbeat mood. Bugs made sense in a way some of the other things about the Southern Reach didn't. In his training as an omnivore in the service, he'd had at least six assignments that involved bugging people or places. Spying on people didn't bring him the kind of vicarious rush it gave some, or if it did, that feeling faded as he came to know his subjects better and invested in a sense of protectiveness meant to shield them. But he did find the actual devices fascinating.

When he thought his search complete, Control amused himself by arranging the bugs across the faded paper of the blotter in what he believed might be chronological order. Some of them glittered silver. Some, black, absorbed the light. There were wires attached to some like umbilical cords. One iteration—disguised within what appeared to be a small, sticky ball of green papier-mâché or colored honeycomb— made him think that a few might even be foreign-made: interlopers drawn by curiosity to the black box that was Area X. Clearly, though, the former director knew and hadn't cared they were there. Or perhaps she had thought it safest to leave them. Perhaps, too, she'd put some there herself.

He wondered if this accounted for her distrust of modern technology.

As for installing his own, he'd have to wait until later: No time now. No time, either, to deploy these bugs for another purpose that had just occurred to him. Control carefully swept them all into a desk drawer and went to find his science guide.

The labs had been buried in the basement on the right side of the U, if you were facing the building from the parking lot out front. They lay directly opposite the sealed-off wing that served as an expedition pre-prep area and currently housed the biologist. Control had been assigned one of the science division's jack-of-all-trades as his tour guide. Which meant that despite seniority—he had been at the agency longer than anyone on staff—Whitby Allen was a push-me-pull-me who, in part due to staff attrition, often sacrificed his studies as a "cohesive naturalist and holistic scientist specializing in biospheres" to type up someone else's reports or run someone else's errands. Whitby reported to the head of the science division, but also to the assistant director. He was the scion of intellectual aristocracy, came from a long line of professors, men and women who had been tenured at various faux-Corinthian-columned private colleges. Perhaps to his family, he had become an outlaw: The dropout art-school student who went wandering and only later got a proper degree.

Whitby was dressed in a blue blazer with a white shirt and an oddly unobtrusive burgundy bow tie. He looked much younger than his age, with eternal brown hair and the kind of tight, pinched face that allows a fifty-something to look a boyish thirty-two from afar. His wrinkles had come in as tiny hairline fractures. Control had seen him in the cafeteria at lunch next to a dozen dollar bills fanned out on the table beside him for no good reason. Counting them? Making art? Designing a monetary biosphere?

Whitby had an uncomfortable laugh and bad breath and teeth that clearly needed some work. Up close, Whitby also looked as if he hadn't slept in years: a youth wizened prematurely, all the moisture leached from his face, so that his watery blue eyes seemed too large for his head. Beyond this, and his fanciful attitude toward money, Whitby appeared competent enough, and while he no doubt had the ability to engage in small talk, he lacked the inclination. This was as good a reason as any, as they threaded their way through the cafeteria, for Control to question him.

"Did you know the members of the twelfth expedition before they left?"

"I wouldn't say 'know,'" Whitby said, clearly uncomfortable with the question.

"But you saw them around."

"Yes."

"The biologist?"

"Yes, I saw her."

They cleared the cafeteria and its high ceiling and stepped into an atrium flooded with fluorescent light. The crunchy chirp of pop music dripped, distant, out of some office or another.

"What did you think of her? What were your impressions?"

Whitby concentrated hard, face rendered stern by the effort. "She was distant. Serious, sir. She outworked all of the others. But she didn't seem to be working at it, if you know what I mean."

"No, I don't know what you mean, Whitby."

"Well, it didn't matter to her. The work didn't matter. She was looking past it. She was seeing something else." Control got the sense that Whitby had subjected the biologist to quite a bit of scrutiny.

"And the former director? Did you see the former director interact with the biologist?"

"Twice, maybe three times."

"Did they get along?" Control didn't know why he asked this question, but fishing was fishing. Sometimes you just had to cast the line any place at all to start.

"No, sir. But, sir, neither of them got along with anyone." He said this last bit in a whisper, as if afraid of being overheard. Then said, as if to provide cover, "No one but the director wanted that biologist on the twelfth expedition."

"No one?" Control asked slyly.

"Most people."

"Did that include the assistant director?"

Whitby gave him a troubled look. But his silence was enough.

The director had been embedded in the Southern Reach for a long time. The director had cast a long shadow. Even gone, she had a kind of influence. Perhaps not entirely with Whitby, not really. But Control could sense it anyway. He had already caught himself having a strange thought: That the director looked out at him through the assistant director's eyes.

The elevators weren't working and wouldn't be fixed until an expert from the army base dropped by in a few days, so they took the stairs. To get to the stairs, you followed the curve of the U to a side door that opened onto a parallel corridor about fifty feet long, the floor adorned with the same worn green carpet that lowered the property value of the rest of the building. The stairs awaited them at the corridor's end, through wide swinging doors more appropriate for a slaughterhouse or emergency room. Whitby, out of character, felt compelled to burst through those double doors as if they were rock stars charging onto a stage—or, perhaps, to warn off whatever lay on the other side—then stood there sheepishly holding one side open while Control contemplated that first step.

"It's through here," Whitby said.

"I know," Control said.

Beyond the doors, they were suddenly in a kind of free fall, the green carpet cut off, the path become a concrete ramp down to a short landing with a staircase at the end—which then plunged into shadows created by dull white halogens in the walls and punctuated by blinking red emergency lights. All of it under a high ceiling that framed what, in the murk, seemed more a human-made grotto or warehouse than the descent to a basement. The staircase railing, under the shy lights, glittered with luminous rust spots. The coolness in the air as they descended reminded him of a high-school field trip to a natural history museum with an artificial cave system meant to mimic the modern day, the highlight of which had been non sequiturs: mid-lunge reproductions of a prehistoric giant sloth and giant armadillo, mega fauna that had taken a wrong turn.

"How many people in the science division?" he asked when he'd acclimated.

"Twenty-five," Whitby said. The correct answer was nineteen.

"How many did you have five years ago?"

"About the same, maybe a few more." The correct answer was thirty-five.

"What's the turnover like?"

Whitby shrugged. "We have some stalwarts who will always be here. But a lot of new people come in, too, with their ideas, but they don't really change anything." His tone implied that they either left quickly or came around . . . but came around to what?

Control let the silence elongate, so that their footsteps were the only sound. As he'd thought, Whitby didn't like silences. After a moment, Whitby said, "Sorry, sorry. I didn't mean anything by that. It's just sometimes frustrating when new people come in and want to change things without knowing . . . our situation. You feel like if they just read the manual first . . . if we had a manual, that is."

Control mulled that, making a noncommittal sound. He felt as if he'd come in on the middle of an argument Whitby had been having with other people. Had Whitby been a new voice at some point? Was *he* the new Whitby, applied across the entire Southern Reach rather than just the science division?

Whitby looked paler than before, almost sick. He was staring off into the middle distance while his feet listlessly slapped the steps. With each step, he seemed more ill at ease. He had stopped saying "sir."

Some form of pity or sympathy came over Control; he didn't know which. Perhaps a change of subject would help Whitby.

"When was the last time you had a new sample from Area X?"

"About five or six years ago." Whitby sounded more confident about this answer, if no more robust, and he was right. It had been six years since anything new had come to the Southern Reach from Area X. Except for the forever changed members of the eleventh expedition. The doctors and scientists had exhaustively tested them and their clothing, only to find . . . nothing. Nothing at all out of the ordinary. Just one anomaly: the cancer.

No light reached the basement except for what the science division created for itself: They had their own generator, filtration system, and food supply. Vestiges, no doubt, of some long-ago imperative that boiled down to "in an emergency, save the scientists." Control found it hard to imagine those first days, when behind closed doors the government had been in panic mode, and the people who worked in the Southern Reach believed that whatever had come into the world along the forgotten coast might soon turn its attentions inland. But the invasion hadn't happened, and Control wondered if something in that thwarting of expectation had started the Southern Reach's decline.

"Do you like working here, Whitby?"

"Like? Yes. I must admit it's often fascinating, and definitely challenging." Whitby was sweating now, beads breaking on his forehead.

It might indeed be fascinating, but Whitby had, according to the records, undergone a sustained spasm of transfer requests about three years ago—one every month and then every two months like an intermittent SOS, until it had trailed off to nothing, like a flatlined EKG. Control approved of the initiative, if not the sense of desperation embedded in the number of attempts. Whitby didn't want to be stuck in a backwater and just as clearly the director or someone hadn't wanted him to leave.

Perhaps it was his utility-player versatility, because it was clear to Control that, just like every department in the Southern Reach, the science division had been "stripped for parts," as his mother would have put it, by antiterrorism and Central. According to the personnel records, there had once been one hundred and fifteen scientists in-house, representing almost thirty disciplines and several subdepartments. Now there were only sixty-five people in the whole haunted place. There had even been talk, Control knew, about relocating, except that the building was too close to the border to be used for anything else.

The same cheap, rotting scent came to him again just then, as if the janitor had unlimited access to the entire building.

"Isn't that cleaning smell a bit strong?"

"The smell?" Whitby's head whipped around, eyes made huge by the circles around them.

"The rancid honey smell."

"I don't smell anything."

Control frowned, more at Whitby's vehemence than anything else. Well, of course. They were used to it. Tiniest of his tasks, but he made a note to authorize changing cleaning supplies to something organic.

When they curved down at an angle that seemed unnecessarily precipitous, into a spacious preamble to the science division, the ceiling seeming higher than ever, Control was surprised. A tall metal wall greeted them, and a small door within it with a sophisticated security system blinking red.

Except the door was open.

"Is this door always open, Whitby?" he asked.

Whitby seemed to believe hazarding a guess might be perilous, and hesitated before saying, "This used to be the back end of the facilities—they only added a door a year or two ago."

Which made Control wonder what this space had been used for back then. Dance hall? Weddings and bar mitzvahs? Impromptu court-martials?

They both had to stoop to enter, only to be greeted by two space-program-quality air locks, no doubt to protect against contamination. The portal doors had been cantilevered open and from within glowed an intense white light that, for whatever reason, refused to peek out beyond the unsecured security door.

Along the walls, at shoulder height, both rooms were lined with flaccid long black gloves that hung in a way that Control could only think of as dejected. There was a sense that it had been a long time since they had been brought to life by hands and arms. It was a kind of mausoleum, entombing curiosity and due diligence.

"What are those for, Whitby? To creep out guests?"

"Oh, we haven't used those for ages. I don't know why they've left them in here."

It didn't really get much better after that.

003: PROCESSING

Later, back in his office, having left Whitby in his world, Control made one more sweep for bugs. Then he prepared to call the Voice, who required reports at regular intervals. He had been given a separate cell phone for this purpose, just to make his satchel bulkier. The dozen times he'd talked to the Voice at Central prior to coming to the Southern Reach, s/he could have been somewhere nearby. S/he could have been observing him through hidden cameras the whole time. Or been a thousand miles away, a remote operative used just to run one agent.

Control didn't recall much beyond the raw information from those prior times, but talking to the Voice made him nervous. He was sweating through his undershirt as he punched the number, after having first checked the hallway and then locked the door. Neither his mother nor the Voice had told him what might be expected from any report. His mother had said that the Voice could remove him from his position without consulting with her. He doubted that was true but had decided to believe it for now.

The Voice was, as ever, gruff and disguised by a filter. Disguised purely for security or because Control might recognize it? "You'll likely never know the identity of the Voice," his mother had said. "You need to put that question out of your head. Concentrate on what's in front of you. Do what you do best."

But what was that? And how did it translate into the Voice thinking he had done a good job? He already imagined the Voice as a megalodon or other leviathan, situated in a think tank filled with salt water in some black-op basement so secret and labyrinthine that no one now remembered its purpose even as they continued to reenact its rituals. A sink tank, really. Or a stink tank. Control doubted the Voice or his mother would find that worth a chuckle.

The Voice used Control's real name, which confused him at first, as if he had sunk so deeply into "Control" that this other name belonged to someone else. He couldn't stop tapping his left index finger against the blotter on his desk.

"Report," the Voice said.

"In what way?" was Control's immediate and admittedly inane response.

"Words would be nice," the Voice said, sounding like gravel ground under boots.

Control launched into a summary of his experience so far, which started as just a summary of the summary he had received on the state of things at the Southern Reach.

But somewhere in the middle he started to lose the thread or momentum—had he already reported the bugs in his office?—and the Voice interrupted him. "Tell me about the scientists. Tell me about the science division. You met with them today. What's the state of things there?"

Interesting. Did that mean the Voice had another pair of eyes inside the Southern Reach?

So he told the Voice about the visit to the science division, although couching his opinions in diplomatic language. If his mother had been debriefing him, Control would have said the scientists were a mess, even for scientists. The head of the department, Mike Cheney, was a short, burly, fifty-something white guy in a motorcycle jacket, T-shirt, and jeans, who had close-cropped silver hair and a booming, jovial voice. An accent that had originated in the north but at times relaxed into an adopted southern drawl. The lines to the sides of his mouth conspired with plunging eyebrows to make of his face an X, a fate he perpetually fought against by being the kind of person who smiled all the time.

His second-in-command, Deborah Davidson, was also a physicist: A skinny jogger type who had actually smoked her way to weight loss. She creaked along in a short-sleeved red plaid shirt and tight brown corduroy pants cinched with a thick, overlarge leather belt. Most of this hidden by a worn black business jacket whose huge shoulder pads revealed its age. She had a handshake like a cold, dead fish, from which Control could not at first extricate himself.

Control's ability to absorb new names, though, had ended with Davidson. He gave vague nods to the research chemist, as well as the staff epidemiologist, psychologist, and anthropologist who had also been stuffed into the tiny conference room for the meeting. At first Control felt disrespected by that space, but halfway through he realized he'd gotten it wrong. No, they were like a cat confronted by a predator—just trying to make themselves look bigger to him, in this case by scaling down their surroundings.

None of the extras had much to add, although he had the sense they might be more forthcoming one-on-one. Otherwise, it was the Cheney and Davidson show, with a few annotations from the anthropologist. From the way they spoke, if their degrees had been medals, they would all have had them pinned to some kind of quasi-military scientist uniform—like, say, the lab coats they all lacked. But he understood the impulse, understood that this was just part of the ongoing narrative: What once had been a wide territory for the science division had, bit by bit, been taken away from them.

Grace had apparently told them—ordered them?—to give Control the usual spiel, which he took as a form of subterfuge or, at best, a possible waste of time. But they didn't seem to mind this rehash. Instead, they relished it, like overeager magicians in search of an audience. Control could tell that Whitby was embarrassed by the way he made himself small and insignificant in a far corner of the room.

The "piece of resistance," as his father used to joke, was a video of white rabbits disappearing across the invisible border: something they must have shown many times, from their running commentary.

The event had occurred in the mid-1990s, and Control had come across it in the data pertaining to the invisible border between Area X and the world. As if in a reflexive act of frustration at the lack of progress, the scientists had let loose two thousand white rabbits about fifty feet from the border, in a clear-cut area, and herded them right into the border. In addition to the value of observing the rabbits' transition from here to there, the science division had had some hope that the simultaneous or near-simultaneous breaching of the border by so many "living bodies" might "overload" the "mechanism" behind the border, causing it to short-circuit, even if "just locally." This supposed that the border *could* be overloaded, like a power grid.

They had documented the rabbits' transition not only with standard video but also with tiny cameras strapped to some of the rabbits' heads. The resulting montage that had been edited together used split screen for maximum dramatic effect, along with slow motion and fast-forward in ways that conveyed an oddly flippant quality when taken in aggregate. As if even the video editor had wanted to make light of the event, to somehow, through an embedded irreverence, find a way to unsee it. In all, Control knew, the video and digital library contained more than forty thousand video segments of rabbits vanishing. Jumping. Squirming atop one another as they formed sloppy rabbit pyramids in their efforts not to be pushed into the border.

The main video sequence, whether shown at regular speed or in slow motion, had a matter-of-fact and abrupt quality to it. The rabbits were zigging and zagging ahead of humans in baggy contamination suits, who had corralled them in a semicircle. The humans looked weirdly like anonymous white-clad riot police, holding long white shields linked together to form a wall to hem in and herd the rabbits. A neon red line across the ground delineated the fifteen-foot transition zone between the world and Area X.

A few rabbits fled around the lip of the semicircle or in crazed jumps found trajectories that brought them over the riot wall as they were pushed forward. But most could not escape. Most hurtled forward and, either running or in mid-jump, disappeared as they hit the edge of the border. There was no ripple, no explosion of blood and organs. They just disappeared. Close-up slow motion revealed a microsecond of transition in which a half or quarter of a rabbit might appear on the screen, but only a captured frame could really chart the moment between *there* and not-there. In one still, this translated into staring at the hindquarters of about four dozen jostling rabbits, most in mid-leap, disembodied from their heads and torsos.

The video the scientists showed him had no sound, just

a voice-over, but Control knew from the records that an awful screaming had risen from the herded rabbits once the first few had been driven across the border. A kind of keening and a mass panic. If the video had continued, Control would have seen the last of the rabbits rebel so utterly against being herded that they turned on the herders and fought, leaping to bite and scratch . . . would have seen the white of the shields stained red, the researchers so surprised that they mostly broke ranks and a good two hundred rabbits went missing.

The cameras were perhaps even less revealing. As if the abandoned rushes from an intense movie battle scene, they simply showed the haunches and the underside of the hind paws of desperately running rabbits and some herky-jerky landscape before everything went dark. There were no video reports from rabbits that had crossed over the border, although the escapees muddied the issue, the swamps on either side looking very similar. The Southern Reach had spent a good amount of time in the aftermath tracking down escapees to rule out that they were receiving footage from across the border.

Nor had the next expedition to Area X, sent in a week after the rabbit experiment, found any evidence of white rabbits, dead or alive. Nor had any similar experiments, on a far smaller scale, produced any results whatsoever. Nor had Control missed a finicky note in one file by an ecologist about the event that read, "What the hell? This is an invasive species. They would have *contaminated* Area X." Would they have? Would whatever had created Area X have allowed that? Control tried to push away a ridiculous image of Area X, years later, sending back a human-size rabbit that could not remember anything but its function. Most of the magicians were all snickering at inappropriate places anyway, as if showing him how they'd done their most notorious trick. But he'd heard nervous laughter before; he was sure that, even at such a remove, the video disturbed many of them.

Some of the individuals responsible had been fired and others reassigned. But apparently adding the passage of time to a farce left you with an iconic image, because here was the noble remnant of the science division, showing him with marked enthusiasm what had been deemed an utter failure. They had more to show him—data and samples from Area X under glass—but it all amounted to nothing more than what was already in the files, information he could check later at his leisure.

In a way, Control didn't mind seeing this video. It was a relief considering what awaited him. The videos from the first expedition, the members of which had died, save one survivor, would have to be reviewed later in the week as primary evidence. But he also couldn't shake the echo of a kind of frat-boy sensibility to the current presentation, the underlying howl of "Look at this shit we sent out into the border! Look at this stunt we pulled!" Pass the cheap beer. Do a shot every time you see a white rabbit.

When Control left, they had all stood there in an awkward line, as if he were about to take a photograph, and shook his hand, one by one. Only after he and Whitby were back on the stairs, past the horrible black gloves, did he realize what was peculiar about that. They had all stood so straight, and their expressions had been so serious. They must have thought he was there to cull yet more from their department. That he was there to judge them. Later still, scooping up some of the bugs from his desk on his way to carry out a bad deed before calling the Voice, he wondered if instead they were afraid of something else entirely.

Most of this Control told the Voice with a mounting sense of futility. Not a lot of it made much sense or would be news; he was just pushing words around to have something to say. He didn't tell the Voice that some of the scientists had used the words *environmental boon* to describe Area X, with a disturbing and demoralizing subtext of "Should we be fighting this?" It was "pristine wilderness," after all, human-made toxins now absent.

"GODDAMMIT!" the Voice screamed near the end of Control's science report, interrupting the Voice's own persistent mutter in the background . . . and Control held the cell phone away from his ear for a moment, unsure of what had set that off, until he heard, "Sorry. I spilled coffee on myself. Continue." Coffee somewhat spoiled the image of the megalodon in Control's head, and it took him a moment to pick up the thread.

When he was done, the Voice just dove forward, as if they were starting over: "What is your mental state at this moment? Is your house in order? What do you think it will take?"

Which question to answer? "Optimistic? But until they have more direction, structure, and resources, I won't know."

"What is your impression of the prior director?"

A hoarder. An eccentric. An enigma. "It's a complicated situation here and only my first full da—"

"WHAT IS YOUR IMPRESSION OF THE PRIOR

DIRECTOR?" A howl of a shout, as if the gravel had been lifted up into a storm raining down.

Control felt his heart rate increase. He'd had bosses before who had anger-management issues, and the fact that this one was on the other end of a cell phone didn't make it any better.

It all spilled out, his nascent opinions. "She had lost all perspective. She had lost the thread. Her methods were eccentric toward the end, and it will take a while to unravel—"

"ENOUGH!"

"But, I—"

"Don't disparage the dead." This time a pebbled whisper. Even with the filter, a sense of mourning came through, or perhaps Control was just projecting.

"Yes, sorry, it's just that—"

"Next time," the Voice said, "I expect you to have something more interesting to tell me. Something I don't know. Ask the assistant director about the biologist. For example. The director's plan for the biologist."

"Yes, that makes sense," Control agreed, but really just hoping to get off the line soon. Then a thought occurred. "Oh—speaking of the assistant director . . ." He outlined the issue that morning with sending the anthropologist and surveyor away, the problem of Grace seeming to have contacts at Central that could cause trouble.

The Voice said, "I'll look into it. I'll handle it," and then launched into something that sounded prerecorded because it was faintly repetitious: "And remember, I am always watching. So really *think* about what it might be that I don't know."

Click.

———

One thing the scientists told him had been useful and unexpected, but he hadn't told the Voice because it seemed to qualify as Common Secret Knowledge.

In trying to redirect away from the failed white rabbits experiment, Control had asked for their current theories about the border, no matter how outrageous.

Cheney had coughed once or twice, looked around, and then spoken up. "I wish I could be more definite about this, but, you know, we argue about it a lot, because there are so many unknowns . . . but, well, I personally don't believe that the border necessarily comes from the same source as whatever is transforming Area X."

"What?"

Cheney grimaced. "A common response, I don't blame you. But what I mean is—there's no evidence that the . . . presence . . . in Area X also generated the border."

"I understood that, but . . ."

Davidson had spoken up then: "We haven't been able to test the border in the same way as the samples taken from inside Area X. But we have been able to take readings, and without boring you with the data, the border is different enough in composition to support that theory. It may be that one Event occurred to create Area X and then a second Event occurred to create the invisible border, but that—"

"They aren't related?" Control interrupted, incredulous.

Cheney shook his head. "Well, only in that Event Two is almost certainly a reaction to Event One. But maybe someone else"—Control noted, once again, the reluctance to say "alien" or "some*thing*"—"created the border."

"Which means," Control said, "that it's possible this second entity was trying to contain the fallout from Event One?"

"Exactly," Cheney said.

Control again suppressed a strong impulse to just get up and leave, to walk out through the front doors and never come back.

"And," he said, drawing out the word, working through it, "what about the way into Area X, through the border? How did you create that?"

Cheney frowned, gave his colleagues a helpless glance, then retreated into the X of his own face when none of them stepped into the breach. "We didn't create that. We found it. One day, it was just . . . there."

An anger rose in Control then. In part because Grace's initial briefing had been too vague, or he'd made too many assumptions. But mostly because the Southern Reach had sent expedition after expedition in through a door they hadn't created, into God knew what—hoping that everything would be all right, that they would come home, that those white rabbits hadn't just evaporated into their constituent atoms, possibly returned to their most primeval state in agonizing pain.

"Entity One or Entity Two?" he asked Cheney, wishing there were some way the biologist could have sat in on this conversation, already thinking of new questions for her.

"What?"

"Which Event creator opened a door in the border, do you think?"

Cheney shrugged. "Well, that's impossible to say, I'm afraid. Because we don't know if its main purpose was to let something in or to allow something out."

Or both. Or Cheney didn't know what he was talking about.

AUTHORITY

Control caught up with the assistant director while navigating his way through one of the many corridors he hadn't quite connected one to the other. He was trying to find HR to file paperwork but still couldn't see the map of the building entire in his head and remained a little off-balance from the phone call with the Voice.

The scraps of overheard conversation in the hallways didn't help, pointing as they did to evidence for which he as yet had no context. "How deep do you think it goes down?" "No, I don't recognize it. But I'm not an expert." "Believe me or don't believe me." Grace didn't help, either. As soon as he came up beside her, she began to crowd him, perhaps to make the point that she was as strong and tall as him. She smelled of some synthetic lavender perfume that made him stifle a sneeze.

After fielding an inquiry about the visit with the scientists, Control turned and bore down on her before she could veer off. "Why didn't you want the biologist on the twelfth expedition?"

She stopped, put some space between them to look askance at him. Good—at least she was willing to engage.

"What was on your mind back then? Why didn't you want the biologist on that expedition?"

Personnel were passing by them on either side. Grace lowered her voice, said, "She did not have the right qualifications. She had been fired from half a dozen jobs. She had some raw talent, some kind of spark, yes, but she was not qualified. Her husband's position on the prior expedition— that compromised her, too."

"The director didn't agree."

"How is Whitby working out, anyway?" she asked by way of reply, and he knew his expression had confirmed his source. Forgive me, Whitby, for giving you up. Yet this also told him Grace was concerned about Whitby talking to him. Did that mean Whitby was Cheney's creature?

He pressed forward: "But the director didn't agree."

"No," she admitted. Control wondered what kind of betrayal that had been. "She did not. She thought these were all *pluses*, that we were too concerned about the usual measurements of suitability. So we deferred to her."

"Even though she had the bodies of the prior expedition disinterred and reexamined?"

"Where did you hear that?" she asked, genuinely surprised.

"Wouldn't that speak to the director's own suitability?"

But Grace's surprise had already ossified back into resistance, which meant she was on the move again as she said curtly, "No. No, it would not."

"She suspected something, didn't she?" Control asked, catching up to her again. Central thought the files suggested that even if the unique mind-wiped condition of the prior expedition didn't signal a kind of shift in the situation in Area X, it might have signaled a shift in the director.

Grace sighed, as if tired of trying to shake him. "She suspected that they might have . . . changed since the autopsies. But if you're asking, you know already."

"And had they? Had they changed?" Disappeared. Been resurrected. Flown off into the sky.

"No. They had decomposed a little more rapidly than might be expected, but no, they hadn't changed."

Control wondered how much that had cost the director

in respect and in favors. He wondered if by the time the director had told them she was attaching herself to the twelfth expedition some of the staff might have felt not alarm or concern but a strange sort of guilty relief.

He had another question, but Grace was done, had already pivoted to veer off down a different corridor in the maze.

There followed some futile, halfhearted efforts to rearrange his office, along with a review of some basic reports Grace had thrown at him, probably to slow his progress. He learned that the Southern Reach had its own props design department, tasked with creating equipment for the expeditions that didn't violate protocols. In other words, fabrication of antiquated technology. He learned that the security on the facilities that housed returning expedition members was undergoing an upgrade; the outdated brand of surveillance camera they'd been using had suffered a systemic meltdown. He'd even thrown out a DVD given to him by a "life-cycle biologist" that showed a computer-generated cross section of the forgotten coast's ecosystem. The images had been created as a series of topographical lines in a rainbow of colors. It was very pretty but the wrong level of detail for him.

At day's end, on his way out, he ran into Whitby again, in the cafeteria around which the man seemed to hover, almost as if he didn't want to be down in the dungeon with the rest of the scientists. Or as if they sent him on perpetual errands to keep him away. A little dark bird had become trapped inside, and Whitby was staring up at where it flew among the skylights.

Control asked Whitby the question he'd wanted to ask Grace before her maze-pivot.

"Whitby, why are there so few returning journals from the expeditions?" Far, far fewer than returnees.

Whitby was still mesmerized by the flight of the bird, his head turning the way a cat's does to follow every movement. There was an intensity to his gaze that Control found disconcerting.

"Incomplete data," Whitby said. "Too incomplete to be sure. But most returnees tell us they just don't think to bring them back. They don't believe it's important, or don't feel the need to. Feeling is the important part. You lose the need or impetus to divulge, to communicate, a bit like astronauts lose muscle mass. Most of the journals seem to turn up in the lighthouse anyway, though. It hasn't been a priority for a while, but when we did ask later expeditions to retrieve them, usually they didn't even try. You lose the impetus or something else intercedes, becomes more crucial and you don't even realize it. Until it's too late."

Which gave Control an uncomfortable image of someone or something in Area X entering the lighthouse and sitting atop a pile of journals and reading them *for* the Southern Reach. Or writing them.

"I can show you something interesting in one of the rooms near the science division that pertains to this," Whitby said in a dreamy tone, still following the path of the bird. "Would you like to see it?" His disconnected gaze clicked into hard focus and settled on Control, who had a sudden jarring impression of there being two Whitbys, one lurking inside the other. Or even three, nestled inside one another.

"Why don't you just tell me about it?"

"No. I have to show you. It's a little strange. You have to see it to understand it." Whitby now gave the impression of not caring if Control saw the odd room, and yet caring entirely too much at the same time.

Control laughed. Various people had been showing him bat-shit crazy things since his days working in domestic terrorism. People had said bat-shit crazy things to him today.

"Tomorrow," he said. "I'll see it tomorrow." Or not. No surprises. No satisfaction for the keepers of strange secrets. No strangeness before its time. He had truly had enough for one day, would gird his loins overnight for a return encounter. The thing about people who wanted to show you things was that sometimes their interest in granting you knowledge was laced with a little voyeuristic sadism. They were waiting for the Look or the Reaction, and they didn't care what it was so long as it inflicted some kind of discomfort. He wondered if Grace had put Whitby up to this after their conversation, whether it was some odd practical joke and he'd been meant to stick his hand into a space only to find his hand covered in earthworms, or open a box only for a plastic snake to spring out.

The bird now swooped down in an erratic way, hard to make out in the late-afternoon light.

"You should see it now," Whitby said, in a kind of wistfully hurt tone. "Better late than never."

But Control had already turned his back on Whitby and was headed for the entrance and then the (blessed) parking lot.

Late? Just how late did Whitby think he was?

004: REENTRY

The car offered a little breathing room, a chance to decompress and transform from one thing to another. The town of Hedley was a forty-minute drive from the Southern Reach. It lay against the banks of a river that, just twenty miles later, fed into the ocean. Hedley was large enough to have some character and culture without being a tourist trap. People moved there even though it fell just short of being "a good town to raise a family in." Between the sputtering shops huddled at one end of the short river walk and the canopy roads, there were hints of a certain quality of life obscured in part by the strip malls that radiated outward from the edges of the city. It had a small private college, with a performing arts center. You could jog along the river or hike greenways. Still, though, Hedley also partook of a certain languor that, especially in the summers, could turn from charming to tepid overnight. A stillness when the breeze off the river died signaled a shift in mood, and some of the bars just off the waterfront had long been notorious for sudden, senseless violence—places you didn't go unless you could pass for white, or maybe not even then. A town that seemed trapped in time, not much different from when Control had been a teenager.

Hedley's location worked for Control. He wanted to be close to the sea but not on the coast. Something about the uncertainty of Area X had created an insistence inside of him on that point. His dream in a way forbid it. His dream told him he needed to be at a remove. On the plane down to his new assignment, he'd had strange thoughts about the inhabitants of those coastal towns to either side of Area X being somehow mutated under the skin. Whole communities no longer what they once were, even though no one could tell this by looking. These were the kinds of thoughts you had to both keep at bay and fuel, if you could manage that trick. You couldn't become devoured by them, but you had to heed them. Because in Control's experience they reflected something from the subconscious, some instinct you didn't want to go against. The fact was, the Southern Reach knew so little about Area X, even after three decades, that an irrational precaution might not be unreasonable.

And Hedley was familiar to him. This was the city to which he and his friends had come for fun on weekends once some of them could drive, even knowing it was kind of a shithole, too, just not as small a shithole as where they lived. Landlocked and forlorn. His mother had even alluded to it the last time he'd seen her. She'd flown in at his old job up north, which had been gradually reduced from analysis and management to a more reactive and administrative role. Due to his own baggage, he guessed. Due to the fact it always started out well, but then, if he stayed too long . . . sometimes something happened, something he couldn't quite define. He became too invested. He became too empathic, or less so. It confused him when it all went to shit because he couldn't remember the point at which it had started to go bad—was still convinced he could get the formula right.

But his mother had come from Central and they'd met in a conference room he knew was probably bugged. Had the Voice traveled with her, been set up in a saltwater tank in the adjoining room?

It was cold outside and she wore a coat, an overcoat, and a scarf over a professional business suit and black high heels. She took off the overcoat and held it in her lap. But she didn't take off the scarf. She looked as if she could surge from her chair at any moment and be out the door before he could snap his fingers. It had been five years since he'd seen her—predictably unreachable when he'd tried to get a message to her about her ex-husband's funeral—but she had aged only a little bit, her brown hair just as fashion-model huge as ever and eyes a kind of calculating blue peering out from a face on which wrinkles had encroached only around the corners of the eyes and, hidden by the hair, across her forehead.

She said, "It will be like coming home, John, won't it?" Nudging him, wanting him to say it, as if he were a barnacle clinging to a rock and she were a seagull trying to convince him to release his grip. "You'll be comfortable with the setting. You'll be comfortable with the people."

He'd had to suppress anger mixed with ambivalence. How would she know whether she was right or wrong? She'd rarely been there, even though she'd had visitation rights. Just him and his father, Dad beginning to fall apart by then, to eat too much, to drink a little too much, during a succession of flings once the divorce was final . . . then redirecting himself to art no one wanted. Getting his house in order and going off to college had been a guilty relief, to not live in that atmosphere anymore.

"And, comfortably situated in this world I know so well, what would I do?"

She smiled at him. A genuine smile. He could tell the difference, having suffered so many times under the dull yellow glow of a fake one that tried to reheat his love for her.

When she really smiled, when she meant it, his mother's face took on a kind of beauty that surprised anyone who saw it, as if she'd been hiding her true self behind a mask. While people who were always sincere rarely got credit for that quality.

"It's a chance to do better," she said. "It's a chance to erase the past."

The past. Which part of the past? The job up north had been his tenth posting in about fifteen years, which made the Southern Reach his eleventh. There were a number of reasons, there were always reasons. Or one reason, in his case.

"What would I have to do?" If he had to pull it out of her, he knew it might not be something he wanted. But he was already tired of the repetitive nature of his current position, which had turned out to be less about fixing and more about repainting facades. He was tired of the office politics, too. Maybe that had always been his problem, at heart.

"You've heard of the Southern Reach?"

He had, mostly through a couple of colleagues who had worked there at one time. Vague allusions, keeping to the cover story about environmental catastrophe. Rumors of a chain of command that was eccentric at best. Rumors of significant variation, of there being more to the story. But, then, there always was. He didn't know, on hearing his mother say those words, whether he was excited or not.

"And why me?"

The smile that prefaced her response was tinged with a bit of sadness or regret or something else that made Control look away. When she'd been on assignment, before she'd left for good, she'd had a short period when she'd been good at writing long, handwritten letters to him—almost as good as he had been at not finding the time or need to read them. But now he almost wished she was writing to him about the Southern Reach in a letter, not telling him about it in person.

"Because they're downsizing this department, although you might not know that, and you'll be on the chopping block. And this is the right fit for you."

That lurch in the pit of his stomach. Another change. Another city. Never any chance to catch his balance. The truth was that after Control had joined up, he had rarely felt like a flash of light. He had often felt heavy, and realized his mother probably felt heavy, too. That she had been feigning a kind of aloofness and lightness, hiding from him the weight of information, of history and context. All of the things that wore you down, even as that was balanced by the electric feeling of being on the side of a border where you knew things no one else knew.

"Is it the only option?" Of course it was, since she hadn't mentioned any other options. Of course it was, since she hadn't traveled all this way just to say hello. He knew that he was the black sheep, that his lack of advancement reflected poorly on her. Had no idea what internecine battles she fought at the higher levels of clandestine departments so far removed from his security clearance that they might as well exist in the clouds, among the angels.

"It might not be fair, John, I know that. But this might be your last chance," she said, and now she wasn't smiling. Not smiling at all. "At least, it's the last chance I can get for you."

For a permanent posting, an end to his nomadic lifestyle, or in general? For keeping a foothold in the agency?

He didn't dare ask—the cold roiling fear she'd put into him was too deep. He hadn't known he needed a last chance. The fear ran so deep that it pushed most other questions out of his head. He hadn't had a moment then to wonder if, perhaps, she wasn't just there to do her son a favor. That perhaps she *needed* him to say yes.

The teasing hook, to balance his fear, delivered light-heartedly and at the perfect moment: "Don't you want to know more than I know? You will if you take this position."

And nothing he could do about his response. It was true. He did.

She hugged him when he said yes to the Southern Reach, which surprised him. "The closer you are, the safer you are," she whispered in his ear. Closer to what?

She smelled vaguely of an expensive perfume, the scent a bit like the plum trees in the backyard of the house they'd all shared up north. The little orchard he'd forgotten about until just this moment. The swing set. The neighbor's mala-mute that always halfheartedly chased him up the sidewalk.

By the time the questions arose within him, it was too late. She had put on the overcoat and was gone as if she'd never been there.

Certainly there was no record of her ever signing in or signing out.

Dusk, the start of the nightly reprieve from the heat, had settled over Hedley by the time he pulled into the driveway. The place he'd rented sat about a mile up a gentle slope of the hills that eventually ended below at the banks of the river. A small, 1,300-square-foot cedar house painted light blue, with the white shutters on the windows slightly heat-warped. It had two bathrooms, a master bedroom, a living room, a galley kitchen, and an office, with a screened-in patio in back. The interior decoration was all in a cloying yet comfortable "heirloom chic." In front, a garden of herbs and petunias that transitioned to a short stretch of lawn next to the driveway.

As he walked up the steps to the front door, El Chorizo jumped out from the bushes to the side and got underfoot. El Chorizo was a huge black-and-white cat, a draft horse of a cat, named by his father. The family had had a pig named El Gato growing up, so this was his father's way of making a joke. Control had taken him as a pet about three years ago, when the cancer had gotten bad enough that El Chorizo had become a burden. He'd always been an indoor-outdoor cat, and Control had decided to let him be that in his new surroundings, too. Apparently it had been the right decision; El Chorizo, or "Chorry" as Control called him, looked alert and confident, even if his long hair was already tangled and dirty.

Together they went inside, and Control put out some wet food in the kitchen, petted him for a few minutes, then listened to his messages, the landline just for "civilians." There was only one message: from Mary Phillips, his girlfriend until they'd broken up about six months ago, checking in to make sure the move had gone okay. She had threatened to come visit, although he hadn't told her his precise location and had just gotten used to sleeping alone again. "No hard feelings," and he couldn't even really remember if he had broken up with her or she with him. There rarely were hard feelings—which felt odd to him and wrong. Shouldn't there be? There had been almost as many girlfriends as postings; they usually didn't survive the moves, or his circumspection, or his odd hours, or maybe he just hadn't found the right person. He couldn't be sure, tried as the cycle kept repeating to wring as much intensity and intimacy out of the early months, having a sense of how it would end. "You're a strange kind of player," the one-night stand before Mary had said to him as he was going down on her, but he wasn't really a player. He didn't know what he was.

Instead of returning the call, he slipped into the living room and sat on the couch. Chorry promptly curled up next to him, and he absentmindedly rubbed the cat's head. A wren or some such rooted around outside the window. There came, too, the call of a mockingbird and a welcome chitter of bats, which weren't as common anymore.

It was so close to everything he knew from his teenage years that he decided to let that be a comfort, along with the house, which helped him believe that this job was going to last. But "always have an exit strategy" was something his mother had repeated ad nauseam from his first day of training, so he had the standard packet hidden in a false bottom to a suitcase. He'd brought more than just his standard sidearm, one of the guns stored with the passports and money.

Control had already unpacked, the idea of leaving his things in storage painful. On the mantel over a brick fireplace that was mostly for show, he had placed a chessboard with the little brightly colored wooden figurines that had been his father's last redoubt. His father had sold them in local crafts shops and worked in a community center after his career had stalled. Occasionally during the last decade of his father's life, an art collector would buy one of the huge art installations rusting under tarps in the backyard, but that was more like receiving a ghost, a time traveler, than anything like a revival of interest. The chessboard, frozen in time, reflected the progress of their last game together.

He pulled himself off the couch, went into the bedroom, and changed into his shorts and T-shirt and running shoes. Chorry looked up at him as if he wanted to come along.

"I know, I know. I just got home. But I'll be back."

He slipped out the front door, deciding to leave Chorry inside, put on his headphones, turned on some of the classical music he loved, and lit out along the street and its dim streetlamps. By now full dusk had arrived and there was just a haze of dark blue remaining over the river below and the lights of homes and businesses, while above the reflected glow of the city pushed the first stars farther into the heavens. The heat had dropped away, but the insistent low chiseling noise of crickets and other insects brought back its specter.

Something immediately felt tight in his left quad, but he knew it would work itself out. He started slowly, letting himself take in the neighborhood, which was mostly small houses like his, with rows of high bushes instead of fences and streets that ran parallel to the ridge of the hill, with some connector streets running straight down. He didn't mind the winding nature of it—he wanted a good three to five miles. The thick smell of honeysuckle came at him in waves as he ran by certain homes. Few people were still out except for some swing-sitters and dog-walkers, a couple of skateboarders. Most nodded at him as he passed.

As he sped up and established a rhythm, headed ever downward toward the river, Control found himself in a space where he could think about the day. He kept reliving the meetings and in particular the questioning of the biologist. He kept circling back to all of the information that had flooded into him, that he had let keep flooding into him. There would be more of it tomorrow, and the day after that, and no doubt new information would keep entering him for a while before any conclusions came back out.

He could try to not get involved at this level. He could try to exist only on some abstract level of management and administration, but he didn't believe that's really what the Voice wanted him to do—or what the assistant director would *let* him do. How could he be the director of the Southern Reach if he didn't understand in his gut what the personnel there faced? He had already scheduled at least three more interviews with the biologist for the week, as well as a tour of the entry point into Area X at the border. He knew his mother would expect him to prioritize based on the situation on the ground.

The border in particular stuck with him as he jogged. The absurdity of it coexisting in the same world as the town he was running through, the music he was listening to. The crescendo of strings and wind instruments.

The border was invisible.

It did not allow half measures: Once you touched it, it pulled you in (or across?).

It had discrete boundaries, including to about one mile out to sea. The military had put up floating berms and patrolled the area ceaselessly.

He wondered, as he jumped over a low wall overgrown with kudzu and took a shortcut between streets across a crumbling stone bridge. He wondered for a moment about those ceaseless patrols, if they ever saw anything out there in the waves, or if their lives were just an excruciation of the same gray-blue details day after day.

The border extended about seventy miles inland from the lighthouse and approximately forty miles east and forty miles west along the coast. It ended just below the stratosphere and, underground, just above the asthenosphere.

It had a door or passageway through it into Area X.

The door might not have been created by whatever had created Area X.

He passed a corner grocery store, a pharmacy, a neighborhood bar. He crossed the street and narrowly missed running into a woman on a bicycle. Abandoned the sidewalk for the side of the road when he had to, wanting now to get to the river soon, not looking forward to the run back up the hill.

You could not get under the border by any means on the seaward side. You could not tunnel under it on the landward side. You could not penetrate it with advanced instrumentation or radar or sonar. From satellites peering down from above, you would see only wilderness in apparent real time, nothing out of the ordinary. Even though this was an optical lie.

The night the border had come down, it had taken ships and planes and trucks with it, anything that happened to be on or approaching that imaginary but too-real line at the moment of its creation, and for many hours after, before anyone knew what was going on, knew enough to keep distant. Before the army moved in. The plaintive groan of metal and the vibration of engines that continued running as they disappeared . . . into something, somewhere. A smoldering, apocalyptic vision, the con towers of a destroyer, sent to investigate with the wrong intel, "sliding into nothing" as one observer put it. The last shocked transmissions from the men and women on board, via video and radio, while most ran to the back in a churning, surging wave that, on the grainy helicopter video, looked like some enormous creature leaping off into the water. Because they were about to disappear and could do nothing about it, all of it complicated by the fog. Some, though, just stood there, watching as their ship disintegrated, and then they crossed over or died or went somewhere else or . . . Control couldn't fathom it.

The hill leveled out and he was back on sidewalks, this time passing generic strip malls and chain stores and people crossing at stoplights and people getting into cars in parking lots . . . until he reached the main drag before the river—a blur of bright lights and more pedestrians, some of them drunk—crossed it, and came into a quiet neighborhood of mobile homes and tiny cinder-block houses. He was sweating a lot by now, despite the coolness. Someone was having a barbecue and they all stopped to watch him as he ran by.

His thoughts turned again to the biologist. To the need to know what the biologist had seen and experienced in Area X. Aware of the fact the assistant director might do more than threaten to take her away. Aware that the assistant director wanted to use that uncertainty to get him to make unsound decisions.

A one-way road fringed with weeds and strewn with gravel from potholes led him down to the river. He emerged from a halo of branches onto a rickety pontoon dock, bent his knees to keep his balance. Finally came to a stop there, at the end of the dock, next to a speedboat lashed to it. Few lights across the river, just little clusters here and there, nothing compared to the roaring splash of lights to his left, where the river walk waited under the deliberate touristy feature of stupid faux-Victorian lampposts topped with globes full of blurry soft-boiled eggs.

Somewhere across the river and off to the left lay Area X—many miles away but still visible somehow as a weight, a shadow, a glimmering. Expeditions would have been coming back or not coming back while he was still in high school. The psychologist would have been transitioning to director at some point as well. A whole secret history had been playing out while he and his friends drove into Hedley, intent on scoring some beers and finding a party, not necessarily in that order.

He'd had a phone call with his mother the day before he'd boarded the plane, headed for the Southern Reach. They'd talked a little bit about his connection to Hedley. She'd said, "I only knew the area because you were there. But you don't remember that." No, he didn't. Nor had he known that she had worked briefly for the Southern Reach, a fact that both did and didn't surprise him. "I worked there to be closer to you," she said, and something in his heart loosened, even as he wasn't sure whether to believe her.

Because it was so hard to tell. At that time he would have been receiving her time-lapse stories from earlier assignments. He tried to fast-forward, figure out when, if ever, she'd told him a disguised version of the Southern Reach. He couldn't find the point, or his memory just didn't want to give it to him. "What did you do there?" he'd asked, and the only word back had been a wall: "Classified."

He turned off his music, stood there listening to the croaking of frogs, the lap and splash of water against the side of the speedboat as a breeze rippled across the river. The dark was more complete here, and the stars seemed closer. The flow of the river had been faster back in the day, but the runoff from agribusiness had generated silt that slowed it, stilled it, and changed what lived in it and where. Hidden by the darkness of the opposite shore lay paper mills and the ruins of earlier factories, still polluting the groundwater. All of it coursing into seas ever-more acidic.

There came a distant shout across the river, and an even-more distant reply. Something small snuffled and quorked its way through the reeds to his right. A deep breath of fresh air was limned by a faint but sharp marsh smell. It was the kind of place where he and his father would have gone canoeing when he was a teenager. It wasn't true wilderness, was comfortingly close to civilization, but existed just enough apart to create a boundary. This was what most people wanted: to be *close to* but not *part of*. They didn't want the fearful unknown of a "pristine wilderness." They didn't want a soulless artificial life, either.

Now he was John Rodriguez again, "Control" falling away. John Rodriguez, son of a sculptor whose parents had come to this country looking for a better life. Son of a woman who lived in a byzantine realm of secrets.

By the time he started back up the hill, he was thinking about whether he should just pursue an exit strategy now. Load everything in the car and leave, not have to face the assistant director again, or any of it.

It always started well.

It might not end well.

But he knew that when morning came, he would rise as Control and that he would go back to the Southern Reach.

RITES

005: THE FIRST BREACH

What is it? Is it on me? Where is it on me? Is it on me? Where on me? Can you see it on me? Can you see it? Where is it on me?"

Morning, after a night filled with dreams from atop the cliff, staring down. Control stood in the parking lot of a diner with his to-go cup of coffee and his breakfast biscuit, staring from two cars away at a thirtysomething white woman in a purple business suit. Even gyrating to find the velvet ant that had crawled onto her, she looked like a real estate agent, with careful makeup and blond hair in a short pageboy cut. But her suit didn't fit well, and her fingernails were uneven, her red nail polish eroded, and he felt her distress extended well back beyond the ant.

The ant was poised on the back of her neck, unmoving for a moment. If he'd told her, she would have smacked it dead. Sometimes you had to keep things from people just so they wouldn't do the first thing that came into their heads.

"Hold still," he told her as he set his coffee and biscuit atop the trunk of his car. "It's harmless, and I'll get it off you." Because no one else seemed of any use. Most were ignoring her, while some, as they got into or out of their cars and SUVs, were laughing at her. But Control wasn't laughing. He didn't find it amusing. He didn't know where Area X was on him, either, and all the questions in his head seemed in that moment as frenetic and useless as the woman's questions.

"Okay, okay," she said, still upset as he curled around and brought his hand down level with the ant, which, after a bit of gentle prodding, climbed on board. It had been struggling to progress across the field of golden hairs on the woman's neck. Red-banded and soft yet prickly, it roamed across his hand in an aimless fashion.

The woman shook her head, craned her neck as if trying to see behind her, gave him a hesitant smile, and said, "Thanks." Then bolted for her car as if late for an appointment, or afraid of him, the strange man who had touched her neck.

Control took the ant into the fringe of vegetation lining the parking lot and let it crawl from his thumb onto the wood chips there. The ant quickly got its bearings and walked off with purpose toward the green strip of trees that lay between the parking lot and the highway, governed by some sense of where it was and where it needed to be that was beyond Control's understanding.

"So long as you don't tell people you don't know something, they'll probably think you know it." That from his father, not his mother, surprisingly. Or perhaps not. His mother knew so much that maybe she thought she didn't need to pretend.

Was he the woman with no clue where the ant was or the ant, unaware it was on the woman?

Control spent the first fifteen minutes of his morning searching for the key to the locked desk drawer. He wanted to solve that mystery before his appointment with the greater mystery posed by the biologist. His stale breakfast biscuit, cooling cup of coffee, and satchel lay graceless to the side of his computer. He didn't feel particularly hungry anyway; the rancid cleaning smell had invaded his office.

When he found the key, he sat there for a moment, staring at it, and then at the locked drawer and the earthy stain across the bottom left corner. As he turned the key in the lock, he suppressed the ridiculous thought that he should have someone else present, Whitby perhaps, when he opened it.

There was something dead inside—and something living.

A plant grew in the drawer, had been growing there in the dark this whole time, crimson roots attached to a nodule of dirt. As if the director had pulled it out of the ground and then, for whatever reason, placed it in the drawer. Eight slender leaves, a deep almost luminous green, protruded from the ridged stem at irregular intervals to form a pleasing circular pattern when viewed from above. From the side, though, the plant had the look of a creature trying to escape, with a couple of limbs, finally freed, reflexively curled over the edge of the drawer.

At the base, half-embedded in the clump of dirt, lay the desiccated corpse of a small brown mouse. Control couldn't be certain the plant hadn't been feeding on it somehow. Next to the plant lay an old first-generation cell phone in a battered black leather case, and underneath both plant and phone he found stacked sedimentary layers of water-damaged file folders. Almost as if someone had, bizarrely, come in and watered the plant from time to time. With the director gone, who had been doing that? Who had done that rather than remove the plant, the mouse?

Control stared at the mouse corpse for a moment, and then reluctantly reached beside it to rescue the phone— the case looked a little melted—and, with the tip of a pen, teased open the edges of a file or two. These weren't official files, from what he could tell, but instead were full of hand-written notes, scraps of newspaper, and other secondary materials. He caught glimpses of words that alarmed him, let the pages fall back into place.

The effect was oddly as if the director had been creating a compost pile for the plant. One full of eccentric intel. Or some ridiculous science project: "mouse-powered irrigation system for data relay and biosphere maintenance." He'd seen weirder things at high-school science fairs, although his own lack of science acumen meant that when extra credit had been dangled in front of him, he'd stuck to time-honored classics, like miniature volcanoes or growing potatoes from other potatoes.

Perhaps, Control conceded as he rummaged a bit more, the assistant director had been correct. Perhaps he would have been better off taking a different office. Sidling out from behind his desk, he looked for something to put the plant in, found a pot behind a stack of books. Maybe the director had been searching for it, too.

Using a few random pages from the piles stacked

around his desk—if they held the secret to Area X, so be it—
Control carefully removed the mouse from the dirt and tossed
it in the garbage. Then he lifted the plant into the pot and
set it on the edge of his desk, as far away from him as possible.

Now what? He'd de-bugged and de-moused the office.
All that was left beyond the herculean task of cleaning up
the stacks and going through them was the closed second
door that led nowhere.

Fortifying himself with a sip of bitter coffee, Control went
over to the door. It took a few minutes to clear the books and
other detritus from in front of it.

Right. Last mystery about to be revealed. He hesitated
for a moment, irritated by the thought that all of these little
peculiarities would have to be reported to the Voice.

He opened the door.

He stared for several minutes.

After a while, he closed it again.

006: TYPOGRAPHICAL ANOMALIES

Same interrogation room. Same worn chairs. Same un-
certain light. Same Ghost Bird. Or was it? The residue
of an unfamiliar gleam or glint in her eyes or her expression, he couldn't figure out which. Something he hadn't
caught during their first session. She seemed both softer
and harder-edged than before. "If someone seems to have
changed from one session to another, make sure you haven't

changed instead." A warning from his mother, once upon a time, delivered as if she'd upended a box of spy-advice fortune cookies and chosen one at random.

Control casually set the pot on the table to his left, placed her file between them as the ever-present carrot. Was that a slightly raised eyebrow in response to the pot? He couldn't be sure. But she said nothing, even though a normal person might have been curious. On a whim, Control had retrieved the mouse from the trash and placed it in the pot with the plant. In that depressing place it looked like trash.

Control sat. He favored her with a thin smile, but still received no response. He had already decided not to pick up where they had left off, with the drowning, even though that meant he had to fight off his own sudden need to be direct. The words Control had found scrawled on the wall beyond the door kept curling through his head in an unpleasant way. *Where lies the strangling fruit that came from the hand of the sinner I shall bring forth the seeds of the dead* . . . A plant. A dead mouse. Some kind of insane rant. Or some kind of prank or joke. Or continued evidence of a downward spiral, a leap off the cliff into an ocean filled with monsters. Maybe at the end, before she shoehorned herself into the twelfth expedition, the director had been practicing for some perverse form of Scrabble.

Nor could the assistant director be entirely innocent of this devolution. Another reason Control was happy she wouldn't be watching from behind the one-way glass. Stealing a trick he'd learned from a colleague who had done it to him at his last job, Control had given Grace an afternoon time for the session. Then he had walked down to the expedition holding area, spoken to the security guard, and had the biologist brought to the debriefing room.

As he dove in, without preamble this time, Control ignored the water stains on the ceiling that resembled variously an ear and a giant subaqueous eye staring down.

"There's a topographical anomaly in Area X, fairly near base camp. Did you or any members of your expedition find this topographical anomaly? If so, did you go inside?" In actual fact, most of those who encountered it called it a tower or a tunnel or even a pit, but he stuck with "topographical anomaly" in hopes she would give it a more specific name on her own.

"I don't remember."

Her constant use of those words had begun to grate, or perhaps it was the words on the wall that grated, and the consistency of her stance was just pushing that irritation forward.

"Are you sure?" Of course she was sure.

"I think I would remember forgetting that."

When Control met her gaze now, it was always to the slightly upraised corners of her mouth, eyes that had a light in them so different from the last session. For reasons he couldn't fathom, that frustrated him. This was not the same person. Was it?

"This isn't a joke," he said, deciding to see how she would react if he seemed irritated. Except he really was irritated.

"I do not remember. What else can I say?" Each word said as if he were a bit slow and hadn't understood her the first time.

A vision of his couch in his new home, of Chorry curled

up on his lap, of music playing, of a book in hand. A better place than here.

"That you do remember. That you are holding something back." Pushing. Some people wanted to please their questioners. Others didn't care or deliberately wanted to obstruct. The thought had occurred, from the first session and the transcripts of three other sessions before he'd arrived, that the biologist might float back and forth between these extremes, not know her own mind or be severely conflicted. What could he do to convince her? A potted mouse had not moved her. A change of topic hadn't, either.

The biologist said nothing.

"Improbable," he said, as if she had denied it again. "So many other expeditions have encountered this topographical anomaly." A mouthful, topographical anomaly.

"Even so," she said, "I don't remember a tower."

Tower. Not tunnel or pit or cave or hole in the ground.

"Why do you call it a tower?" he asked, pouncing. Too eager, he realized a moment later.

A grin appeared on Ghost Bird's face, and a kind of remote affection. For him? Because of some thought that his words had triggered?

"Did you know," she replied, "that the phorus snail attaches the empty shells of other snails onto its own shell. As a result, the saltwater phorus snail is very clumsy. It staggers and tumbles about because of these empty shells, which offer camouflage, but at a price."

The deep well of secret mirth behind the answer stung him.

———

Perhaps, too, he had wanted her to share his disdain for the term *topographical anomaly*. It had come up during his initial briefing with Grace and other members of the staff. As some "topographical anomaly" expert had droned on about its non-aspects, basically creating an outline for what they didn't know, Control had felt a heat rising. A whole monologue rising with it. Channeling Grandpa Jack, who could work himself into a mighty rage when he wanted to, especially when confronted by the stupidities of the world. His grandpa would have stood and said something like, "Topological anomaly? Topological anomaly? Don't you mean *witchcraft*? Don't you mean the end of civilization? Don't you mean some kind of spooky thing that we know nothing, absolutely fucking nothing about, to go with everything else we don't know?" Just a shadow on a blurred photo, a curling nightmare expressed by the notes of a few unreliable witnesses—made more unreliable through hypnosis, perhaps, no matter Central's protestations. A spiraling thread gone astray that might or might not be made of something else entirely—not even as scrutable in its eccentricity as a house-squatter of a snail that stumbled around like a drunk. No hope of knowing what it was, or even just blasting it to hell because that's what intelligent apes do. Just some thing in the ground, mentioned as casually, as matter-of-factly, as *manhole cover* or *water faucet* or *steak knives. Topographical anomaly.*

But he had said most of this to the bookshelves in his office on Tuesday—to the ghost of the director while at a snail's pace beginning to sort through her notes. To Grace and the rest of them, he had said, in a calm voice, "Is there anything else you can tell me about it?" But they couldn't.

Any more, apparently, than could the biologist.

Control just stared at her for a moment, the interrogator's creepy prerogative, usually meant to intimidate. But Ghost Bird met his stare with those sharp green eyes until he looked away. It continued to nag at him that she was different today. What had changed in the past twenty-four hours? Her routine was the same, and surveillance hadn't revealed anything different about her mental state. They'd offered her a carefully monitored phone call with her parents, but she'd had nothing to say to them. Boredom from being cooped up with nothing but a DVD player and a censored selection of movies and novels could not account for it. The food she ate was from the cafeteria, so Control could commiserate with her there, but this still did not provide a reason.

"Perhaps this will jog your memory." Or stop you lying. He began to read summaries of accounts from prior expeditions.

"An endless pit burrowing into the ground. We could never get to the bottom of it. We could never stop falling."

"A tower that had fallen into the earth that gave off a feeling of intense unease. None of us wanted to go inside, but we did. Some of us. Some of us came back."

"There was no entrance. Just a circle of pulsing stone. Just a sense of great depth."

Only two members of that expedition had returned, but they had brought their colleagues' journals. Which were filled with drawings of a tower, a tunnel, a pit, a cyclone, a series of stairs. Where they were not filled with images of more mundane things. No two journals the same.

Control did not continue for long. He had begun the recitations aware that the selected readings might contaminate the edges of her amnesia . . . if she actually suffered from memory loss . . . and that feeling had quickly intensified. But it was mostly his own sense of unease that made him pause, and then stop. His feeling that in making the tower-pit more real in his imagination, he was also making it more real in fact.

But Ghost Bird either had not or had picked up on his tiny moment of distress, because she said, "Why did you stop?"

He ignored her, switched one tower for another. "What about the lighthouse?"

"What about the lighthouse?" First thought: She's mimicking me. Which brought back a middle school memory of humiliation from bullies before the transformation in high school as he'd put his efforts into football and tried to think of himself as a spy in the world of jocks. Realized that the words on the wall had thrown him off. Not by much, but just enough.

"Do you remember it?"

"I do," she said, surprising him.

Still, he had to pull it out of her: "What do you remember?"

"Approaching it from the trail through the reeds. Looking in the doorway."

"And what did you see?"

"The inside."

It went that way for a while, with Control beginning to lose track of her answers. Moving on to the next thing she said she couldn't remember, letting the conversation fall into a rhythm, one that she might find comfortable. He told himself he was trying to get a sense of her nervous tics, of anything that might give away her real state of mind or her real agenda. It wasn't actually dangerous to stare at her. It wasn't dangerous at all. He was Control, and he was in control.

Where lies the strangling fruit that came from the hand of the sinner I shall bring forth the seeds of the dead to share with the worms that gather in the darkness and surround the world with the power of their lives while from the dim-lit halls of other places forms that never could be writhe for the impatience of the few who have never seen or been seen. In the black water with the sun shining at midnight, those fruit shall come ripe and in the darkness of that which is golden shall split open to reveal the revelation of the fatal softness in the earth. The shadows of the abyss are like the petals of a monstrous flower that shall blossom within the skull and expand the mind beyond what any man can bear . . . And on and on it went, so that Control had the impression that if the director hadn't run out of space, hadn't added a map of Area X, she wouldn't have run out of words, either.

At first he had thought the wall beyond the door was covered in a dark design. But no, someone had obliterated it with a series of odd sentences written with a remarkably thick black pen. Some words had been underlined in red and others boxed in by green. The weight of them had made him take a step back, then just stand there, frowning.

Initial theory, abandoned as ridiculous: The words

were the director's psychotic ode to the plant in her desk drawer. Then he was drawn to the slight similarities between the cadence of the words and some of the more religious anti-government militias he had monitored during his career. Then he thought he detected a faint murmur of the tone of the kinds of sloth-like yet finicky lunatics who stuck newspaper articles and Internet printouts to the walls of their mothers' basements. Creating—glue stick by glue stick and thumbtack by thumbtack—their own single-use universes. But such tracts, such philosophies, rarely seemed as melancholy or as earthy yet ethereal as these sentences.

What had burned brightest within Control as he stared at the wall was not confusion or fear but the irritation he had brought into his session with the biologist. An emotion that manifested as surprise: cold water dumped into an unsuspecting empty glass.

Inconsequential things could lead to failure, one small breach creating another. Then they grew larger, and soon you were in free fall. It could be anything. Forgetting to enter field notes one afternoon. Getting too close to a surveillance subject. Skimming a file you should have read with your full attention.

Control had not been briefed on the words on the director's wall, and he had seen nothing about them in any of the files he had so meticulously read and reread. It was the first indication of a flaw in his process.

When Control thought the biologist was truly comfortable and feeling pleased with herself and perhaps even very clever, he said, "You say your last memory of Area X was of drowning in the lake. What do you remember specifically?"

The biologist was supposed to blanch, gaze turning inward, and give him a sad smile that would make him sad, too, as if she had become disappointed in him for some reason. That somehow he'd been doing so well and now he'd fucked up. Then she would protest, would say, "It wasn't the lake. It was in the ocean," and all of the rest would come spilling out.

But none of that happened. He received no smile of any kind. Instead, she locked everything away from him, and even her gaze withdrew to some far-off height—a lighthouse, perhaps—from which she looked down at him from a safe distance.

"I was confused yesterday," she said. "It wasn't in Area X. It was my memory from when I was five, of almost drowning in a public fountain. I hit my head. I had stitches. I don't know why, but that's what came back to me, in pieces, when you asked that question."

He almost wanted to clap. He almost wanted to stand up, clap, and hand over her file.

She had sat in her room last night, bored out of her mind from lack of stimuli, and she had anticipated this question. Not only had she anticipated it, Ghost Bird had decided to turn it into an egg laid by Control. Give away a less personal detail to protect something more important. The fountain incident was a well-documented part of her file, since she'd had to go to the hospital for stitches. It might confirm for him that she remembered something of her childhood, but nothing more.

It occurred to him that perhaps he wasn't entitled to her memories. Perhaps no one was. But he pushed himself away from that thought, like an astronaut pushing off from the side of a space capsule. Where he'd end up was anyone's guess.

"I don't believe you," he said flatly.

"I don't care," she said, leaning back in her chair. "When do I get out of here?"

"Oh, you know the drill—you've got to take one for the team," he said, using clichés to breeze past her question, trying to sound ignorant or dumb. Not so much a strategy as to punish himself for not bringing his A game. "You signed the agreement; you knew the debriefing might take a while." You knew, too, that you might come back with cancer or not come back at all.

"I don't have a computer," she said. "I don't have any of the books I requested. I'm being kept in a cell that has a tiny window high up on the wall. It only shows the sky. If I'm lucky, I see a hawk wheel by every few hours."

"It's a room, not a cell." It was both.

"I can't leave, so it's a cell. Give me books at least."

But he couldn't give her the books she wanted on memory loss. Not until he knew more about the nature of her memory loss. She had also asked for all kinds of texts about mimicry and camouflage—he'd have to question her about that at some point.

"Does this mean anything to you?" he asked to deflect her attention, pushing the potted plant–mouse across the table to her.

She sat straight in her chair, seemed to become not

just taller but wider, more imposing, as she leaned in toward him.

"A plant and a dead mouse? It's a sign you should give me my fucking books and a computer." Perhaps it wasn't amusement that made her different today. Maybe it was a sense of recklessness.

"I can't."

"Then you know what you can do with your plant and your mouse."

"All right then."

Her contemptuous laughter followed him out into the hall. She had a nice laugh, even when she was using it as a weapon against him.

007: SUPERSTITION

Twenty minutes later, Control had contrived to cram Whitby, Grace, and the staff linguist, Jessica Hsyu, into cramped quarters in front of the revealed section of wall with the director's peculiar handwritten words scrawled across it. Control hadn't bothered to move books or much of anything else. He wanted them to have to sit in close, uncomfortable proximity—let us bond in this phone booth, with our knees shoved up against one another's. Little fabric sounds, mouth-breathing, shoe-squeaks, unexpected smells, all would be magnified. He thought of it as a bonding experience. Perhaps.

Only the assistant director had gotten a regular-size

chair. That way she could hold on to the illusion that she was in charge; or, rather, he hoped he could forestall any complaint from her later that he was being petty. He had already ignored Grace's pointed "I am so thankful that this is correct on the schedule," which meant she already knew he'd moved up his interrogation of the biologist. She'd kept him waiting while she joked with someone in the hall, which he took as a micro-retaliation.

They were huddled around the world's smallest conference table/stool, on which Control had placed the pot with the plant and mouse. Everything in its time and place, although the director's cell phone would not be part of the conversation—Grace had already confiscated it.

"What is this," he said, pointing to the wall of words, "in my office?" Not quite willing to concede the unspoken point that continued to radiate from Grace like a force field: It was still the former director's office.

"This" included not just the words but the crude map of Area X drawn beneath the words, in green, red, and black, showing the usual landmarks: lighthouse, topographical anomaly, base camp . . . and also, farther up the coast, the island. A few stray words had been scribbled with a ballpoint pen out to the sides—incomprehensible—and there were two rather daunting slash marks about half a foot above Control's head, with dates about three years apart. One red. One green. With the director's initials beside them, too. Had the director been *checking her height*? Of all of the strange things on the wall, that seemed the strangest.

"I thought you said you had read all the files," Grace replied.

Nothing in the files had mentioned a door's worth of

peculiar text, but he wouldn't argue the point. He knew it was unlikely he had uncovered something unknown to them.

"Humor me."

"The director wrote it," Grace said. "These are words found written on the walls of the tunnel."

Control took a moment to digest that information.

"But why did you leave it there?" For an intense moment the words and the rotting honey smell combined to make him feel physically ill.

"A memorial," Whitby said quickly, as if to provide an excuse for the assistant director. "It seemed too disrespectful to take it down." Control had noticed Whitby kept giving the mouse strange glances.

"Not a memorial," Grace said. "It's not a memorial because the director isn't dead. I don't believe she's dead." She said this in a quiet but assured way, causing a hush from Whitby and Hsyu, as if Grace had shared an opinion that was an embarrassment to her. Control's careful manipulation of the thermostat meant they were sweating and squirming a bit anyway.

"What does it mean?" Control asked, to move past the moment. Beyond Grace's obstructionism, he could see a kind of pain growing in her that he had no wish to exploit.

"That's why we brought the linguist," Whitby said charitably, even though it was clear that Hsyu's presence had surprised the assistant director. But Hsyu had ever more influence as the Southern Reach shrank; soon enough, they might have a situation where subdepartments consisted of one person writing themselves up for offenses, giving themselves raises and bonuses, celebrating their own birthdays with custom-made Southern Reach–shaped carrot cakes.

Hsyu, a short, slender woman with long black hair, spoke.

"First of all, we are ninety-nine point nine percent certain that this text is by the lighthouse keeper, Saul Evans." A slight uprising inflection to her voice imbued even the blandest or most serious statement with optimism.

"Saul Evans . . ."

"He's right up there," Whitby said, pointing to the wall of framed images. "In the middle of that black-and-white photo." The one in front of the lighthouse. So that was Saul. He'd known that already, somewhere in the back of his mind.

"Because you found it printed somewhere else?" Control asked Hsyu. He hadn't had time to do more than glance at the file on Evans—he'd been too busy familiarizing himself with the staff of the Southern Reach and the general outline of the situation in Area X.

"Because it matches his syntax and word choice in a few of his sermons we have on audiotape."

"What was he doing preaching if he was a lighthouse keeper?"

"He was retired as a preacher, actually. He left his ministry up north very suddenly, for no documented reason, then came south and took the lighthouse keeper position. He'd been there for five years when the border came down."

"Do you think he brought whatever caused Area X with him?" Control ventured, but no one followed him into the hinterlands.

"It's been checked out," Whitby said. For the first time a sliver of condescension had entered his tone when addressing Control.

"And these words were found within the topographical anomaly?"

"Yes," Hsyu said. "Reconstructed from the reports of several expeditions, but we've never gotten a useful sample of the material the words are made of."

"Living material," Control said. Now it was coming back to him, a bit. The words hadn't been part of the summary, but he'd seen reports of words written on the tower walls in living tissue. "Why weren't these words in the files?"

The linguist again, this time with some reluctance: "To be honest, we don't like to reproduce the words. So it might have been buried in the information, like in a summary in the lighthouse keeper's file."

Grace had nothing to add, apparently, but Whitby chimed in: "We don't like to reproduce the words because we still don't know exactly what triggered the creation of Area X . . . or why."

And yet they'd left the words up behind the door that led nowhere. Control was struggling to see the logic there.

"That's superstition," Hsyu protested. "That's complete and utter superstition. You shouldn't say that." Control knew her parents were very traditional and came from a culture in which spirits manifested and words had a different significance. Hsyu did not share these beliefs—vehemently did not, practicing a lax sort of Christian faith, which brought with it inexplicable elements and phantasmagoria all its own. But he still agreed with her assessment, even if that antipathy might be leaking into her analysis.

She would have continued with a full-blown excoriation of superstition, except that Grace stopped her.

"It's not superstition," she said.

They all turned to her, swiveling on their stools.

"It is superstition," she admitted. "But it might be true."

How could a superstition be true? Control pondered that later, as he turned his attention to his trip to the border along with a cursory look at a file Whitby had pulled for him titled simply "Theories." Maybe "superstition" was what snuck into the gaps, the cracks, when you worked in a place with falling morale and depleted resources. Maybe superstition was what happened when your director went missing in action and your assistant director was still mourning the loss. Maybe that was when you fell back on spells and rituals, the reptile brain saying to the rest of you, "I'll take it from here. You've had your shot." It wasn't even unreasonable, really. How many invisible, abstract incantations ruled the world beyond the Southern Reach?

But not everyone believed in the same versions. The linguist still believed in the superstition of logic, for example, perhaps because she had only been at the Southern Reach for two years. If the statistics held true, she would burn out within the next eighteen months; for some reason, Area X was very hard on linguists, almost as hard as it was on priests, of which there were none now at the Southern Reach.

So perhaps she was only months removed from converting to the assistant director's belief system, or Whitby's, whatever that might be. Because Control knew that belief in a scientific process only took you so far. The ziggurats of illogic erected by your average domestic terrorist as he or she bought the fertilizer or made a detonator took on their own teetering momentum and power. When those towers crashed to the earth, they still existed whole in the perpetrator's mind, and everyone else's too—just for different reasons.

But Hsyu had been adamant, for reasons that didn't make Control any more comfortable about Area X.

Imagine, she had told Control next, that language is only part of a method of communication. Imagine that it isn't even the important part but more like the pipeline, the highway. A conduit only. *Infrastructure* was the word Control would use with the Voice later.

The real core of the message, the meaning, would be conveyed by the combinations of living matter that composed the words, as if the "ink" itself was the message.

"And if a message is half-physical, if a kind of coding is half-physical, then words on a wall don't mean that much at all, really, in my opinion. I could analyze those words for years—which is, incidentally, what I understand the director may have done—and it wouldn't help me to understand anything. The type of conduit helps decide how fast the message arrives, and perhaps some context, but that's all. Further"—and here Control recognized that Hsyu had slipped into the rote routine of a lecture given many times before, possibly accompanied by a PowerPoint presentation— "if someone or something is trying to jam information inside your head using words you understand but a meaning you don't, it's not even that it's not on a bandwidth you can receive, it's much worse. Like, if the message were a knife and it created its meaning by cutting into meat and your head is the receiver and the tip of that knife is being shoved into your ear over and over again . . ."

She didn't need to say more for Control to think of the expeditions come to grief before they had banned names and modern communication technology. What if the fate of the first expedition in particular had been sealed by a kind of *interference* they had brought with them that had made them simply unable to listen, to perceive?

He returned to the lighthouse keeper. "So we think that Saul Evans wrote all of this long ago, right? He can't possibly be writing anything now, though. He'd be ancient at this point."

"We don't know. We just don't know."

This, unhelpfully, from Whitby, while they all gave him a look like animals caught in the middle of the road late at night with a car coming fast.

008: THE TERROR

An hour or so later, it was time to visit the border, Grace telling him that Cheney would take him on the tour. "He wants to, for some reason." And Grace didn't, clearly. Down the corridor again to those huge double doors, led by Whitby, as if Control had no memory—only to be greeted by a cheerful Cheney, whose brown leather jacket seemed not so much ubiquitous or wedded to him as a part of him: a beetle's carapace. Whitby faded into the background, disappearing through the doors with a conspicuous and sharp intake of breath as if about to dive into a lake.

"I thought I'd come up and spare you the dread gloves," Cheney exclaimed as he shook Control's hand. Control wondered if there was some cunning to his affability, or if that was just paranoia spilling over from his interactions with Grace.

"Why keep them there?" Control asked as Cheney led him via a circuitous "shortcut" past security and out to the parking lot.

"Budget, I'm afraid. Always the answer around here," Cheney said. "Too expensive to remove them. And then it became a joke. Or, we made it into a joke."

"A joke?" He'd had enough of jokes today.

At the entrance, Whitby miraculously awaited them at the wheel of an idling army jeep with the top down. He looked like a silent-movie star, the person meant to take the pratfalls, and his pantomimed unfurling of his hand to indicate they should get on board only intensified the impression. Control gave Whitby an eye roll and Whitby winked at him. Had Whitby been a member of the drama club in college? Was he a thwarted thespian?

"Yes, a joke," Cheney continued, agreeable, as they jumped into the back; Whitby or someone had conspicuously put a huge file box in the front passenger seat so no one could sit there. "As if whatever's strange and needs to be analyzed comes to us from inside the building, not from Area X. Have you *met* those people? We're a bunch of lunatics." A bullfrog-like smile—another joke. "Whitby—take the scenic route."

But Control was hardly listening; he was wrinkling his nose at the unwelcome fact that the rotting honey smell had followed them into the jeep.

For a long time, Whitby spoke not at all and Cheney said things Control already knew, playing tour guide and apparently forgetting he was repeating things from the bunny briefing just the day before. So Control focused most of his attention on his surroundings. The "scenic route" took them the usual way Control had seen on maps: the winding road, the roadblocks, the trenches like remnants from an ancient war. Where possible, the swamp and forest had been retained as natural cover or barriers. But odd bald patches of drained swamp and clear-cut forest appeared at intervals, sometimes with guard stations or barracks placed there but often just turned into meadows of yellowing grass. Control got a prickling on his neck that made him think of snipers and remote watchers. Maybe it helped flush out intruders for the drones. Most army personnel they passed were in camouflage, and it was hard for him to judge their numbers. But he knew everyone they passed outside the last checkpoint thought what lay beyond was an area rendered hazardous due to environmental contamination.

In "cooperation with" the Southern Reach, the army had been tasked with finding new entry points into Area X, and relentlessly—or, perhaps, with growing boredom—monitored the edges for breaches. The army also still tested the border with projectiles from time to time. He knew, too, that nukes were locked in on Area X from the nearest silos, military satellites keeping watch from above.

But the army's primary job was to work hard to keep people out while maintaining the fiction of an ecological disaster area. Annexing the land that comprised Area X, and double again around it, as a natural expansion of a military base farther up the coast had helped in that regard. As did the supposed "live fire ranges" dotting the area. The army's role had arguably become larger as the Southern Reach had been downsized. All medical staff and engineers now re-sided with army command, for example. If a toilet broke down at the Southern Reach, the plumber came over from the military base to fix it.

Whitby whipped the jeep from side to side on a rough stretch of road, bringing Cheney alarmingly close. On further inspection, Cheney displayed the remnants of a body builder's physique, as if he had once been fit, but that this condition, like all human conditions, had receded—and then reconstituted itself in the increased thickness around his waist—but in receding had left behind a still-solid chest, jutting forward through the white shirt, out from the brown jacket, in a triumphant way that almost gave cover to his gut. He was also, according to his file, "a first-rate scientist partial to beer," the kind of mind Control had seen before. It needed dulling to slow it down or to distance itself from the possibility of despair. Beer versus scientist represented a kind of schism between the banality of speech versus the originality of thought. An ongoing battle.

Why would Cheney play the buffoon to Control when he was in fact a mighty brain? Well, maybe he was a buffoon, outside of his chosen field, but then Control wasn't exactly anyone's first invitee to a cocktail party, either.

Once they'd put the distraction of the major checkpoints behind them and entered the stretch of fifteen miles of gravel road—which seemed to take all of Whitby's attention, so he continued to say little—Control asked, "Is this the route that the expedition would take to the border, too?"

The longer they had been traveling, the more the image in his head, of the progress of the expeditions down this very road, each member quiet, alone in the vast expanse of their thoughts, had been interrupted by the stage business of lurching to a stop at so many checkpoints. The destruction of solace.

"Sure," Cheney said. "But in a special bus that doesn't need to stop."

A special bus. No checkpoints. No limousine for the expeditions, not on this road. Were they allowed last-meal requests? Was the night before often a drunken reverie or more of a somber meditation? When was the last time they were allowed to see family or friends? Did they receive religious counsel? The files didn't say; Central descended on the Southern Reach like a many-limbed über-parasite to coordinate that part.

Loaded down or unencumbered? "And already with their backpacks and equipment?" he asked. He was seeing the biologist on that special bus, sans checkpoints, fiddling with her pack, or sitting there silent with it beside her on the seat. Nervous or calm? No matter what her state of mind at that point, Control guessed she would not have been talking to her fellow expedition members.

"No—they'd get all of that at the border facility. But they'd know what was in it before that—it'd be the same as their training packs. Just fewer rocks." Again, the look that meant he was supposed to laugh, but, always considerate, Cheney chuckled for him yet again.

So: Approaching the border. Was Ghost Bird elated, indifferent? It frustrated him that he had a better sense of what she wouldn't be than what she was.

"We used to joke," Cheney said, interrupted by a pothole poorly navigated by Whitby, "we used to joke that we ought to send them in with an abacus and a piece of flint. Maybe a rubber band or two."

In checking Control's reaction to his levity, Cheney must have seen something disapproving or dangerous, because he added, "Gallows humor, you know. Like in an ER." Except he hadn't been the one on the gallows. He'd stayed behind and analyzed what they'd brought back. The ones who did come back. A whole storeroom of largely useless samples bought with blood and careers, because hardly any of the survivors went on to have happy, productive lives. Did Ghost Bird remember Cheney, and if so, what was her impression of him?

The endless ripple of scaly brown tree trunks. The smell of pine needles mixed with a pungent whiff of decay and the exhaust from the jeep. The blue-gray sky above, through the scattered canopy. The back of Whitby's swaying head. Whitby. Invisible and yet all too visible. The cipher who came in and out of focus, seemed both near and far.

"The terror," Whitby had said during the morning meeting, staring at the plant and the mouse. *"The terror."* But oddly, slurring it slightly, and in a tone as if he were imparting information rather than reacting or expressing an emotion.

Terror sparked by what? Why said with such apparent enthusiasm?

But the linguist talked over Whitby and soon pushed so far beyond the moment that Control couldn't go back to it at the time.

"A name conveys a whole series of related associations,"

Hsyu had said, launching some more primordial section of her PowerPoint, created during a different era and perhaps initially pitched to an audience of the frozen megafauna Control remembered so vividly from the natural history museum. "A set of related ideas, facts, etc. And these associations exist not just in the mind of the one named—form their identity—but also in the minds of the other expedition members and thus accessible to whatever else might access them in Area X. Even if by a process unknown to us and purely speculative in nature. Whereas 'biologist'—that's a function, a subset of a full identity." Not if you did it right, like Ghost Bird, and you were totally and wholly your job to begin with. "If you can be your function, then the theory is that these associations narrow or close down, and that closes down the pathways into personality. Perhaps."

Except Control knew that wasn't the only reason to take away names: It was to strip personality away for the starker purpose of instilling loyalty and to make conditioning and hypnosis more effective. Which, in turn, helped mitigate or stave off the effects of Area X—or, at least, that was the rationale Control had seen in the files, as put forward in a note by James Lowry, the only survivor of the first expedition and a man who had stayed on at the Southern Reach despite being damaged and taking years to recover.

Overtaken by some sudden thought she chose not to share, Hsyu then performed her own pivot, like Grace through the hallway maze: "We keep saying 'it'—and by 'it' I mean whatever initiated these processes and perhaps used Saul Evans's words—is like this thing or like that thing. But it isn't—it is only itself. Whatever it is. Because our minds process information almost solely through analogy and categorization, we are often defeated when presented with something that fits no category and lies outside of the realm of our analogies." Control imagined the PowerPoint coming to a close, the series of marbled borders giving way to a white screen with the word *Questions?* on it.

Still, Control understood the point. It echoed, in a different way, things the biologist had said during their session. In college, what had always stuck with him in Astronomy 101 was that the first astronomers to think of points of light not as part of a celestial tapestry revolving around the earth but as individual planets had had to wrench their imaginations—and thus their analogies and metaphors—out of a grooved track that had been running through everyone's minds for hundreds and hundreds of years.

Who at the Southern Reach had the kind of mind needed to see something new? Probably not Cheney at this point. Cheney's roving intellect had uncovered nothing new for quite some time, possibly through no real fault of its own. Yet Control came back to one thought: Cheney's willingness to keep banging his head against a wall—despite the fact that he would never publish any scientific papers about any of this—was, in a perverse way, one of the best reasons to assume the director had been competent.

Gray moss clinging to trees. A hawk circling a clear-cut meadow under skies growing darker. A heat and humidity to the air that was trying to defeat the rush of wind past them.

The Southern Reach called the last expedition the twelfth, but Control had counted the rings, and it was actually the thirty-eighth iteration, including six "eleventh" expeditions. The hagiography was clear: After the true fifth expedition, the Southern Reach had gotten stuck like a jammed CD, with nearly the same repetitions. Expedition 5 became X.5.A, followed by X.5.B and X.5.C, all the way to an X.5.G. Each expedition number thereafter adhered to an particular set of metrics and introduced variables into the equation with each letter. For example, the eleventh expedition series had been composed of all men, while the twelfth, if it continued to X.12.B and beyond, would continue to be composed of all women. He wondered if his mother knew of any parallel in special ops, if secret studies showed something about gender that escaped him in considering the irrelevance of this particular metric. And what about someone who didn't identify as male or female?

Control still couldn't tell from his examination of the records that morning if the iterations had started as a clerical error and become codified as process (unlikely) or been initiated as a conscious decision by the director, sneakily enacted below the radar of any meeting minutes. It had just popped up as if always there. A need to somehow act as if they weren't as far along without concrete results or answers. Or the need to describe a story arc for each set of expeditions that didn't give away how futile it was fast becoming.

During the fifth, too, the Southern Reach had started lying to the participants. No one was ever told they were part of Expedition 7.F or 8.G, or 9.B, and Control wondered how anyone had kept it straight, and how the truth might have eaten away at morale rather than buoyed it, brought into the Southern Reach a kind of cynical fatalism. How peculiar to keep prepping the "fifth" expedition, to keep roll-ing this stone up this hill, over and over.

Grace had just shrugged when asked about the transi-tion from X.11.K to X.12.A during orientation on Monday, which already felt a month away from Wednesday. "The biologist knew about the eleventh expedition because her husband was careless. So we moved on to the twelfth." Was that the only reason?

"A lot of accommodations were made for the biologist," Control observed.

"The director ordered it," Grace said, "and I stood be-hind her." That was the end of that line of inquiry, Grace no longer willing to admit that there might have been any dis-tance between her and the director.

And, as often happened, one big lie had let in a series of little lies, under the guise of "changing the metrics," of alter-ing the experiment. So that as they got diminishing returns, the director fiddled more and more with the composition of the expeditions, and fiddled with what information she told them, and who knew if any of it had helped anything at all? You reached a certain point of desperation, perhaps thought the train was coming faster than others did, and you'd use whatever you found hidden under the seats, whether a weapon or just a bent paper clip.

If you quacked like a scientist and waddled like a scientist, soon, to nonscientists, you became the subject under dis-cussion and not a person at all. Some scientists lived within this role, almost embraced it, transformed into walking theses or textbooks. This couldn't be said about Cheney, though, despite lapses into jargon like "quantum entanglements."

At a certain point on the way to the border, Control began to collect Cheneyisms. Much of it came to Control unsolicited because he found that Cheney, once he got warmed up, hated silence, and threw into that silence a strange combination of erudite and sloppy syntax. All Control had to do, with Whitby as his innocent accomplice, was not respond to a joke or comment and Cheney would fill up the space with his own words. Jesus, it was a long drive.

"Yeah, there's a lot of enabling of each other's dip-shittery. It's almost all we've got."

"We don't even understand how every organism on our planet works. Haven't even identified them all yet. What if we just don't have the language for it?"

"Are we obsolete? I think not, I think not. But don't ask the army's opinion of that. A circle looks at a square and sees a badly made circle."

"As a physicist, what do you do when you're faced by something that doesn't care what you do and isn't affected by your actions? Then you start thinking about dark energy and you go a little nuts."

"Yeah, it's something we think about: How do you know if something is out of the ordinary when you don't know if your instruments would register the progressions? Lasers, gravitational-wave detectors, X-rays. Nothing useful there. I got this spade here and a bucket and some rubber bands and duct tape, you know?"

"Hardly any scientists at Central, either. Am I right?"

"I guess it's kind of strange. To practically live next to this. I guess I could say that. But then you go home and you're home."

"Do you know any physics? No of course you don't. How could you?"

"Black holes and waves have a similar structure, you know? Very, very similar as it turns out. Who would've expected that?"

"I mean, you'd expect Area X to cooperate at least a little bit, right? I'd've staked my reputation on it cooperating with us enough to get some accurate readings at least, an abnormal heat signature or something."

Later, a refinement of this statement: "There is some agreement among us now, reduced though we may be, that to analyze certain things, an object must allow itself to be analyzed, must agree to it. Even if this is just simply by way of *some* response, some reaction."

These last two utterances, jostling elbows, Cheney had offered up a bit plaintively because, in fact, he had staked his reputation to Area X—in the general sense that the Southern Reach had become his career. The initial glory of it, of being chosen, and then the constriction of it, like a great snake named Area X was suffocating him, and then also what he had to know in his innermost thoughts, or even coursing across the inner rind of his brain. That the Southern Reach had indeed destroyed his career, perhaps even been the reason for his divorce.

"How do you feel about all of the misinformation given to the expedition?" Control asked Cheney, if only to push back against the flood of Cheneyisms. He knew Cheney had had some influence in shaping that misinformation.

Cheney's frown made it seem as if Control's question were akin to criticizing the paint job on a car that had been involved in a terrible accident. Was Control a killjoy to want to snuff out Cheney's can-do, his can't-help-it brand of the jowly jovial? But jovial grated on Control most of the time. "Jovial" had always been a pretext, from the high school football team's locker room on—the kind of hearty banter that covered up greater and lesser crimes.

"It wasn't—isn't—really misinformation," Cheney said, and then went dark for a moment, searching for words. Possibly he thought it was a test. Of loyalty or attitude or moral rigor. But he found words soon enough: "It's more like creating a story or a narrative to guide them through the narrows. An anchor."

Like a lighthouse that distracted them from topographical anomalies, a lighthouse that seemed by its very function to provide safety. Maybe Cheney told himself that particular story about the tale, or tale about the story, but Control doubted the director had seen it that way, or even a biologist with only partial memory.

"Jesus, this is a long drive," Cheney said into the silence.

009: EVIDENCE

Finally they had addressed the mouse in the room, and the plant, during their meeting about the wall beyond his door.

"What about this mouse, this plant?" Control had

demanded, to see what that shook loose. "Is this a memorial, too?"

Plant and mouse still resided inside the pot, had not yet leapt out and gone for their throats even though Hsyu had kept a keen eye on the pot during the entire meeting. Whitby, though, wouldn't even acknowledge it with a glance, looked like a cat ready to leap off in the opposite direction at the slightest sign of impending pot-activated danger.

"No, not really," Grace conceded after a pause. "She was trying to kill it."

"What?"

"It wouldn't die." She said it with contempt, as if breaking the natural order of things wasn't a miracle but an affront.

The assistant director made Whitby embark upon a summary of hair-raising attempts at destruction that included stabbings, careful burnings, deprivation of soil and water, introduction of parasites, general neglect, the emanation of hateful vibes, verbal and physical abuse, and much more. Whitby reenacted some of these events with overly manic energy.

Clippings had been rushed to Central, and perhaps even now scientists labored to unlock the plant's secrets. But Central had sent no information back, and nothing the director had done could kill it, not even sticking it in a locked drawer. Except, someone had taken pity on the plant and watered it, perhaps even stuck in a dead mouse for nutritional value. Control looked with suspicion upon both Whitby and Grace. The idea that one of them had been merciful only made him like them both a little more.

Hsyu had then piped up: "She took it from the samples

rooms, I believe. It was from Area X originally. A very common plant, although I'm not a botanist."

Then, by all means, lead the way to the samples rooms.

Except that Hsyu, as a linguist, didn't have security clearance.

A few miles from the border the landscape changed, and Whitby had to slow down to about ten miles an hour as the road narrowed and became more treacherous. The dark pines and the patches of swamp gave way to a kind of subtropical rain forest. Control could see the curling question marks of fiddlehead ferns and a surprising density of delicate black-winged mayflies as the jeep passed over several wooden bridges that crossed a welter of creeks. The smell of the land had changed from humid and cloying to something as questing as the ferns: a hint of freshness caused by a thicker canopy of leaves. They were, he realized, making their way along the periphery of a huge sinkhole, the kind of "topographical anomaly" that created an entirely different habitat. Sinkhole parks in the area were, for whatever reason, favorite teen hangouts, and sometimes after leaving Hedley with their ill-gotten six-packs they had headed for rendezvous with girls there. The sinkholes he remembered had been litter grounds of crushed beer cans and a scattering of condom wrappers. The kinds of places the local police kept an eye on because it was a rare weekend someone didn't get into a fight there.

More surprising still, white rabbits could be seen, nimbly negotiating the edges of pools of standing water and brown-leaf-littered moist spaces where the rotting of the earth proceeded apace and red-tipped mushrooms rose primordial.

Which caused Control to interrupt one of Cheney's stutter-step monologues: "Are those what I think they are?"

Cheney, clearly relieved that Control had said something: "Yes, those are the true descendants of the experiment. The ones that got away. They breed . . . well, just like rabbits. There was an eradication effort, but it was taking up too many resources, so we just let it happen now."

Control followed the progress of one white brute, larger than his fellows—or larger than her fellows—who sought the higher ground in limitless leaps and bounds. There was something defiant in its stride. Or Control was projecting that onto the animal, just as he was projecting onto most of the other rabbits a peculiar stillness and watchfulness.

Whitby chimed in unexpectedly: "Rabbits have three eyelids and can't vomit." For a moment Control, startled that Whitby had spoken, assigned more significance to the statement than it deserved.

"You know, it's a good reminder to be humble," Cheney said, like a rumbling steamroller intent on paving over Whitby, "to be humbled. A humbling experience. Something like that."

"What if some of them are returnees?" Control asked.

"What?"

Control thought Cheney had heard, but he repeated the question.

"You mean from across the border—they got across and came back? Well, that would be bad. That would be sloppy.

Because we know that they've spread fairly far. The ones savvy enough to survive. And as happens, some of them have gotten out of the containment zone and been trapped by enterprising souls and sold to pet stores."

"So you're saying that it's possible that some of the progeny of your fifteen-year-old experiment are now residing in people's homes? As pets?" Control was astonished.

"I wouldn't put it quite that way, but that's the gist, I guess," Cheney conceded.

"Remarkable" was Control's only comment, aghast.

"Not really," Cheney replied, pushing back gently but firmly. "Way of the world. Or at least of invasive species everywhere. I can sell you a python from the dread peninsula that's got the same motivations."

Whitby, a few moments later, the most he said in one gulp during the whole trip: "The few white-and-brown ones are the offspring of white rabbits mating with the native marsh rabbits. We call them Border Specials, and the soldiers shoot and eat them. But not the pure white ones, which I don't think makes sense. Why shoot any of them?"

Why not shoot *all* of them? Why *eat* any of them?

Fifty thousand samples languished in the long rooms that formed the second floor of the left-hand side of the U, assuming an approach from the parking lot. They'd gone before lunch, left Hsyu behind. They had to don white biohazard suits with black gloves, so that Control was actually wearing a version of the gloves that had so unsettled him down in the science division. This was his revenge, to plunge his hands into them and make them his puppets, even if he didn't like their rubbery feel.

The atmosphere was like that inside a cathedral, and as if the science division had been some kind of rehearsal for this event, the sequence of air locks was the same. An ethereal, heavenly music should have been playing, and the way the light struck the air meant that in certain pools of illumination Control could see floating dust motes, and certain archways and supporting walls imbued the rooms with a numinous feeling, intensified by the high ceilings. "This is my favorite place in the Southern Reach," Whitby told him, face alight through his transparent helmet. "There's a sense of calm and safety here."

Did he feel unsafe in the other sections of the building? Control almost asked Whitby this question, but felt that doing so would break the mood. He wished he had his neoclassical music on headphones for the full experience, but the notes played on in his mind regardless, like a strange yearning.

He, Whitby, and Grace walked through in their terrestrial space suits like remote gods striding through a divinely chosen terrain. Even though the suits were bulky, the lightweight fabric didn't seem to touch his skin, and he felt buoyant, as if gravity operated differently here. The suit smelled vaguely of sweat and peppermint, but he tried to ignore that.

The rows of samples proliferated and extended, the effect enhanced by the mirrors that lined the dividing wall between each hall. Every kind of plant, pieces of bark, dragonflies, the freeze-dried carcasses of fox and muskrat, the dung of coyotes, a section from an old barrel. Moss, lichen, and fungi. Wheel spokes and the glazed eyes of tree frogs staring blindly up at him. He had expected, somehow, a Frankenstein laboratory of two-headed calves in formaldehyde and some hideous manservant with a hunchback lurching ahead of them and explaining it all in an incomprehensible bouillabaisse of good intentions and slurred syntax. But it was just Whitby, and it was just Grace, and in that cathedral neither felt inclined to explain anything.

Analysis by Southern Reach scientists of the most recent samples, taken six years ago and brought back by expedition X.11.D, showed no trace of human-created toxicity remained in Area X. Not a single trace. No heavy metals. No industrial runoff or agricultural runoff. No plastics. Which was impossible.

Control peeked inside the door the assistant director had just opened for him. "There you are," she said, inanely he thought. But there he was, in the main room, with an even higher ceiling and more columns, looking at endless rows and rows of shelves housed inside of a long, wide room.

"The air is pure here," Whitby said. "You can get high just from the oxygen levels."

Not a single sample had ever shown any irregularities: normal cell structures, bacteria, radiation levels, whatever applied. But he had also seen a few strange comments in the reports from the handful of guest scientists who had passed the security check and come here to examine the samples, even as they had been kept in the dark about the context. The gist of these comments was that when they looked away from the microscope, the samples changed; and when they stared again, what they looked at had reconstituted itself to appear normal. "There you are." To Control, in that brief glance, staring across the vast litter of objects spread out before him, it mostly looked like a cabinet of curiosities: desiccated beetle husks, brittle starfish, and other things in jars, bottles, beakers, and boxes of assorted sizes.

"Has anyone ever tried to eat any of the samples?" he asked Grace. If they'd just devoured the undying plant, Control was fairly sure it wouldn't have come back.

"Shhhh," she said, exactly as if they were in church and he had spoken too loudly or received a cell-phone call. But he noticed Whitby looking at him quizzically, head cocked to one side within his helmet. Had *Whitby* sampled the samples? Despite his terror?

Parallel to this thought, the knowledge that Hsyu and other non-biologists had never seen the samples cathedral. He wondered what they might have read in the striations of the fur of a dead swamp rat or in the vacant glass eyes of a marsh hawk, its curved beak. What susurrations or utterances might verbalize all unexpected from a cross section of tree moss or cypress bark. The patterns to be found in twigs and leaves.

It was too absurd a thought to give words to, not when he was so new. Or, perhaps, even when he was old in this job, should he be that lucky or unlucky.

So there he was.

When the assistant director closed the door and they moved on to the next section of the cathedral, Control had to bite his thumb to stop a giggle from escaping. He'd had a vision of the samples starting to dance behind that door, freed of the terrible limitations of the human gaze. "Our banal, murderous imagination," as the biologist had put it in a rare unguarded moment with the director before the twelfth expedition.

———

In the corridor afterward, with Whitby, a little drained by the experience: "Was that the room you wanted me to see?"

"No," Whitby said, but did not elaborate.

Had he insulted the man with his prior refusal? Even if not, Whitby had clearly withdrawn his offer.

Glimpses of towns now under kudzu and other vines, moldering in the moss: a long-abandoned miniature golf course with a pirate theme. The golf greens had been buried in leaves and mud. The half decks of corsairs' ships rose at crazy angles as if from choppy seas of vegetation, masts cracked at right angles and disappearing into the gloom as it began to rain. A crumbling gas station lay next door, the roof caved in by fallen trees, the pavement so cracked by gnarled roots that it had crumbled into water-ripe pieces with the seeming texture and consistency of dark, moist brownies. The fuzzy, irregular shapes of houses and two-story buildings through the trees proved that people had lived here before the evacuation. This close to the border as little as possible was disturbed, and so these abandoned places could only be broken down by the natural process of decades of rain and decay.

The final stretch to the border had Whitby circling ever lower until Control was certain they were below sea level, before they came up again slightly to a low ridge upon which sat a drab green barracks, a more official-looking brick building for army command and control, and the local Southern Reach outpost.

According to a labyrinthine hierarchical chart that resembled several thick snakes fucking one another, the Southern

Reach was under the army's jurisdiction here, which might be why the Southern Reach facility, closed down between expeditions, looked a bit like a row of large tents that had been made of lemon meringue. Which is to say, it looked like any number of the churches Control had become familiar with in his teenage years, usually because of whatever girl he was dating. The calcification of revivalists and born-agains often took this form: as of something temporary that had hardened and become permanent. And thus it was either a series of white permafrost tents that greeted them or the white swell of huge waves, frozen forever. The sight was as out of place and startling as if the facility had resembled a fossilized herd of huge MoonPies, a delicacy of those youthful years.

Army HQ was in a dome-shaped section of the barracks after the final checkpoint, but no one seemed to be around except a few privates standing in the churned mud bath that was the unofficial parking lot. Loitering with no regard for the light rain falling on them, talking in a bored but intense way while smoking cherry-scented filtered cigarettes. "Whatever you want." "Fuck off." They had the look of men who had no idea what they guarded, or knew but had been trying to forget.

Border commander Samantha Higgins—who occupied a room hardly larger than a storage closet and just as depressing—was AWOL when they called on her. Higgins's aide-de-camp—"add the camp" as his punning father would've put it—relayed an apology that she'd had to "step out" and couldn't "receive you personally." Almost as if he were a special-delivery signature-required package.

Which was just as well. There had been awkwardness between the two entities after the final eleventh expedition had turned up back home—procedures changed, the security tapes scrutinized again and again. They had rechecked the border for other exit points, looking for heat signals, fluctuations in air flow, anything. Found nothing.

So Control thought of "border commander" as a useless or misleading title and didn't really care that Higgins wasn't there, no matter how Cheney seemed to take it as a personal affront: "I told her this was important. She knew this was important."

While Whitby took the opportunity to fondle a fern, revealing a hitherto unobserved sensitivity to texture.

Control had felt foolish asking Whitby what he meant by saying "the terror," but he also couldn't leave it alone. Especially after reading over the theories document Whitby had handed him that morning, which he also wanted to talk about. Control thought of the theories as "slow death by," given the context: Slow death by aliens. Slow death by parallel universe. Slow death by malign unknown time-traveling force. Slow death by invasion from an alternate earth. Slow death by wildly divergent technology or the shadow biosphere or symbiosis or iconography or etymology. Death by this and by that. Death by indifference and inference. His favorite: "Surface-dwelling terrestrial organism, previously unknown." Hiding where all of these years? In a lake? On a farm? At slots in a casino?

But he recognized his bottled-up laughter for the onset

of hysteria, and his cynicism for what it was: a defense mechanism so he wouldn't have to think about any of it.

Death, too, by arched eyebrow: a fair amount of implied or outright "your theory is ridiculous, unwarranted, useless." Some of the ghosts of old interdepartmental rivalries resurrected, and coming through in odd ways across sentences. He wondered how much fraternization had taken place over the years—if an archaeologist's written wince at an environmental scientist's seemingly reasonable assertion represented a fair opinion or meant he was seeing an endgame playing out, the final consequence of an affair that had occurred twenty years earlier.

So before the trip to the border, giving up his lunchtime, Control had summoned Whitby to his office to have it out with him about "the terror" and talk about the theories. Although as it turned out they barely touched on the theories.

Whitby had perched on the edge of the chair opposite Control and his huge desk, intent and waiting. He was almost vibrating, like a tuning fork. Which made Control reluctant to say what he had to say, even though he still said it: "Why did you say 'the terror' earlier? And then you repeated it."

Whitby wore an expression of utter blankness, then lit up to the extent that he seemed to levitate for a moment. He had the busy look of a hummingbird in the act of pollination as he said, "Not 'terror.' Not 'terror' at all. *Terroir.*" And this time he drew out and corrected the pronunciation of the word, so Control could tell it was not "terror."

"What is . . . terroir then?"

"A wine term," Whitby said, with such enthusiasm that it made Control wonder if the man had a second job as a sommelier at some upscale Hedley restaurant along the river walk.

Somehow, though, the man's sudden animation animated Control, too. There was so much obfuscation and so much rote recital at the Southern Reach that to see Whitby excited by an idea lifted him up.

"What does it mean?" he asked, although still unsure whether it was a good idea to encourage Whitby.

"What doesn't it mean?" Whitby said. "It means the specific characteristics of a place—the geography, geology, and climate that, in concert with the vine's own genetic propensities, can create a startling, deep, original vintage."

Now Control was both confused and amused. "How does this apply to our work?"

"In all ways," Whitby said, his enthusiasm doubled, if anything. "Terroir's direct translation is 'a sense of place,' and what it means is the sum of the effects of a localized environment, inasmuch as they impact the qualities of a particular product. Yes, that can mean wine, but what if you applied these criteria to thinking about Area X?"

On the cusp of catching Whitby's excitement, Control said, "So you mean you would study everything about the history—natural and human—of that stretch of coast, in addition to all other elements? And that you might—you just might—find an answer in that confluence?" Next to the idea of terroir, the theories that had been presented to Control seemed garish and blunt.

"Exactly. The point of terroir is that no two areas are the same. That no two wines can be exactly the same because no combination of elements can be exactly the same. That certain varietals cannot occur in certain places.

But it requires a deep understanding of a region to reach conclusions."

"And this isn't being done already?"

Whitby shrugged. "Some of it. Some of it. Just not all of it considered together, in my opinion. I feel there is an over-emphasis on the lighthouse, the tower, base camp—those discrete elements that could be said to jut out of the landscape—while the landscape itself is largely ignored. As is the idea that Area X could have formed nowhere else . . . although that theory would be highly speculative and perhaps based mostly on my own observations."

Control nodded, unable now to shake a sturdy skepticism. Would terroir really be more useful than another approach? If something far beyond the experience of human beings had decided to embark upon a purpose that it did not intend to allow humans to recognize or understand, then terroir would simply be a kind of autopsy, a kind of admission of the limitations of human systems. You could map the entirety of a process—or, say, a beachhead or an invasion—only after it had happened, and still not know the *who* or the *why*. He wanted to say to Whitby, "Growing grapes is simpler than Area X," but refrained.

"I can provide you with some of my personal findings," Whitby said. "I can show you the start of things."

"Great," Control said, nodding with exaggerated cheeriness, and was relieved that Whitby took that single word as closure to the conversation and made a fairly rapid exit, less relieved that he seemed to take it as undiluted affirmation.

Grand unified theories could backfire—for example, Central's overemphasis on trying to force connections between unconnected right-wing militia groups. Recalled that his father had made up stories about how one piece in his ragtag sculpture garden commented on that one, and how they were all part of a larger narrative. They had all occupied the same space, were by the same creator, but they had never been meant to communicate, one to another. Just as they had never been meant to molder and rust in the backyard. But that way at least his father could rationalize them remaining out there together, under the hot sun and in the rain, even if protected by tarps.

The border had come down in the early morning, on a day, a date, that no one outside of the Southern Reach remembered or commemorated. Just that one inexplicable event had killed an estimated fifteen hundred people. How did you factor ghosts into any terroir? Did they deepen the flavor, or did they make things dry, chalky, irreconcilable? The taste in Control's mouth was bitter.

If terroir meant a confluence, then the entrance through the border into Area X was the ultimate confluence. It was also the ultimate secret, in that there were no visual records of that entry point available to anyone. Unless you were there, looking across at it, you could never experience it. Nor did it help if you were peering at it through a raging thunderstorm, shoes filling up with mud, with only one umbrella between the three of you.

They stood, soaked and cold, near the end of a path that wound from the barracks across the ridge above the giant sinkhole and then on to more stable land. They were looking at the right side of a tall, sturdy, red wooden frame that delineated the location, the width and height, of the entrance beyond. The path ran parallel to a paint line perpetually refreshed to let you know the border lay fifteen feet beyond. If you went ten feet beyond the line, the lasers from a hidden security system would activate and turn you into cooked meat. But otherwise, the army had left as small a footprint as possible; no one knew what might change the terroir. Here the toxicity levels almost matched those inside of Area X, which was to say: nil, nada, nothing.

As for terror, his personal level had been intensified by deltas of lightning that cracked open the sky and thunder that sounded like a giant in a bad mood ripping apart trees. Yet they had persevered, Cheney holding the blue-and-white-striped umbrella aloft, arm fully extended toward the sky, and Control and Whitby huddled around him, trying to shuffle in a synchronized way along the narrow path without tripping. All of it useless against the slanted rain.

"The entrance isn't visible from the side," Cheney said in a loud voice, his forehead flecked with bits of leaf and dirt. "But you'll see it soon. The path circles around to meet it head-on."

"Doesn't it project light?" Control smacked away something red with six legs that had been crawling up his pants.

"Yes, but you can't see it from the side. From the side it doesn't appear to be there at all."

"It is twenty feet high and twelve feet wide," Whitby added.

"Or, as I say, sixty rabbits high and thirty-six rabbits wide," Cheney said.

Control, struck by a sudden generosity, laughed at that one, which he imagined brought a flush of happiness to

Cheney's features although they could barely recognize each other in the slop and mire.

The area had the aspect of a shrine, even with the downpour. Especially because the downpour cut off abruptly at the border even though the landscape continued uninterrupted. Somehow Control had expected the equivalent of the disconnect when a two-page spread didn't quite line up in a coffee-table book. But instead it just looked like they were slogging through a huge terrarium or greenhouse with invisible glass revealing a sunny day on the grounds beyond.

They continued to the end amid a profusion of lush plant life and an alarmingly crowded landscape of birdlife and insects, with deer visible in the middle distance through the veil of rain. Hsyu had said something during their meeting about making assumptions about terminology, and he had replied, to a roaring silence, "You mean like calling something a 'border'?" Tracking back from stripping names from expedition members: What if when you accreted personality and other details around mere function, a different picture emerged?

After a few minutes of sloshing through mud, they curved around to come to a halt in front of the wooden structure.

He had not expected any of it to be beautiful, but it was beautiful.

Beyond the red wooden frame, Control could see a roughly rectangular space forming an arch at the top, through which swirled a scintillating, questing white light, a light that fizzed and flickered and seemed always on the point of being snuffed out but never was . . . there was a kind of spiraling effect to it, as it continually circled back in on itself. If you blinked quickly it almost looked as if the light consisted of eight or ten swiftly rotating spokes, but this was an illusion.

The light was like nothing he had ever seen. It was neither harsh nor soft. It was not twee, like faery lite from bad movies. It was not the darkish light of hucksters and magicians or anyone else looking to define light by use of shadows. It lacked the clarity of the all-revealing light of the storage cathedral, but it wasn't murky or buttery or any other descriptor he could think of right then. He imagined trying to tell his father about it, but, really, it was his father who could have described the quality of that light to him.

"Even though it's such a tall corridor and so wide, you have to crawl with your pack as close to the middle as possible. As far away from the sides as possible." Cheney, confirming what Control had already read in summaries. Like cats with duct tape on their backs, slinking forward on their bellies. "No matter how you feel about enclosed or open spaces, it'll be strange in there, because you will feel simultaneously as if you are progressing across a wide open field and as if you're on a narrow precipice without guardrails and could fall off at any moment. So you exist in a confined and limitless space all at once. One reason we put the expedition members under hypnosis."

Not to mention—and Cheney never did—that the expedition leader in each case had to endure the experience without benefit of hypnosis, and that some experienced strange visions while inside. "It was like being in one of those aquariums with the water overhead, but murkier, so that I could not really tell what was swimming there. Or it wasn't the water that was murky but instead the creatures." "I saw constellations and everything was near and far all at once."

"There was a vast plain like where I grew up, and it just kept expanding and expanding, until I had to look at the ground because I was getting the sense of being filled up until I would have burst." All of which could just as easily have occurred inside the subjects' minds.

Nor did the length of the passageway correspond to the width of the invisible border. Some reports from returning expeditions indicated that the passageway meandered, while others described it as straight. The point was, it varied and the time to travel through it into Area X could not be estimated except within a rough parameter of a "norm" of three hours to ten hours. Indeed, because of this, one of the earliest fears of Central had been that the entry point might disappear entirely, even if other opinions differed. Among the files on the border, Control had found a relevant quote from James Lowry: ". . . the door when I saw it looked like it had always been there, and would always be there even if there was no Area X."

The director had apparently thought the border was advancing, but there was no evidence to support that view. An interceding note in the files from far up the chain of command had offered the comment that perhaps the director was just trying to get attention and money for a "dying agency." Now that he saw the entrance, Control wondered how anyone would know what an "advance" meant.

"Don't stare at it directly for too long," Whitby offered. "It tends to draw you in."

"I'll try not to," Control said. But it was too late, his only solace that surely if he started walking toward it, Whitby or Cheney would stop him. Or the lasers would.

The swirling light defeated his attempts to conjure up

the biologist. He could not get her to stand beside him, to follow the other three members of the twelfth expedition into that light. By then, by the time she had arrived at this spot, she would already have been under hypnotic influence. The linguist would already have left the expedition. There would have been just the four of them, with their packs, about to crawl through that impossible light. Only the director would have been seeing it all with clear eyes. If Control went through her scribbled notes, if he excavated the sedimentary layers and got to the core of her . . . could he come back here and reconstruct her thoughts, her feelings, at that moment?

"How did the members of the last eleventh and the twelfth get out of Area X without being seen?" Control asked Cheney.

"There must be another exit point we haven't been able to find." The object, observed, still not cooperating with him. A vision of his father in the kitchen when he was fourteen, shoving rotting strawberries into the bottom of a glass and then adding a cone of curled-up paper over the top, to trap the fruit flies that had gotten into the house.

"Why can we see the corridor?" Control asked.

"Not sure what you mean," Cheney said.

"If it's visible, then we were meant to see it." Maybe. Who really knew? Every off-the-cuff comment Control made came, or so he thought, with a built-in echo, as if the past banal observations of visitors and new employees lingered in the air, seeking to merge, same with same, and finding an exact match far too often.

Cheney sucked on his cheek a second, grudgingly admitted, "That's a theory. That's definitely a theory, all right. I can't say it isn't."

AUTHORITY

Staggering thought: What might come out into the world down a corridor twenty feet tall by twelve feet wide?

They stood there for long moments, bleeding time but not acknowledging it, heedless of the rain. Whitby stood apart, letting the rain soak him, contemptuous of the umbrella. Behind them, through the thunder, the hard trickle of water from the creeks gurgling back down into the sinkhole beyond the ridge. Ahead, the clarity of a cloudless summer day.

While Control tried to stare down that sparkling, that dancing light.

010: FOURTH BREACH

The terroir" infiltrated his thoughts again, when, late in the day, drying off, Control received the transcripts from his morning session with the biologist, the trip to the border kaleidoscoping through his head. He had just reluctantly re-tossed the mouse into the trash and repatriated the plant with the storage cathedral. It had taken an effort of will to do that and to close the door on the weird sermon scrawled on his wall. He hated to engage in superstition, but the doubt remained—that he had made a mistake, that the director had left both mouse and plant in her desk drawer for a reason, as a kind of odd protection against . . . what?

He still didn't know as he performed an Internet search on Ghost Bird's reference to the phorus snail, which revealed she was quoting almost word for word from an old book by an obscure amateur "parson-naturalist." Something she would have encountered in college, with whatever associated memories that, too, might bring. He didn't believe it had significance, except for the obvious one: The biologist had been comparing him to an awkward snail.

Then he thumbed through the transcript, which he found comforting. At one point during the session, fishing, Control had pivoted away from both tower and lighthouse, back to where she had been picked up.

Q: *What did you leave at the empty lot?*

What if, he speculated there at his desk—still ignoring the water-stained pages in the drawer next to him—the empty lot was a terroir related to the terroir that was Area X? What if some confluence of person and place meant something more than just a return home? Did he need to order a complete historical excavation of the empty lot? And what about the other two, the anthropologist and the surveyor? Mired in the arcana of the Southern Reach, he wouldn't have time to check on them for another few days. Grudging gratitude to Grace for simplifying his job by sending them away.

Meanwhile, the biologist was answering his question on the page.

A: *Leave? Like, what? A necklace with a crucifix? A confession?*
Q: *No.*
A: *Well, why don't you tell me what you thought I might've left there?*
Q: *Your manners?*

That had earned him a chuckle, if a caustic one, followed by a long, tired sigh that seemed to expel all the air from her lungs.

A: *I've told you that nothing happened there. I woke up as if from an endless dream. And then they picked me up.*
Q: *Do you ever dream? Now, I mean.*
A: *What would be the point?*
Q: *What do you mean?*
A: *I'd just dream of being out of this place.*
Q: *Do you want to hear about my dreams?*

He didn't know why he had said this to her. He didn't know what he'd tell her. Would he tell her about the endless falling into the bay, into the maw of leviathans?

To his surprise, she said:

A: *What do you dream of, John? Tell me.*

It was the first time she'd used his name, and he tried to hate how it had sent a kind of spark through him. *John.* She had brought her feet up onto the chair so she was hugging her knees and peering at him almost impishly.

Sometimes you had to adjust your strategy, give up something to get something. So he did tell her his dream, even though he felt self-conscious and hoped Grace wouldn't see it in the official record, use it against him somehow. But if he'd lied, if he'd made something up, Control believed that Ghost Bird would know, that even as he'd been trying to interpret her tells, she had been processing *him* the whole time. Even when he asked the questions he was hemorrhaging data. He had a sudden image of information floating out the side of his head in a pixelated blood-red mist. These are my relatives. This is my ex-girlfriend. My father was a sculptor. My mother is a spy.

But she had relented, too, during the conversation, for a moment.

> A: *I woke in the empty lot and I thought I was dead. I thought I was in purgatory, maybe, even though I don't believe in an afterlife. But it was quiet and so empty . . . so I waited there, afraid to leave, afraid there might be some reason I was meant to be there. Not sure I wanted to know anything else. Then the police came for me, and then the Southern Reach after that. But I still believed I wasn't really alive.*

What if the biologist had just that morning decided she was alive, not dead? Perhaps that accounted for the change in her mood.

When he had finished reading, he could feel Ghost Bird still staring at him, and she would not let his gaze drop, held him there, or he let her do it. For whatever reason.

On the way back from the border, a silence had come over Control, Whitby, and Cheney, perhaps overloaded by the contrast between sun/heat and rain/cold. But it had seemed to Control like the companionable silence of shared experience, as if he had been initiated into membership in an exclusive club without having been asked first. He was wary of that feeling; it was a space where shadows crept in that shouldn't creep in, where people agreed to things that they did not actually agree with, believing that they were of one purpose and intent. Once, in such a space, a fellow agent had called him "homey" and made an offhand comment about him "not being your usual kind of spic."

When they were about a mile from the Southern Reach, Cheney said, too casually, "You know, there's a rumor about the former director and the border."

"Yes?" Here it came. There it was. How comfort led to overreach or to some half reveal of what should be hidden.

"That she went over the border by herself once," Cheney said, staring off into the distance. Even Whitby seemed to want to distance himself from that statement, leaning forward in his seat as he drove. "Just a rumor," Cheney added. "No idea if it's true."

But Control didn't care about that, despite the addition being disingenuous. The truth clearly didn't worry Cheney, or he already knew it was true and wanted Control on the scent.

"Does this rumor include when this might have happened?" Control asked.

"Before the final eleventh expedition."

Part of him had wanted to take that to the assistant director and see what she might or might not know. Another part decided that was a premature idea. So he'd chewed on the information, wondering why Cheney had fed it to him, especially in front of Whitby. Did that mean Whitby had the spine, despite the evidence, to withhold even when Grace wanted him to share?

"Have you ever been over the border, Cheney?"

An explosive snort. "No. Are you crazy? No."

In the parking lot at day's end, Control sat behind the wheel, keys in the ignition, and decompressed for a moment. The rain had passed, leaving oily puddles and a kind of verdant sheen on the grass and trees. Only Whitby's purple electric car remained, at an angle across two spaces, as if it had washed up there.

Time to call the Voice and file his report. Getting it over with was better than letting work bleed into his evening.

The phone rang and rang.

The Voice finally answered with a "Yes—what?" as if Control had called at a bad time.

He had meant to ask about the director's clandestine border trip, but the Voice's tone threw him off. Instead, he started off with the plant and the mouse: "I found something odd in the director's desk . . ."

Control blinked once, twice, three times. As they were talking, he had noticed something. It was the smallest thing, and yet it rattled him. There was a squashed mosquito on the inside of his windshield, and Control had no idea how it had gotten there. He knew it hadn't been there in the morning, and he had no memory of swatting one anyway. Paranoid thought: Carelessness on the part of someone searching his car . . . or did someone want him to know he was being watched?

Attention divided, Control became aware of wobbles in his conversation with the Voice. Almost like air pockets that pushed an airplane up and forward, while the passenger inside, him, sat there strapped in and alarmed. Or as if he were watching a TV show where the cable hiccupped and brought him five seconds forward every few minutes. Yet the conversation picked up where it had left off.

The Voice was saying, with more than usual gruffness, "I'll get you more information—and don't you worry, I'm still working on the goddamn assistant director situation. Call me tomorrow."

A ridiculous image snuck into his head of the assistant director walking into the parking lot while he was at the border, forcing the lock, rummaging through his glove box, sadistically squashing the mosquito.

"I don't know if that's a good idea at this point, about Grace," Control said. "It might be better to . . ."

But the Voice had already hung up, leaving Control to wonder how it had gotten dark so quickly.

Control contemplated the tangled geometry of blood and delicate limbs. He couldn't stop staring at the mosquito. He had meant to say something else to the Voice, but he'd forgotten it because of the mosquito and now it would have to wait until tomorrow.

Was it possible he *had* squashed the mosquito reflexively and didn't remember? He found that unlikely. Well, just in case he hadn't, he'd leave the damn thing there, along with its splotch of blood. That might send some kind of message back. Eventually.

At home, Chorry waited on the step. Control let him inside, put out some cat food he'd bought at the store along with a chicken sandwich, ate in the kitchen, even though Chorry's meal made the space stink of greasy salmon. He watched the cat chow down but his thoughts were elsewhere, on what he considered the failures of his day. He felt as if most of his passes had been behind his receivers and his high school coach was yelling at him. The wall behind the door had thrown him off. The wall and the meetings had taken up too much of his time. Even the border trip hadn't put things right, just stabilized them while opening new lines of inquiry. The idea that the director had been across the border before the final eleventh expedition had returned to worry at him. Cheney, during their border trip: "I never had the idea that the director agreed with us much, you know? Or, she kept her own counsel, or had some other council, along with Grace. Or I don't know much about people. Which is possible, I guess."

Control reached into his satchel for some of his notes from the border trip, and in doing so was shocked to find three cell phones there instead of two—the sleek one used for communication with the Voice, the other one for regular use, and another, bulkier. Frowning, Control pulled them out. The third was the old, nonfunctioning phone from the director's desk. He stared at it. How had it gotten in there? Had Grace put it in there? An old black beetle of a phone, the rippled, pitted burn across the leather cover a bit like a carapace. Grace couldn't have done it. She must have left it in his office after all and he must have absentmindedly picked it up. But then why hadn't he noticed it in the parking lot, after he finished talking to the Voice?

He set the phone on the kitchen counter, giving it a wary stare or two before he settled into the living room. What was he missing?

After a few sets of halfhearted push-ups, he turned on the television. Soon he was being bombarded by a montage of reality shows, news of another school massacre, a report on another garbage zone in the ocean, and some announcer screaming out the prelims of an MMA match. He dithered between a cooking show and a mystery, two of his favorites, because they didn't require him to think, before deciding on the mystery, the cat purring on his lap like a revving engine.

As he watched the TV, he remembered a lecture in his second year of college by a professor of environmental science. The gist had been that institutions, even individual departments in governments, were the concrete embodiments of not just ideas or opinions but also of attitudes and emotions. Like hate or empathy, statements such as "immigrants need to learn English or they're not really citizens" or "all mental patients deserve our respect." That in the workings of, for example, an agency, you could, with effort, discover not just the abstract thought behind it but the concrete emotions. The Southern Reach had been set up to investigate (and contain) Area X, and yet despite all the signs and symbols of that mission—all of the talk and files and briefs and analysis—some other emotion or attitude also existed within the agency. It frustrated him that he could not quite put his finger on it, as if he needed another sense, or a sensitivity, that he lacked. And yet as Grace had said, once he became too comfortable within the Southern Reach, once he was cocooned by its embrace, he would be too indoctrinated to perceive it.

That night, he did not dream. He did remember being woken well before dawn by something small crawling across the roof in fits and starts, but soon enough it stopped moving. It hadn't been enough to wake the cat.

012: SORT OF SORTING

In the morning, back at work, he discovered that a fluorescent rod had burned out in his office, dulling the light. Control's chair and desk in particular lay under a kind of gloom. He moved a lamp from the bookcases and set it up on a shelf jutting out toward the desk on his left. The better to see that Whitby had followed through on his threat and left a thick, somewhat worn-looking document on his desk entitled "Terroir and Area X: A Complete Approach." Something about the rust on the massive paper clip biting into the title page, the yellowing nature of the typed pages, the handwritten annotations in different-color pens, or maybe the torn-out taped-in images, made him reluctant to go down that particular rabbit hole. It would have to wait its turn, which might at this point mean next week or even next month. He had another session with the biologist, as well as a meeting with Grace about his agency recommendations, and then, on Friday, an appointment to view the videos from the first expedition. Among other pressing things on his mind . . . like a little redecorating. Control opened the door with the words hidden behind it. He took some photographs. Then, using a can of white paint and a brush requisitioned from maintenance, he meticulously painted over all of it: every last word, every detail of the map. Grace and the others would have to get by without a memorial because he couldn't live with the pressure of those words pulsing out from behind the door. Also the height measurements, if that's what they were. Two coats, three, until only a shadow remained, although the height marks, written using a different kind of pen, continued to shine through. If they were height marks, then the director had grown by a quarter inch between measurements, unless she'd been wearing higher heels the second time.

After painting, Control set out two of his father's carvings from the chessboard at home, meaning for them to replace the missing talismans of plant and mouse. A tiny red rooster and a moon-blue goat, they came from a series entitled simply *Mi Familia*. The rooster had the name of one of his uncles, the goat an aunt. His dad had photographs from his youth of playing in the backyard with his friends and cousins, surrounded by chickens and goats, a garden stretching out of sight along a wooden fence. But Control only remembered his father's chickens—generously put, tradition or legacy chickens, named and never slaughtered. "Homage chickens" as Control had teased his father.

Chess was a hobby he had developed that could be shared during his father's chemo treatments and that his father could ponder and worry at when Control wasn't there in the room. Their shared affliction before the cancer had been pool, at which they were both mediocre, even though they enjoyed it. But his dad's physical ailments had outstripped the mental deterioration, so that hadn't been an option. Books as a salve to the boredom of TV? No, because the bookmark just began to separate one sea of unread words from another. But with a reminder of whose turn it was, chess left some evidence of its past even when his dad got confused toward the end.

Control had press-ganged his dad's carvings into being pieces; they were a motley bunch that didn't much correlate to their function, since they were being twice reinterpreted— first as people into animals and then into chess pieces. But he became a better player, his interest raised because abstraction had been turned into something real, and the results, although comical to them, seemed to matter more. "Abuela to bishop" as a move had set them both to giggling. "Cousin Humberto to La Sobrina Mercedez."

Now these carvings were going to help him. Control set the rooster on the far left corner of his desk and the goat on the right, with the rooster facing out and the goat staring back at him. He had glued to each a nearly invisible nano-camera that would transmit wirelessly to his phone and laptop. If nothing else, he meant for his office to be secure, to make of it a bastion, to take from it all unknowns, and to substitute only that which might be a comfort to him. Who knew what he might discover?

He was then free to consider the director's notes.

The preamble to reading the director's notes had much of the ritual of a spring cleaning. He cleared all of the chairs except his own from the office, setting them up in the hallway. Then he started to make piles in the middle of the floor. He tried to ignore the ambivalent stains revealed on the carpet. Coffee? Blood? Gravy? Cat vomit? Clearly the janitor and any cohorts had been banned from the director's office for quite some time. He had a vision of Grace ordering that the office be kept as is, in much the same way that on cop shows the parents of slain children allowed not a single new dust mote to enter the hallowed ground of their lost ones' bedrooms. Grace had kept it locked until his arrival, had held on to the spare key, and yet he didn't think she'd be showing up on his surveillance video.

So he sat on a stool, his favorite neoclassical composer playing on his laptop, and let the music fill the room and create a kind of order out of chaos. Skipping no step, Grandpa, even if there was a skip to his step. He already had received files that morning from Grace—conveyed via a third-party administrative assistant so they could avoid talking to each other. These files detailed all of the director's official memos and reports—against which he would have to check every doodle and fragment. An "inventory list" as Control thought of it. He had considered asking Whitby to sort through the notes, but with each item the security clearance fluctuated from secret to top secret to what-the-fuck-is-this-secret like some volatile stock market dealing in futures.

Grace's title for the list was too functional: DIRECTOR FILES—DMP OF MAJOR AND MINOR MEMOS AND REPORTS. DMP, or Data Management Program, referred to the proprietary imaging and viewing system the Southern Reach had paid for and implemented in the nineties. Control would have gone with something pithier than Grace had, like THE DIRECTOR DOCUMENTS, or more dramatic, like TALES FROM A FORGOTTEN AGENCY or THE AREA X DOSSIER.

The piles had to be organized by topic so that they would at least loosely match up to Grace's DMP: border, light-house, tower, island, base camp, natural history, unnatural history, general history, unknown. He also decided to make a pile for "irrelevant," even though what might seem irrele-vant to him might to someone else be the Rosetta stone—if such a stone, or the pebble version, even existed among all the debris.

This was a comfortable place for him, a comfortable task, familiar as penance during a period of shame and demo-tion, and he could lose himself in it almost as thoughtlessly as doing the dishes after dinner or making the bed in the morning—emerge in some ways refreshed.

But with the crucial difference that these piles looked in part as if he had tracked in dirt on his shoes from outside. The former director was making him into a new kind of urban farmer, building compost piles with classified mate-rial that had originated out in the world, bringing with it a rich backstory. Oak and magnolia trees had provided some of the raw material in the form of leaves, to which the direc-tor had added napkins, receipts, even sometimes toilet paper, creating a thick mulch.

The diner where Control ate breakfast had yielded sev-eral noteworthy receipts, as did a corner grocery store, where the former director had at various times shopped as a conve-nient last resort. The receipts indicated straggler items, not quite a formal outing for groceries. A roll of paper towels

and beef jerky one time, fruit juice and breakfast cereal another time, hot dogs, a quart of skim milk, nail scissors, and
a greeting card the next. The napkins, receipts, and advertis-
ing brochures from a barbecue place in her hometown of
Bleakersville figured prominently, and induced in Control a
hunger for ribs. Bleakersville was only about fifteen minutes
from the Southern Reach, right off the highway that led to
Hedley. According to Grace, the house there had been swept
clean of anything related to the Southern Reach, the results
catalogued in a special DIRECTOR'S HOUSE section of
the DMP file.

Panicked thought after about an hour: What if the seemingly random surfaces on which the director had written her
notes had significance? What if the words were not the whole
message, just as the lighthouse keeper's deranged sermon
wasn't the whole story? The storage cathedral came to mind,
and although it seemed improbable he wondered, paranoid,
if some of the leaves came from Area X, then dismissed the
thought as speculative and counterproductive.

No, the director's vast array of textures revealed "only"
that she had been absorbed in her task, as if she had been
desperate to write down her observations in the moment,
had wanted neither to forget nor to have an internal editor
interrupt her search for understanding. Or no hacker to peer
into the inner workings of her mind, distilled down to a DMP
or otherwise.

He had, as a result, to sort through not just piles of primary "documents" but also a haphazard record of the director's life and her wanderings through the world outside of the
Southern Reach buildings. This helped, because he had
only dribs and drabs from the official file—either due to

Grace's interference or because the director herself had managed to winnow it terse. She had no siblings and had grown up with her father in the Midwest. She had studied psychology at a state college, been a consultant for about five years. She had then applied for the Southern Reach through Central, where she had endured a grueling schedule designed to force her to prove herself over and over—and thus make up for her undistinguished career to date. The Southern Reach must have seemed a more attractive posting back then—and where the sparse information turned into the roiling mass of notes in her office. His request for further intel had been offered up to the labyrinthine and terse maw of Central, which had clamped shut on it. Someday a file might be spat out in his direction.

So he was left with trying to build a true terroir vision of the director—her motivations and knowledge base—from everything he was sorting through and by creating a whole layering of other, non-DMP categories in his mind. She had a subscription to a table television guide, as well as a selection of culture and art magazines, judging not just from torn pages but from subscription renewal forms. She had owed the dentist $72.12 at one point for a cleaning not covered by her insurance and didn't care who knew it. A bowling alley outside of town was a frequent haunt. She got birthday cards from an aunt, but either wasn't sentimental about cards or wasn't that close to the woman. She liked pork chops and shrimp with grits. She liked to dine alone, but one receipt from the barbecue place had two dinner orders on it. Company? Perhaps, like him, she sometimes ordered food to go so she'd have a lunch for the next day.

There was not much about the border in her notes, but that white spiral, that enormous space, did not leave him completely. There was an odd synchronicity as he worked that linked the spiral to his mother's flash of light across the sky, the literal and the metaphoric joined together across an expanse of time and context so vast that only thoughts could bridge the gap.

The sedimentary layers that had existed under the plant and mouse proved the most difficult to separate out. Some pages were brittle and thin, and the scraps of paper and ragged collages of leaves had a tendency to stick together, while being infiltrated and bound more tightly by the remains of translucent roots touched by lines of crimson left behind by the plant. As Control painstakingly separated one page from another, a musty smell that had lain dormant rose up, became strong and pungent. He tried not to compare it to the stench of dirty socks.

The layers continued to support that the director liked both nature and a cold breakfast. As he liberated the proof of purchase cut out of a box of bran flakes from an oak leaf stained blue by words thickened into almost unreadable ink blots, he knew that the cardboard had never before been unwedded from its brittle bride. "Review transcripts from X.10.C, esp. anthro on LH landing" read the cardboard. "Recommend discontinuing use of black boxes for conditioning purposes" read the leaf. He placed the oak leaf on the unknown pile, as in "unknown value."

Other intriguing fragments revealed themselves, too, some peeking out between books on the stacks or just shoved roughly between pages, less like bookmarks and more as if she had become irritated with them and was punishing the very words she had scribbled down. It was between the pages of a basic college biology textbook that looked worn enough to have been the director's own that Control found, on real paper, bizarrely printed on a dot matrix printer despite a date of only eighteen months ago, a note on the twelfth expedition.

In the note, which hadn't made it into Grace's DMP file, the director called the surveyor "someone with a strong sense of reality, a good, bracing foil to the others." The linguist discarded in the border prep area she called "useful but not essential; possibly a dangerous addition, a sympathetic but narrow character who might deflect attention." Sympathetic to whom? Deflect attention from what? And was this deflection desirable or . . . ? The anthropologist was referred to by her first name, which confused Control until he suddenly recognized it. "Hildi will be on board, will understand." He stared at that note for a while. On board with what? Understand what?

Beyond a frustrating lack of context, the notes conveyed a sense that the director had been casting a play or movie. Notes for actors. Teams needed cohesion, but the director didn't seem as concerned with morale and the group dynamic as with . . . some other quality.

The note on the biologist was the most extensive and caused Control to vibrate with additional questions.

Not a very good biologist. In a traditional sense. Empathic more toward environments than people. Forgets the reasons she went, who is paying her salary. But becomes embedded to an extraordinary extent. Would know Area X better than I do from almost the first moment sets foot there. Experience with similar settings. Self-sufficient. Unburdened. Connection through her husband. What would she be in Area X? A signal? A flare? Or invisible? Exploit.

Another note, found nearby in volume 2 of a slim three-pamphlet set on xenobiology, came to mind: "bio: expo to TA contam?" Biologist exposure to topographical anomaly contamination was his best guess—an easy guess. But without a date, he could not even be sure it pertained to the same expedition. Similarly, when had "Keep from L" and "L said no—no surprise" been written on two separate scraps, and did "L" stand for Lowry or in some esoteric and less likely way mean "lighthouse keeper"?

He let all of this settle in, knew he had to be patient. There were a lot of notes, and a lot of pages to Grace's DMP file, nothing yet on a prior trip by the director across the border. But already he was getting the sense of undercurrents, was finding now in Whitby's terroir theory something that might apply more to the Southern Reach than to Area X, perhaps framed by a single mind. The idea that a dysfunctional thought could take root in a vacuum, the individual anonymous and wraithlike, unknowable because, especially at first, he or she had no interaction with other people. Because more and more in the modern Internet era you came across isolated instances of a mind virus or worm: brains that self-washed, bathed in received ideologies that came down from on high, ideologies that could remain dormant or hidden for years, silent as death until they struck. Almost anything could happen now, and did. The government could not investigate every farmer's purchase of fertilizer and fireworks—could not self-police every deviant brain within its own ranks.

The thought had occurred while sorting through the scraps that if you ran an agency devoted to understanding and combating a force that constituted an insurgency, and you believed the border was, in some sense at least, advancing, then you might deviate from official protocols. That if your supervisors and colleagues did not agree with your assessment, you might come up with an alternative plan and begin to enact it on your own. That, wary and careful, you might then and only then reach out to recruit the help of others who did believe you, or at least weren't hostile, to implement that plan. Whether you let them in on the details or not. Just possibly, you might begin to work out this plan on the back of receipts from your favorite restaurants, while watching TV or reading a magazine.

When it came time to leave for his appointment with Grace, Control looked up to realize he had boxed himself in with piles of paper and stacked folders. Once past that, the doorway full of chairs and a small collapsible table required so much effort to navigate that he wondered if he'd subconsciously been trying to keep something out.

013: RECOMMENDATIONS

Control had wanted to impose himself on Grace's territory, to show her he was comfortable there, but that meant when he arrived she was in the middle of a ridiculously cheerful conversation with her administrative assistant.

While he waited, Control reviewed the basics, the basics being all that had been given to him, for whatever reason. Grace Stevenson. *Homo sapiens.* Female. Family originally from the West Indies. She was third-generation in this country and the eldest of three daughters. The parents had worked hard to put all three through college, and Grace had graduated valedictorian of her class with dual degrees in political science and history, followed by training at Central. Then, during a special op, she'd injured her leg—no details on how—and washed up on the shores of the Southern Reach. No, that wasn't right. The director had picked her name out of a hat? Cheney had made some noises to that effect at one point on their border trip.

But she had to have harbored larger ambitions at some point, so what had kept her here—just the director? For from the start of her stint at the Southern Reach, Grace Stevenson had entered a kind of holding pattern, if not a slow slide into stagnation—the personal depths of that pit probably her messy, drawn-out divorce almost eight years ago, that event timed almost to the month of the college graduation of her twin boys. A year later she had informed Central about her relationship with a Panamanian national—a woman—so that she could again be fully vetted and deemed no security risk, which she wasn't. A planned mess, then, but still traumatic. Her boys were doctors now, and also immortalized in a desk photo of them at a soccer game. Another photo showed her arm in arm with the director. The director was a big woman, with the kind of frame where you couldn't tell if she ran to fat or was muscular. They were at some Southern Reach company picnic, a barbecue station jutting into the frame from the left and people in flowery beach shirts in the backgrouund. The idea of agency social events struck Control as absurd for some reason. Both photos were already familiar to him.

After the divorce, the assistant director's fate had been ever more joined to that of the director, whom she'd had to cover for several times, if he was reading between the lines correctly. The story ended with the director's disappearance and Grace landing the booby prize: getting to be the Assistant Director for Life.

Oh, yes, and as a result of all of this, and more, Grace Stevenson fostered an overwhelming sense of hostility toward him. An emotion he sympathized with, although only to a point, which was probably his failing. "Empathy is a losing game," his father had liked to say, sometimes worn down by the casual racism he encountered. If you had to think about it, then you were doing it wrong.

The assistant finally gone, Control sat down opposite Grace while she held the printout of his initial list of recommendations at arm's length, not so much because it smelled or was otherwise offensive but because she refused to get progressive lenses.

Would she take the recommendations as a challenge? They were deliberately premature, but he hoped so. Although it certainly didn't bode well that a mini tape recorder lay whirring in front of him, her response to his presence in her space. But he had practiced his mannerisms in the mirror that morning, just to see how nonverbal he could be.

In truth, most of his admin and managerial recommendations could apply to any organization that had been rudderless—or to be generous, operating with half a rudder—for a few years. The rest were stabs in the dark, but whatever they cut was as likely to flense lard as hamstring anyone. He wanted the flow of information to go in multiple directions, so that, for example, Hsyu the linguist had access to classified information from other agency departments. He also wanted to approve long-forbidden overtime and nighttime working hours, since the electricity in the building had to stay on twenty-four hours a day anyway. He had noticed most of the staff left early.

Some other things were unnecessary, but with any luck Grace would waste time and energy fighting him on them.

"That was fast," she said finally, tossing the paper-clipped pages of his list back across the desk at him. The pages slid into his lap before he could catch them.

"I did my homework," Control said. Whatever that meant.

"A conscientious schoolboy. A star pupil."

"The first part." Control half agreed, not sure he liked the way she said it.

Grace didn't bother wasting even an insincere smile in response. "Let me get to the point. Someone has been interfering with my access to Central this week—making inquiries, poking around. But whoever is doing you this favor has no tact—or whatever faction is behind it doesn't have quite enough pull."

"I don't know what you're talking about," Control said,

his nonverbal mannerisms sagging in surprise along with the rest of him, despite his best efforts.

Faction. Despite his daydream about the Voice having a black-ops identity, it had not occurred to him that his mother might be heading up a faction, which led him automatically to the idea of true shadow ops—along with an opposition. It threw him, a little, that Central might be that fragmented. Just how elephantine, how rhinoceroscrutian, had the Voice's efforts been in following up on Control's request? And: What did Grace use her contacts for when she wasn't turning them against him?

Grace's look of disgust told him what she thought about his answer. "Then, in that case, John Rodriguez, I have no comment on your recommendations, except to say that I will begin to implement them in as excruciatingly slow a fashion as possible. You should begin to see a few of them—like, 'buy new floor cleaner,' in place by next quarter. Possibly. Maybe."

He had a vision, again, of Grace spiriting away the biologist, of multiple mutual attempted destructions, until somewhere up in the clouds, atop two vast and blood-drenched escalators, they continued to do battle years from now.

Control's stiff nod—gruffly acknowledging defeat—wasn't the mannerism he'd been hoping to use.

But she wasn't done. Her eyes glittered as she opened a drawer and pulled out a mother-of-pearl jewelry box.

"Do you know what this is?" she asked him.

"A jewelry box?" he replied, confused, definitely back on his heels now.

"This is a box full of accusations," Grace said, holding it toward him like an offering. With this jewelry box, I thee despise.

"What is a box of accusations?" Although he didn't want to know.

With a clink-and-tinkle, the yawning velvet mouth sent a handful of bugs Control recognized all too well rolling and skittering across her blotter at him. Most of them came to a stop before the edge, but a couple followed the list onto his lap. The rotting honey smell had intensified again.

"*That* is a box of accusations."

Attempting a comeback, aware it was feeble: "I see only one accusation there, made multiple times."

"I haven't emptied it yet."

"Would you like to empty it now?"

She shook her head. "Not yet. But I will if you continue to interfere with Central. And you can take your spies with you."

Should he lie? That would defeat the purpose of sending the message.

"Why would I bug you?" With a look that he knew undercut his innocence, even as indignation rose in him as ardently as if he *were* innocent. Because in a way he thought he was innocent: Action bred reaction. Lose a few expedition members, gain a few bugs. She might even recognize some of them.

But Grace persisted: "You did. You also rifled through my files, looked in all of my drawers."

"No, I didn't." This time his anger was backed by something real. He hadn't ransacked her office, only placed the bugs there, but now even that act troubled him the more he thought about it. It was out of character, had served no real purpose, had been counterproductive.

Grace continued on patiently. "If you do it again, I'll file a complaint. I've already changed the pass-key combination on my door. Anything you need to know, you can just ask me."

Easily said, but Control didn't think it was true, so he tested it: "Did you put the director's cell phone in my satchel?" Couldn't bring himself to ask the even more ludicrous question "Did you squash a mosquito in my car?" or anything about the director and the border.

"Now, why would I do that?" she asked, echoing him, but she looked serious, puzzled. "What are you talking about?"

"Keep the bugs as souvenirs," he said. Put them in the Southern Reach Olde Antique Shoppe and sell them to tourists.

"No, I mean it—what are you talking about?"

Rather than respond, Control got up, retreated into the corridor, not sure if he heard laughter from behind him or some distorted echo through the overhead vent.

014: HEROIC HEROES OF THE REVOLUTION

Later, as he was wallowing in the notes, plugging his ears and eyes with them, to forget about Grace—if he hadn't ransacked Grace's office who had?—the expedition wing buzzed him and an excitable-sounding male voice told Control that the biologist was "not feeling good at all— she says she's not up for an interview today." When he asked what was wrong, the man told him, "She's been complaining of cramps and fever. The doctor says it's a cold." A cold? A cold was nothing.

"Hit the ground running." The notes and these sessions were still firmly within his domain. He didn't want to postpone, so he'd go to her. With any luck, he wouldn't bump into Grace. Whitby he could've used help from, but even though he'd buzzed him, the man was making himself scarce.

As he said that he'd stop by soon, Control realized that it might be some ploy—the obvious one of not playing along, but also that by going he might be giving up some advantage or confirming that she held some power over him. But his head was full of scraps of notes and the puzzle of a possible clandestine trip by the director across the border and the deadly echo of muffled interiors of jewelry boxes. He wanted to clear it out, or fill it up with something else for a while.

He left his office, headed down the corridor. Of the smattering of personnel in the hall beyond some were actually in lab coats for once. For his benefit? "Bored?" a pale gaunt man who looked vaguely familiar murmured to the black woman walking beside him as they passed. "Eager to get on with it," came the reply. "You prefer this place, you really do, don't you?" Should he be playing it by the book more? Perhaps. He couldn't deny that the biologist had gotten lodged inside of his head: A faint pressure that made the path leading to the expedition wing narrower, the ceilings lower, the continuous seeking tongue of rough green carpet curling up around him. They were beginning to exist in some transitional space between interrogation and conversation, something for which he could not quite find a name.

"Good afternoon, Director," said Hsyu, head rising unexpected from a water fountain to his left so that it was as if a large puppet or art installation had come to life. "Is everything okay?"

Everything had been fine just a second before. Why would anything be different now? "You just looked very serious." Perhaps *you're* not very serious today; couldn't that be it? But he didn't say it, just smiled and continued on down the hall, already leaving the Lilliputian domain of the linguistics subdepartment.

Every time the biologist spoke something changed in his world, which he found suspicious on some level, resented it for the distraction. But not a flirtation, no, nor even the ordinary emotional bond. He knew with absolute certainty that he would *not* become overly fixated or obsessional, enter into some downward spiral, if they continued to talk, to share the same space. That had no place in his plans, didn't fit his profile.

The expedition wing featured four layers of obvious security, with the debriefing room they usually used perched on the edge of the outer layer—right after you passed through a decontamination zone that scanned you for everything from bacteria to the ghost of that rusty nail that had risen up through your foot on the rocky beach when you were ten. Considering the biologist had stood in a festering empty lot full of weeds, rusted metal, cracked concrete, and dog shit for hours before arriving, this seemed pointless. But still they did it, with an unsmiling and calm efficiency. Beyond that, all was rendered in an almost blinding white that contrasted with the washed-out teal-and-copper textures of the rooms off the corridor. Three more locked doors lay between the rest of the Southern Reach and the "suites," aka the holding areas. A texture and tone that might once have been futurist but now felt retro-futurist clung to white-and-black furniture that had an abstract modernist quality.

This is a version of a chair. This is an approximation of a table, a counter. The "bedeviled" glass partitions, as his dad would have joked, had been etched and frosted into simplistic wilderness scenes, including a row of reeds with an approximation of a marsh hawk hovering above. Like most such efforts, all of this could have come from the set of a low-budget 1970s sci-fi movie. It had none of the fluidity and sense of frozen motion, either, that his father had tried to put into his abstract sculptures.

In the minimalist foyer and rec rooms that served as preamble to the suites you could also find a novel's worth of photographs and portraits that had no relationship to reality. The photographs had been carefully chosen to suggest post-mission success, complete with grins and cheers, when they actually depicted pre-mission prep, often for expeditions gone disastrously wrong, or actors from photoshoots. The portraits, a long procession of them ending at the suites, were worse, in Control's estimation. They depicted all twenty-five "returning" members of the first expedition, the triumphant pioneers who had encountered the "pristine wilderness" that in fact had killed all but Lowry. This was the alternative reality any staff that came into contact with expedition members had to support. This was the fiction that came with its own made-up or tailored stories of bravery and endurance meant to evoke these same qualities in the current expedition. Like some socialist dictatorship's glorious heroes of the revolution.

What did it mean? Nothing. Had the biologist believed it all? Perhaps. The tale wanted to be believed, begged to be believed: a story of good old national can-do pride. Roll up your sleeves and get down to work, and if you try hard enough you'll come back alive and not a broken-down zombie with a distant gaze and cancer in place of a personality and an intact short-term memory.

He found Ghost Bird in her room, on her cot—or, someone other than him might have reported back, her bed. The place combined the ambiance of a whitewashed barracks, a summer camp, and a failing hotel. The same pale walls—although here you could see painted-over graffiti, the same as in a prison cell. The high ceiling included a skylight, and on the side wall a narrow window, too high for the biologist to peer out of it. The bed had been built into the far wall, and opposite it a TV with DVD player: approved movies only and a couple of approved channels. Nothing too realistic. Nothing that might fill in the amnesia. It was mostly ancient science-fiction and fantasy movies or melodramas. Documentaries and news programs were on the No list. Animal shows could go either way.

"I thought I would visit you this time, since you don't feel well," he said, through his surgical mask. The attendant had already said she had given her permission.

"You thought you'd crash my sickness party and take advantage of me not being at full strength," she said. Her eyes were bloodshot and hooded with shadow, her face drawn. She was still wearing the same odd janitorial-military outfit, this time with red socks. Even sick, she looked strong. She must do push-ups and pull-ups at a ferocious rate, was all he could think.

"No," he said, spinning an ovoid plastic chair so, before he'd thought through the visual, he could lean against the back, legs awkwardly splayed to either side. Did they not allow real chairs for the same reason airports only had plastic knives? "No, I was concerned. I didn't want to drag you to the debriefing room." He wondered if the medication for her sickness had made her fuzzy, if he should come back later. Or not at all. He had become uncomfortably aware of the power imbalance between them in this setting.

"Of course. Phorus snails are known for their courtesy."

"If you'd read further in your biology text, you would have discovered this is true."

That earned him half a laugh, but also her turning away from him on the bed-cot as she hugged an extra yellow pillow. Her V of a back faced him, the fabric of her shirt pulled tight, the delicate hairs on the smooth skin of her neck revealed to him with an almost microscopic precision.

"We could go into the common area if you would prefer?"

"No, you should see me in my unnatural environment."

"It seems nice enough," he said, then wished he hadn't.

"The Ghost Bird has a usual daily range of ten to twenty square miles, not a cramped space for pacing of, say, forty feet."

He winced, nodded in recognition, changed the subject. "I thought maybe today we'd talk about your husband and also the director."

"We won't talk about my husband. And *you're* the director."

"Sorry. I meant the psychologist. I misspoke." Cursing and forgiving himself at the same time.

She swiveled enough to give him a raised eyebrow, right eye hidden by the pillow, then fell back into contemplating the wall. "Misspoke?"

"I meant the psychologist."

"No, I think you meant director."

"Psychologist," he said stubbornly. Perhaps with too much irritation. There was something about the casualness of the situation that alarmed him. He should not have come anywhere near her private quarters.

"If you say so." Then, as if playing on his discomfort, she turned again so she was on her side facing him, still clutching the pillow. She peered up at him and said with a kind of sleepy cheekiness, "What if we share information?"

"What do you mean?" He knew exactly what she meant.

"You answer a question and I'll answer a question."

He said nothing, weighing the threat of that versus the reward. He could lie to her. He could lie to her all day long, and she'd never know.

"Okay," he said.

"Good. I'll start. Are you married or ever been married?"

"No and no."

"Zero for two. Are you gay?"

"That's another question—and no."

"Fair enough. Now ask away."

"What happened at the lighthouse?"

"Too general. Be more specific."

"When you went inside the lighthouse, did you climb to the top? What did you find?"

She sat up, back to the wall. "That's two questions. Why are you looking at me that way?"

"I'm not looking at you in any particular way." He'd just become aware of her breasts, which hadn't happened during prior sessions, and now was trying to become unaware of them again.

"But that's two questions." Apparently, he'd given the correct response.

"Yes, you're right about that."

"Which one do you want answered?"

"What did you find?"

"Who says I remember any of it?"

"You just did. So tell me."

"Journals. Lots of journals. Dried blood on the steps. A photograph of the lighthouse keeper."

"A photograph?"

"Yes."

"Can you describe it?"

"Two middle-aged men, in front of the lighthouse, a girl out to the side. The lighthouse keeper in the middle. Do you know his name?"

"Saul Evans," he said without thinking. But couldn't see the harm, was already mulling over the significance of a photograph that hung in the director's office also existing in the lighthouse. "That's your question."

He could tell she was disappointed. She frowned, shoulders slumped. Could tell as readily that the name "Saul Evans" meant nothing to her.

"What else can you tell me about the photo?"

"It was framed, hanging on the wall at the middle landing, and the lighthouse keeper's face was circled."

"Circled?" Who had circled it, and why?

"That's another question."

"Yes."

"Now tell me what your hobbies are."

"What? Why?" It seemed like a question for the wider world, not the Southern Reach.

"What do you do when you're not here?"

Control considered that. "I feed my cat."

She laughed—chortled, actually, ending in a short coughing fit. "That's not a hobby."

"More like a vocation," he admitted. "No, but—I jog. I like classical music. I play chess sometimes. I watch TV sometimes. I read books—novels."

"Nothing very distinctive there," she said.

"I never claimed to be unique. What else do you remember from the expedition?"

She squinted, eyebrows applying pressure to the rest of her face as if that might help her memory. "That's a very broad question, Mr. Director. Very broad."

"You can answer it however you like."

"Oh, thank you."

"I just mean that—"

"I know what you mean," she said. "I almost always know what you mean."

"Then answer the question."

"It's a voluntary game," she explained. "We can stop at any time. Maybe I want to stop now." That recklessness again, or something else? She sighed, crossed her arms. "Something bad happened at the top. I saw something bad. But I'm not quite sure what. A green flame. A shoe. It's confused, like it's in a kaleidoscope. It comes and it goes. It feels as if I'm receiving someone else's memories. From the bottom of a well. In a dream."

"Someone else's memories?"

"It's my turn. What does your mother do?"

"That's classified."

"I bet it is," she said, giving him an appraising look.

———

He ended the session soon thereafter. What was true empathy anyway but sometimes turning away, leaving someone alone? Tired and in her room, she had become not so much less sharp as almost too relaxed.

She was confusing him. He kept seeing sides of her that he had not known existed, that had not existed in the biologist he had known from the files and transcripts. He felt as if he'd been talking to someone younger today, someone more glib and also more vulnerable, if he'd chosen to exploit that. Perhaps it *was* because he had invaded her territory, while she was sick—or perhaps she was, for some reason, trying out personalities. Some part of him missed the more confrontational Ghost Bird.

As he went back through the layers of security, passing the faked portraits and photos, he acknowledged that at least she had admitted some of her memories of the expedition were intact. That was a kind of progress. Although it still felt too slow, felt every now and then as if everything was happening too slow, and that he was taking too long to understand. A ticking clock he couldn't see, that was beyond his power to truly see.

One day her portrait would be up on the wall. When the subject was still alive, did they have to sit for those, or were they created from existing photographs? Would she have to recount some fiction about her experiences in Area X, without ever having a complete memory of what had actually happened?

015: SEVENTH BREACH

Photographs had also been buried in the sedimentary layers of the director's desk. Many were of the lighthouse from different angles, a few from various expeditions but also reproductions of ancient daguerreotypes taken soon after the lighthouse had first been built, along with etchings and maps. The topographical anomaly as well, although fewer of these. Among them was a second copy of one of the photographs that hung on the wall opposite his desk—almost certainly the photograph the biologist had seen. That black-and-white photograph of the last lighthouse keeper, Saul Evans, with one of his assistants to his left, and on the right, hunched over as she clambered up some rocks in the background, a girl whose face was half-obscured by the hood of her jacket. Was her hair black, brown, or blond? Impossible to tell from the few strands visible. She was dressed in a practical flannel shirt and jeans. The photo had a wintry feel to it, the grass in the background faded and sparse, the waves visible beyond the sand and rocks cresting in a cold kind of way. A local girl? As with so many others, they might never know who she had been. The forgotten coast had not been the best place to live if you cared about anyone finding you from census records.

The lighthouse keeper was in his late forties or early fifties, except Control knew you could only serve until fifty, so he must have been in his forties. A weathered face, bearded as you might expect. A sea captain's hat, even though the man had never been any kind of sailor. Control couldn't intuit much from looking at Saul Evans. He looked like a walking, talking cliché, as if he'd tried hard for years to mimic first an eccentric lay preacher whose sermons referenced hellfire and then whatever one might expect from a lighthouse keeper. You could become invisible that way, as Control knew from his few operations in the field. Become a type, no one saw you. Paranoid thought: What better disguise? But disguise for what?

The photo had been taken by a member of the Séance & Science Brigade about a week or two before the Event that had created Area X. The photographer had gone missing when the border came down. It remained the only photo of Saul Evans they had, except for some shots from twenty years earlier, well before he'd come to the coast.

By the late afternoon, Control felt as if he hadn't gotten much further—just given himself a respite from governance of the Southern Reach—although even that was interrupted (again) by the sound of his reconstituted chair barricade being encountered by an apparition who turned out to be Cheney ambitiously leaning forward across the clattery chairs so he could peer around the corner.

". . . Hello, Cheney."

"Hello . . . Control."

Perhaps because of his precarious position, Cheney seemed at a loss, even though he was the intruder. Or as if he had thought the office might be empty, the chairs foreshadowing some shift in hierarchy?

"Yes?" Control said, not wanting to invite Cheney all the way in.

The X of his face tightened, the lines unsuccessfully

trying to break free and become either parallel or one line. "Oh, yes, well, I guess I just wondered if you'd followed up about, you know, the director's *trip*." This last bit delivered in a low voice backed up by a quick glance away down the hall. Did Cheney have a faction, too? That would be tiresome. But no doubt he did: He was the one true hope of the nervous scientists huddled in the basement, waiting to be downsized, plucked one by one from their offices and cubicles by the giant, invisible hand of Central and then tossed into a smoldering pit of indifference and joblessness.

"Since I've got you here, Cheney, here's a question for you: Anything out of the ordinary about the second-to-last eleventh expedition?" Another thing Control hated about the iterations: a metric mouthful to enunciate, harder still to remember the actual number. "X.11.H, it was, right?"

Cheney, stabilized by some crude chair rearrangement, appeared in full, motorcycle jacket and all, in the doorway. "X.11.J. I don't think so. You have the files."

But that was just it. Control had a fairly crude report, including the intel that the director had conducted the exit interviews . . . which were astonishingly vague in their happy-happy nothing-bad-happened message. "Well, it was the expedition before the director's *special trip*. I thought you might have some insight."

Cheney shook his head, seemed now to very much regret his intrusion. "No, nothing much. Nothing that comes to mind." Did the director's office somehow make him uncomfortable? His gaze couldn't seem to fix on one thing, ricocheted from the far wall to the ceiling and then, ever so briefly, like the brush of a moth's wings, touched upon the mounds of unprofessional evidence circling Control. Did

Cheney think of them as piles of gold Control would steal or piles of shit sandwiches he was being forced to eat?

"Let me ask you about Lowry, then," Control said, thinking about the ambiguous "L." notes he'd found and the video he'd be watching all too soon. "How did Lowry and the director get along?"

Cheney seemed just as uncomfortable with this question but more willing to answer. "How does anyone get along, when you think about it, really? Lowry didn't like me personally but we got along fine professionally. He had an appreciation for our role. He knew the value of having good equipment." Which probably meant Lowry had approved every purchase order Cheney ever wrote.

"But what about him and the director?" Control asked. Again.

"Bluntly? Lowry admired her in his way, tried to make her his protégé, but she didn't want to be. She was very much her own person. And I think she thought he got too much credit for just surviving."

"Wasn't he a hero?" A glorious hero of the revolution plastered on a wall, remade in the image created by a camera lens and doctored documents. Rehabilitated from his awful experiences. Made productive. Booted up to Central after a while.

"Sure, sure," Cheney said. "Sure enough. But, you know, maybe overrated. He liked to drink. He liked to throw his weight around. I remember the director once said something unkind, compared him to a prisoner of war who thinks just because he suffered he knows a lot. So, some friction. But they worked together, though. They did work together. Respect in opposition." Quick flash of a smile, as if to say, "We're all comrades here."

"Interesting." Although not really. Another tactical discovery: Evidence of infighting in the Southern Reach, a breakdown in organizational harmony because people weren't robots, couldn't be made to act like robots. Or could they?

"Yes, if you say so," Cheney said, and trailed off.

"Is there anything else?" Control asked, a pointed stare beneath a frozen smile daring Cheney to ask again about his investigation into the director's trip.

"No, I guess not. Nope. Not that I can think of," Cheney said, clearly relieved. He tossed his goodbyes in classic convoluted Cheneyesque fashion as he backed out, amble-stumbling over the chairs and out of sight down the corridor.

After that, Control concentrated on nothing but basic sorting, until all the bits of paper had been accounted for and the piles safely stored in separate filing boxes for further categorizing. Although Control had noticed numerous references to the Séance & Science Brigade, he had found only three brief mentions of Saul Evans to go with the photo. As if the director's interests had led her elsewhere.

He had, however, uncovered and set aside a sheet handwritten by the director, of seemingly random words and phrases, which he eventually realized, by taking a cross-referencing peek at Grace's DMP file, had been used as hypnotic commands on the twelfth expedition. Now *that* was interesting. He almost buzzed Cheney to ask him about it, but something made him put the phone receiver down before punching in the extension.

At a quarter past six, Control felt a compulsion to wander out into the corridor for a good stretch. Everything lay under a hush and even a distant radio sounded like a garbled lullaby. Roaming farther afield, he was crossing the end of the now-empty cafeteria when he heard sounds coming from a storage room close to the corridor that led to the science division. Almost everyone had left, and he'd planned to leave soon himself, but the sounds distracted him. Who was in there? The elusive janitor, he hoped. The horrible cleaning product needed to be switched out. He was convinced it was a health hazard.

So he grasped the knob, receiving a little electric shock as he turned it, and then wrenched outward with all of his strength.

The door flew open, knocking Control back.

A pale creature was crouched in front of shelves of supplies, revealed under the sharp light of a single low-swinging lightbulb.

An unbearable yet beatific agony deformed its features. Whitby.

Breathing heavily, Whitby stared up at Control. The look of agony had begun to evaporate, leaving behind an expression of combined cunning and caution.

Clearly Whitby had just suffered some kind of trauma. Clearly Whitby had just heard that a family member or close friend had died. Even though it was Control who had received the shock.

Control said, idiotically, "I'll come back later," as if they'd had a meeting scheduled in the storage room.

Whitby jumped up like a trap-door spider, and Control flinched and took a step back, certain Whitby was attacking him. Instead Whitby pulled him into the storage room, shutting the door behind them. Whitby had a surprisingly strong grip for such a slight man.

"No, no, please come in," he was saying to Control, as if he hadn't been able to speak and guide his boss inside at the same time, so that now there was a lip-synch issue.

"I really can come back later," Control said, still rattled, preserving the illusion that he hadn't just seen Whitby in extreme distress . . . and also the illusion that this was Whitby's office and not a storage space.

Whitby stared at him in the dull light of the low-hung single bulb, standing close because it was crowded with the two of them in there, narrow with a high ceiling that could not be seen through the darkness above the bulb, a shield directing its light downward only. The shelves to either side of the central space displayed several rows of a lemon-zest cleaning product, along with stacked cans of soup, extra mop heads, garbage bags, and a few digital clocks with a heavy layer of dust on them. A long silver ladder led up into darkness.

Whitby was *still* composing his expression, Control realized, having to consciously wrench his frown toward a smile, wring the last clenched fear from his features.

"I was just getting some peace and quiet," Whitby said. "It can be hard to find."

"You looked like you were having a breakdown, to be honest," Control said, not sure he wanted to continue playing pretend. "Are you okay?" He felt more comfortable saying this now that Whitby clearly wasn't going to have a psychotic break. But he was also embarrassed that Whitby had managed to so easily trap him in here.

"Not at all," Whitby said, a smile finally fitted in place,

and Control hoped the man was responding to the first part of what he had said. "What can I help you with?"

Control went along with this fiction Whitby continued to offer up, if only because he had noticed that the inside lock on the door had been disabled with a blunt instrument. So Whitby had wanted privacy, but he had also been utterly afraid of being trapped in the room, too. There was a staff psychiatrist—a free resource for Southern Reach employees. Control didn't remember seeing anything in Whitby's file to indicate that he had ever gone.

It took Control a moment longer than felt natural, but he found a reason. Something that would run its course and allow him to leave on the right note. Preserve Whitby's dignity. Perhaps.

"Nothing much, really," Control said. "It's about some of the Area X theories."

Whitby nodded. "Yes, for example, the issue of parallel universes," he said, as if they were picking up a conversation from some other time, a conversation Control did not remember.

"That maybe whatever's behind Area X came from one," Control said, stating something he didn't believe and not questioning the narrowing of focus.

"That, yes," Whitby said, "but I've been thinking more about how every decision we make theoretically splits off from the next, so that there are an infinite number of other universes out there."

"Interesting," Control said. If he let Whitby lead, hopefully the dance would end sooner.

"And in some of them," Whitby explained, "we solved the mystery and in some of them the mystery never existed, and there *never was* an Area X." This said with a rising intensity. "And we can take comfort in that. Perhaps we could even be *content* with that." His face fell as he continued: "If not for a further thought. Some of these universes where we solved the mystery may be separated from ours by the thinnest of membranes, the most insignificant of variations. This is something always on my mind. What mundane detail aren't we seeing, or what things are we doing that lead us away from the answer."

Control didn't like Whitby's confessional tone because it felt as if Whitby was revealing one thing to hide another, like the biologist's explanation of the sensation of drowning. This simultaneous with parallel universes of perception opening between him and Whitby as he spoke because Control felt as if Whitby were talking about *breaches*, the same breaches so much on his mind on a daily basis. Whitby talking about breaches angered him in a territorial way, as if Whitby was commenting on Control's past, even though there was no logic to that.

"Perhaps it's your presence, Whitby," Control said. A joke, but a cruel one, meant to push the man away, close down the conversation. "Maybe without you here we would have solved it already."

The look on Whitby's face was awful, caught between knowing that Control had expressed the idea with humor and the certainty that it didn't matter if it was a joke or serious. All of this conveyed in a way that made Control realize the thought was not original but had occurred to Whitby many times. It was too insincere to follow up with "I didn't mean it," so some version of Control just left, running down the hall as fast as he was able, aware that his extraction solution was unorthodox but unable to stop himself. Running down the green carpet while he stood there and apologized/laughed it off/changed the subject/took a pretend phone call . . . or, as he actually did, said nothing at all and let an awkward silence build.

In retaliation, although Control didn't understand it then, Whitby said, "You have seen the video, haven't you? From the first expedition?"

"Not yet," as if he were admitting to being a virgin. That was scheduled for tomorrow.

A silent shudder had passed through Whitby in the middle of delivering his own question, a kind of spasmodic attempt to fling out or reject . . . something, but Control would leave it up to some other, future version of himself to ask Whitby why.

Was there a reality in which Whitby had solved the mystery and was telling it to him right now? Or a reality in which he was throttling Whitby just for being Whitby? Perhaps sometimes, at this moment, he met Whitby in a cave after a nuclear holocaust or in a store buying ice cream for a pregnant wife or, wandering farther afield, perhaps in some scenarios they had met much earlier—Whitby the annoying substitute teacher for a week in his freshman high school English class. Perhaps now he had some inkling as to why Whitby hadn't advanced farther, why his research kept getting interrupted by grunt work for others. He kept wanting to grant Whitby a localized trauma to explain his actions, kept wondering if he just hadn't gotten through enough layers to reach the center of Whitby, or if there was no center to reach and the layers defined the man.

"Is *this* the room you wanted to show me?" Control asked, to change the subject.

"No. Why would you think that?" Whitby's cavernous eyes and sudden expression of choreographed puzzlement made him into an emaciated owl.

Control managed to extricate himself a minute or so later.

But he couldn't get the image of Whitby's agony-stricken face out of his head. Still had no idea why Whitby had hidden in a storage room.

The Voice called a few minutes later, as Control was trying desperately to leave for the day. Control was ready despite Whitby. Or, perhaps, because of Whitby. He made sure the office door was locked. He took out a piece of paper on which he had scribbled some notes to himself. Then he carefully put the Voice on speakerphone at medium volume, having already tested to make sure there was no echo, no sense of anything being out of the ordinary.

He said hello.

A conversation ensued.

They talked for a while. Then the Voice said, "Good," while Control kept looking, at irregular intervals, at his sheet. "Just stabilize and do your job. Paralysis is not a cogent option, either. You will get good sleep tonight."

Stabilize. Paralysis. Cogent. As he hung up, he was alarmed to realize that he did feel as if he *had* been stabilized. That now the encounter with Whitby seemed like a blip, inconsequential when seen in the context of his overall mission.

At the diner counter the next morning, the cashier, a plump gray-haired woman, asked him, "You with the folks working at that government agency on the military base?"

Guarded, still shaking off sleep and a little hungover: "Why do you ask?"

"Oh," she said sweetly, "they all have the same look about them, that's all."

She wanted him to ask "What look is that?" Instead, he just smiled mysteriously and gave her his order. He didn't want to know what look he shared, what secret club he'd joined all unsuspecting. Did she have a chart somewhere so she could check off shared characteristics?

Back in the car, Control noticed that a white mold had already covered the dead mosquito and the dried drop of blood on his windshield. His sense of order and cleanliness offended, he wiped it all away with a napkin. Who would he present the evidence of tampering to, anyway?

The first item on his agenda was the long-awaited viewing of the videotape taken by the first expedition. Those video fragments existed in a special viewing room in an area of the building adjacent to the quarters for expedition members. A massive white console sat against the far wall in that cramped space. It jutted more sharply at the top than the bottom and mimicked the embracing shape of the Southern Reach building. Within that console—dull gray head recessed inside a severe cubist cowl—a television had been embedded that provided access to the video and nothing else. The television was an older model dating back to the time of the first expedition, with its bulky hindquarters recessed into an alcove in the wall. Control's back still retained the groaning memory of a similar ungainly weight as a college student struggling to get a TV into his dorm room.

A low black marble desk with glints of Formica stood in front of the television, old-fashioned buttons and joy sticks allowing for manipulation of the video content—almost like an antiquated museum exhibit or one of those quarter-fed séance machines at the carnival. A phalanx of four black leather conference chairs had been tucked in under the desk. Cramped quarters with the chairs pulled out, although the ceiling extended a good twenty feet above him. That should have alleviated his slight sense of claustrophobia, but it only reinforced it with some minor vertigo, given the slant of the console. The vents above him, he noticed, were filthy with dust. A sharp car-dashboard smell warred with a rusty mold scent.

The names of twenty-four of the twenty-five members of the first expedition had been etched on large gold labels affixed to the side walls.

If Grace denied that the wall of text written by the lighthouse keeper was a memorial for the former director, she could not deny either that this room *did* serve as a memorial for that expedition or that she served as its guardian and curator. The security clearance was so high for the video footage that of the current employees at the Southern Reach only the former director, Grace, and Cheney had access. Everyone else could see photo stills or read transcripts, but even then only under carefully controlled conditions.

So Grace served as his liaison because no one else could, and as she wordlessly pulled out a chair and through some arcane series of steps prepped the video footage, Control realized a change had come over her. She prepared the footage not with the malicious anticipation he might have expected but with loving devotion and at a deliberate pace more common to graveyards than AV rooms. As if this were a neutral space, some cease-fire agreed to between them without his knowledge.

The video would show him dead people who had become darkly legendary within the Southern Reach, and he could see she took her job as steward seriously. Probably in part because the director had, too—and the director had known these people, even if her predecessor had sent them to their fates. After a year of prep. With all of the best high-tech equipment that the Southern Reach could acquire or create, dooming them.

Control realized his heart rate had leapt, that his mouth had become dry and his palms sweaty. It felt as if he were about to take a very important test, one with consequences.

"It's self-explanatory," Grace said finally. "The video is cued up to the beginning and proceeds, with gaps, chronologically. You can move from clip to clip. You can skip around—whatever you prefer. If you are not finished by the end of one hour, I will come in here and your session will be over." They had recovered more than one hundred and fifty fragments, most of the surviving footage lasting between ten seconds and two minutes. Some recovered by Lowry, others by the fourth expedition. They did not recommend watching the footage for more than an hour at any one time. Few had spent that long with it.

"I will also be waiting outside. You can knock on the door if you are done early."

Control nodded. Did that mean he was to be locked in? Apparently it did.

Grace relinquished her seat. Control took her place, and as she left there came an unexpected hand on his shoulder, perhaps putting more weight into the gesture than necessary. Then came the click of the door lock from the outside as she left him alone in a marble vault lined with the names of wraiths.

Control had asked for this experience, but now did not really want it.

The earliest sequences showed the normal things: setting up camp, the distant lighthouse jerkily coming into view from time to time. The shapes of trees and tents showed up dark in the background. Blue sky wheeled across the screen as someone lowered the camera and forgot to turn off the camcorder. Some laughter, some banter, but Control was, like a seer or a time traveler, suspicious already. Were those the expected, normal things, the banal camaraderie displayed by human beings, or instead harbingers of secret communiqués, subcutaneous and potent? Control hadn't wanted the interference, the contamination, of someone else's analysis or opinions, so he hadn't read everything in the files. But he realized right then that he was too armored with foreknowledge anyway, and too cynical about his caution not to find himself ridiculous. If he wasn't careful, everything would be magnified, misconstrued, until each frame carried the promise of menace. He kept in mind the note from another analyst that no other expedition had encountered what he was about to see. Among those that had come back, at least.

A few segments from the expedition leader's video journal followed at dusk—caught in silhouette, campfire behind her—reporting nothing that Control didn't already know. Then about seven entries followed, each lasting four or five seconds, and these showed nothing but blotchy shadow: night shots with no contrast. He kept squinting into that murk hoping some shape, some image, would reveal itself. But in the end, it was just the self-fulfilling prophecy of black dust motes floating across the corners of his vision like tiny orbiting parasites.

A day went by, with the expedition spreading outward in waves from the base camp, with Control trying not to become attached to any of them. Not swayed by the charm of their frequent joking. Nor by the evident seriousness and competence of them, some of the best minds the Southern Reach could find. The clouds stretched long across the sky. A sobering moment when they encountered the sunken remains of a line of military trucks and tanks sent in before the border went down. The equipment had already been covered over in loam and vines. By the time of the fourth expedition, Control knew, all traces of it would be gone. Area X would have requisitioned it for its own purposes, privilege of the victor. But there were no human remains to disturb the first expedition, although Control could see frowns on some faces. By then, too, if you listened carefully, you could begin to hear the disruption of transmissions on the walkie-talkies issued to the expedition members, more and more queries of "Come in" and "Are you there" followed by static.

Another evening, the dawn of another day, and Control

felt as if he were moving along at a rapid clip, almost able to relax into the closed vessel formed by each innocuous moment and to live there in blissful ignorance of the rest. Even though by now the disruption had spread, so that queries via walkie-talkie had become verbal miscues and misunderstandings. Listener and listened-to had begun to be colonized by some outside force but had not yet realized it. Or, at least, not voiced concerns for the camera. Control chose not to rewind these instances. They sent a prickling shiver across the back of his neck, gave him a faint sensation of nausea, increased the destabilizing sense of vertigo and claustrophobia.

Finally, though, Control could no longer fool himself. The famous twenty-second clip had come up, which the file indicated had been shot by Lowry, who had served as both the team's anthropologist and its military expert. Dusk of the second day, with a lisp of sunset. Dull dark tower of the lighthouse in the middle distance. In their innocence, they had not seen the harm in splitting up, and Lowry's group had decided to bivouac on the trail, among the remains of an abandoned series of houses about halfway to the lighthouse. It had hardly been enough to constitute a village, with no name on the maps, but had been the largest population center in the area.

A rustling sound Control associated with sea oats and the wind off the beach, but faint. The wreckage of the old walls formed deeper shadows against the sky, and he could just see the wide line that was the stone path running through. In the clip, Lowry shook a bit holding the camera. In the foreground, a woman, the expedition leader, was shouting, "Get her to stop!" Her face was made a mask by the light from the recorder and the way it formed such severe shadows around her eyes and mouth. Opposite, across a kind of crude picnic table that appeared fire-burned, a woman, the expedition leader, shouted, "Get her to stop! Please stop! Please stop!" A lurk and spin of the camera and then the camera steadied, presumably with Lowry still holding it. Lowry began to hyperventilate, and Control recognized that the sound he had heard before was a kind of whispered breathing with a shallow rattle threading through it. Not the wind at all. He could also just hear urgent, sharp voices from off-camera, but he couldn't make out what they were saying. The woman on the left of the screen then stopped shouting and stared into the camera. The woman on the right also stopped shouting, stared into the camera. An identical fear and pleading and confusion radiated from the masks of their faces toward him, from so far away, from so many years away. He could not distinguish between the two manifestations, not in that murky light.

Then, sitting bolt upright, even knowing what was to come, Control realized it was not dusk that had robbed the setting behind them of any hint of color. It was more as if something had interceded on the landscape, something so incredibly large that its edges were well beyond the camera's lens. In the last second of the videotape, the two women still frozen and staring, the background seemed to shift and keep shifting . . . followed by a clip even more chilling to Control: Lowry in front of the camera this time, goofing off on the beach the next morning, and whoever was behind the camera laughing. No mention of the expedition leader. No sign of her on any of the subsequent video footage, he knew. No explanation from Lowry. It was as if she had been erased from their memories, or as if they had all suffered some vast, unimaginable trauma while off-camera that night.

But the dissolution continued despite their seeming happiness and ease. For Lowry was saying words that had no meaning and the person holding the camera responded as if she could understand him, her own speech not yet deformed.

Carnage followed him from the video screening, when he finally left, escorted by Grace back into the light, or a different kind of light. Carnage might follow him for a while. He wasn't sure, was having difficulty putting things into words, had done little more than mumble and nod to Grace when she asked him if he was okay, while she held his arm as if she were holding him up. Yet he knew that her compassion came with a price, that he might pay for it later. So he extricated himself, insisted on leaving her behind and walking the rest of the way back in solitude.

He had a full day ahead of him still. He had to recover. Next was his scheduled time with the biologist, and then status meetings, and then . . . he forgot what was next. Stumbled, tripped, leaned on one knee, realized he was in the cafeteria area and its familiar green carpet with the arrow pattern pointing in from the courtyard. Caught by the light streaming from those broad, almost cathedral-like windows. It was sunny outside, but he could already see the angry gray in the middle of white clouds that signaled more afternoon showers.

In the black water with the sun shining at midnight, those fruit shall come ripe and in the darkness of that which is golden shall split open to reveal the revelation of the fatal softness in the earth.

A lighthouse. A tower. An island. A lighthouse keeper. A border with a huge shimmering door. A director who might have gone AWOL across that border, through that door. A squashed mosquito on his windshield. Whitby's anguished face. The swirling light of the border. The director's phone in his satchel. Demonic videos housed in a memorial catafalque. Details were beginning to overwhelm him. Details were beginning to swallow him up. No chance yet to let them settle or to know which were significant, which trivial. He'd "hit the ground running" as his mother had wanted, and it wasn't getting him very far. He was in danger of incoming information outstripping his prep work, the knowledge he'd brought with him. He'd exhausted so many memorized files, burned through tactics. And he'd have to dig into the director's notes in earnest soon, and that would bring with it more mysteries, he was sure.

The screaming had gone on and on toward the end. The one holding the camera hadn't seemed human. Wake up, he had pleaded with the members of the first expedition as he watched. Wake up and understand what is happening to you. But they never did. They couldn't. They were miles away, and he was more than thirty years too late to warn them.

Control put his hand on the carpet, the green arrows up close composed of threads of a curling intertwined fabric almost like moss. He felt its roughness, how threadbare it had become over the years. Was it the original carpet, from thirty years ago? If so, every major player in those videos, in the files, had strode across it, had crisscrossed it hundreds and hundreds of times. Perhaps even Lowry, holding his camcorder, joking around before their expedition. It was as worn down as the

Southern Reach, as the agency moved along its appointed grooves on this fun-house ride that was called Area X.

People were staring at him, too, as they crisscrossed the cafeteria. He had to get up.

From the dim-lit halls of other places forms that never could be writhe.

Control went from bended knee to the interrogation room with the biologist—after a brief interlude in his office. He had needed some form of relief, some way to cleanse. He'd called up the information on Rock Bay, the biologist's longest assignment before she'd joined the twelfth expedition. From her field notes and sketches, he could tell it was her favorite place. A rich, northern rain forest with a verdant ecosystem. She'd rented a cottage there, and in addition to photographs of the tidal pools she'd studied, he had shots of her living quarters—Central's routine thorough follow-up. The cot-like bed, the comfortable kitchen, and the black stove in the corner that doubled as a fireplace, the long spout going up into a chimney. There were aspects of the wilderness that appealed to him, that calmed him, but so too did the simple domesticity of the cottage.

Once seated in the room, Control placed a bottle of water and her files between them. A gambit he was bored with, but nevertheless . . . His mother had always said the repetition of ritual made pointing to the thing that had been rendered invisible all the more dramatic. Someday soon he might point to the files and make an offer.

The fluorescent lights pulsed and flickered, something beginning to devolve in them. He didn't care if Grace watched from behind the glass or not. Ghost Bird looked terrible today, not so much sick but like she had been crying, which was how he felt. There was a darkness around her eyes and a slump to her posture. Any recklessness or amusement had been burned away or gone into hiding.

Control didn't know where to start because he didn't want to start at all. What he wanted to talk about was the video footage, but that was impossible. The words would linger, form in his mind, but never become sound, trapped between his need and his will. He couldn't tell any human being, ever. If he let it out, contaminated someone else's mind, he would not forgive himself. A girlfriend who had gleaned some sense of his job had once asked, "Why do you do it?"—meaning why serve such a clandestine purpose, a purpose that could not be shared, could not be revealed. He'd given his standard response, in a portentous manner, to poke fun at himself. To disguise the seriousness. "To know. To go beyond the veil." Across the border. Even as Control said it, he had known that he was also telling her he didn't mind leaving her there, alone, on the other side.

"What would you like to talk about?" he asked Ghost Bird, not because he was out of questions but because he wanted her to take the lead.

"Nothing," she said, listless. The word came out at a muttering slant.

"There must be something." Pleading. Let there be something, to distract from the carnage in my head.

"I am not the biologist."

That brought Control out of himself, forced him to consider what she meant.

"You are not the biologist," he echoed.

"You want the biologist. I'm not the biologist. Go talk to her, not me."

Was this some kind of identity crisis or just meta-phorical?

Either way, he realized that this session had been a mistake.

"We can try again in the afternoon," he said.

"Try what?" she snapped. "Do you think this is *therapy*? Who for?"

He started to respond, but in one violent motion she swept his files and water off the table and grabbed his left hand with both of hers and wouldn't let go. Defiance and fear in her eyes. "What do you want from me? What do you *really* want?"

With his free hand, Control waved off the guards plunging into the room. From the corner of his eye, their retreat had a peculiar suddenness, as if they'd been sucked back into the doorway by something invisible and monstrous.

"Nothing," he said, to see how she'd respond. Her hand was clammy and warm, not entirely pleasant; something was definitely going on beneath her skin. Had her fever gotten worse?

"I won't assist in charting my own pathology," she hissed, breathing hard, shouting: "I am not the biologist!"

He pulled himself loose, pushed away from the table, stood, and watched as she fell back into her seat. She stared down at the table, wouldn't look up at him. He hated to see her distress, hated worse that he seemed to have caused it.

"Whoever you are, we'll pick this up later," he said.

"Humoring me," she muttered, arms folded.

But by the time he'd picked up the bottle of water and his scattered files and made it to the door, something had changed in her again.

Her voice trembled on the cusp of some new emotion. "There was a mating pair of wood storks in the holding pond out back when I left. Are they still there?"

It took a moment to realize she meant when she'd left on the expedition. Another moment to realize that this was almost an apology.

"I don't know," he said. "I'll find out."

What had happened to her out there? What had happened to him in here?

The last fragment of video remained in its own category: "Unassigned." Everyone was dead by then, except for an injured Lowry, already halfway back to the border.

Yet for a good twenty seconds the camera flew above the glimmering marsh reeds, the deep blue lakes, the ragged white cusp of the sea, toward the lighthouse.

Dipped and rose, fell again and soared again.

With what seemed like a horrifying enthusiasm.

An all-consuming joy.

017: PERSPECTIVE

Steps had begun to go missing. Steps had begun to occur out of step. Lunch followed a status meeting that, the moment it was done, Control barely remembered no matter how hard he tried. He was here to solve a puzzle in some ways, but he felt as if it were beginning to solve him instead.

Control had talked for a while, he knew that, about how he wanted to know more about the lighthouse and its relationship to the topographical anomaly. After which Hsyu said something about the patterns in the lighthouse keeper's sermon, while the sole member of the props department, a hunched-over elderly man named Darcy with a crinkly tinfoil voice, added commentary throughout her talk, referring to the "crucial role, now and in the future, of the historical accuracy division."

Trees framed the campfire, the members of the expedition around the campfire. Something so large you couldn't see its outline, crawling or lumbering through the background, obscenely threaded between the trees and the campfire. He didn't like to think about what could be so huge and yet so lithe as to thread like that, to conjure up the idea of a fluid wall of ribbony flesh.

Perhaps he could have continued to nod and ask questions, but he had become more and more repulsed by the way Hsyu's assistant, Amy-something, chewed on her lip. Slowly. Methodically. Without thought. As she scribbled notes or whispered some piece of information in Hsyu's ear. The off-white of her upper left cuspid and incisors would appear, the pink gum exposed as the upper lip receded, and then with almost rhythmic precision, she would nip and pincer, nip and pincer, the left side of her lower lip, which over time became somewhat redder than her lipstick.

Something had *brushed* through or *interceded* across the screen for a moment in the background, while in the middle a man with a beard squatted—not Lowry but a man named

O'Connell. At first, Control had thought O'Connell was mumbling, was saying something in a language he didn't understand. And, trying to find logic, trying to grasp, Control had almost buzzed Grace right then to tell her about his discovery. But by another few frames, Control could tell that the man was actually chewing on his lip, and continued chewing until the blood came, the whole time resolutely staring into the camera because there was, Control slowly realized, no other place safe enough to look. O'Connell was speaking as he chewed, but the words weren't anything unique now that Control had read the wall. It was the most primal and thus most banal message imaginable.

Predictable lunch to follow, in the cafeteria. Stabilizing lunch, he'd thought, but *lunch* repeated too many times became a meaningless word that morphed into *lunge* that became *lunged* that became a leaping white rabbit that became the biologist at the depressing table that became an expedition around a campfire, unaware of what they were about to endure.

Control followed a version of Whitby he was both wary of and concerned about, and who muddled his way through the tables, with Cheney, Hsyu, and Grace trailing behind him. Whitby hadn't been in the status meeting, but Grace had seen him ducking into a side corridor as they'd walked downstairs and roped him into their lunch. Then it had just been a case of everyone deferring to Whitby in his natural habitat. Whitby couldn't like the cafeteria for the food. It had to be the open-air quality of the space, the clear lines of sight. Perhaps it was simply that you could escape in any direction.

Whitby led them to a round faux-wooden table with low

plastic seats—all of it jammed up against the corner farthest from the courtyard, which abutted stairs that led to the largely empty space known as the third level that they had just vacated, really a glorified landing with a few conference rooms. Control realized Whitby had chosen the table so he could cram his slight frame into the semicircle closest to the wall—a wary if improbable gunslinger with his back to the stairs, looking out across the cafeteria to the courtyard and the fuzzy green of a swamp dissolving in humid bubbles of condensation against the glass.

Control sat facing Grace, with Whitby and Hsyu flanking Grace to right and left. Cheney plopped into the seat next to Control, opposite Whitby. Control began to suspect some of them weren't there by chance, or voluntarily, the way Grace seemed to be commandeering the space. The huffing X of Cheney's face leaned in, solicitous as he said, "I'll hold down the fort while you get your food and go after."

"Just get me a pear or an apple and some water, and I'll stay here instead," Control said. He felt vaguely nauseated.

Cheney nodded, withdrew his thick hands from the table with a slap, and left along with the others, while Control contemplated the large framed photo hanging on the wall. Old and dusty, it showed the core of the Southern Reach team at the time. Control recognized some faces from his various briefings, zeroing in on Lowry, come back for a visit from Central, still looking haggard. Whitby was there, too, grinning near the center. The photo suggested that at one time Whitby had been inquisitive, quick, optimistic—perhaps even impishly proactive. The missing director was just a hulking shadow off at the left edge. She loomed, committed to neither a smile nor a frown.

At that time, she would have been a relatively new hire, an apprentice to the staff psychologist. Grace would have joined about five years later. It could not have been easy for either of them to make their way up the hierarchy and hold on to their power. That had taken toughness and perseverance. Perhaps too much. But at least they had both missed the crazier manifestations of the early days, of which the hypnosis was the only surviving remnant. Cryptozoologists, an almost séance, the bringing in of psychics, given the bare facts and asked to produce . . . what? Information? No information could be extracted from their divinations.

The others returned from the buffet, Cheney with a pear on a plate and the asked-for water. Control reflected that if something terrible happened later that day and forensics tried to reconstruct events from the contents of their stomachs, Cheney would look like a fussy bird, Whitby like a pig, Hsyu a health nut, and Grace a mere nibbler. She sat back in her seat, glaring at him now, with her two packets of crackers and coffee arranged in front of her as if she planned to use it as evidence against him. He braced himself, trying to clear his head with a sip of water.

"Status meetings every Thursday or every other Thursday?" he asked, just to test the waters and make conversation. He clamped down on an automatic impulse to use the question to begin a sly exploration of department morale.

But Grace didn't want to make conversation.

"Do you want to hear a story," she said, and it wasn't a question. She looked as if she had made up her mind about something.

"Sure," Control said. "Why not?" While Cheney fidgeted next to him, and Whitby and Hsyu simultaneously seemed to flatten and become smaller, looking away from Grace, as if she'd become a repelling magnet.

Her stare bore down on him and he lost the urge to gnaw on his pear. "It concerns a domestic terrorism operative." Here it comes, there it goes.

"How interesting," Control said. "I was in domestic terrorism for a while."

Continuing on as if Control hadn't said a word: "The story is about a blown field assignment, this operative's third out of training. Not his first or his second, but his third, so no real excuses. What was his job? He was to observe and report on separatist militia members on the northwest coast—based in the mountains but coming down into two key port cities to recruit." Central had believed that the radical cells in this militia had the will and resources to disrupt shipping, blow up a building, many things. "No coherent political views or vision. Just ignorant white men mostly, college age but not in college. A few radicalized women, and then the usual others unaware of what their ignorant men were up to. None of them as stupid as the operative."

Control sat very still. He began to feel as if his face were cracking. He was getting warmer and warmer, a tingling flame spreading slowly throughout his body. Was she trying to tear him down, stone by stone? In front of the few people at the Southern Reach with whom he already had some kind of rapport?

Cheney had gotten in some huffing sounds to express his disapproval of where this might be going. Whitby looked as if a stranger walking toward him from very far away was trying to give him the details of an interesting conversation, but he wasn't quite close enough to hear about it yet—so sorry, not his fault.

"Sounds familiar," Control said, because it did, and he even knew what came next.

"The operative infiltrates the group, or the edges of the group," Grace said. "He gets to know some of the friends of the people at the core of it."

Hsyu, frowning, focused on something of interest on the carpet as she got up with her tray, managed a cheerful if abrupt goodbye, and left the table.

"Not fair, Grace, you know that," Cheney whispered, leaning forward, as if somehow he could direct his words solely to her. "An ambush." But by Control's own reckoning, it *was* fair. Very fair. Given that they hadn't agreed to ground rules ahead of time.

"This operative starts following the friends and, eventually, they lead him to a bar. The girlfriend of the second-in-command likes to have a drink at this bar. She is on the list; he has memorized her photograph. But instead of just observing her and reporting back, this clever, clever operative ignores his orders and starts to talk to her, there in the bar—"

"Do you want me to tell the rest of the story?" Control interrupted. Because he could. He could tell it—wanted to tell it, had a fierce desire to tell it—and felt a perverse gratitude toward Grace, because this was such a human problem, such a banal, human problem compared to all the rest.

"Grace . . ." Cheney, imploring.

But Grace waved them both off, faced Whitby so that Whitby had no choice but to look at her. "Not only does he have a conversation with this woman, Whitby"—Whitby as startled by the complicity of his name as if she had put her arm around him—"but he seduces her, telling himself that he is doing it to help the cause. Because he is an arrogant man. Because he is too far off his leash." Mother had typified that as hearsay, as she had typified a lot of things, but in this case she had been right.

"We used to have forks and spoons in the cafeteria," Whitby said, mournfully. "Now we just have sporks." He turned to the left, then the right, looking either for alternative cutlery or for a quick way to exit.

"Next time you tell this story, you should leave out the seduction, which didn't happen," Control said, a spiral of ash in his head and a faint ringing in his ears. "You could also add that the operative didn't have clear orders from his superior."

"You heard the man. You heard him." The Cheney murmur, as subtle as a donkey burp.

Grace kept speaking directly to Whitby, with Whitby now swiveling toward Cheney, the expression asking Cheney what he should do, and Cheney unable or unwilling to give him guidance. Let it play out to the bitter end. Draw the poison. This was trench warfare. This was always going to continue.

"So the operative beds the girlfriend"—no triumph in her voice at least—"although he knows it is dangerous, knows that the members of the militia might find out. His supervisor does not know what he is doing. Yet. And then one day—"

"One day," Control interrupted, because if she was going to tell this story she should get the rest of it right, godfucking dammit. "One day he goes to the bar—this is only the third time—and gets made by surveillance cameras put in overnight by the boyfriend." Control hadn't spoken to her the second time in the bar. That third and final time, yes. How he wished he hadn't. He couldn't even remember what he'd said to her, or her to him.

"Correct," Grace said, a momentary confused expression adding weight to her face. "Correct."

It was an old scar by now for Control, even if it seemed like a fresh wound to every scavenger that tried to dip their beak or snout into it, to tear away some spoiled meat. The routine of telling the story transformed Control from a person into an actor dramatizing an ancient event from his own life. Every time he had to reenact it, the monologue became smoother, the details less complex and more easily fitted together, the words like stuffing puzzle pieces into his mouth and spewing them out in the perfect order to form a picture. He disliked the performance more each time. But the only other choice was to be blackmailed by a part of his past now more than seventeen years and five months gone by. Even though it followed him around to each new job because his supervisor at the time had decided Control deserved, forever, more punishment than he'd received at the point of impact.

In the worst versions, like the one Grace had started to tell, he'd slept with the girlfriend, Rachel McCarthy, and had compromised operations beyond repair. But the truth had been bad enough. He had come out of private college as his mother's protégé; excellent grades, a kind of unthinking swagger, and completion of training at Central with high marks. He'd had great success in the field the first two times out, tracking good ole boys across flat plains and gentle hills in the middle of the country—pickups and chewing tobacco and lonely little town squares, snacking on fried okra while he watched guys in baseball caps load suspicious boxes into the backs of vans.

"I made a terrible mistake. I think about it every day. It guides me in my job now. It makes me humble and keeps me focused." But he didn't think about it every day. You didn't think about it every day or it would rise up and consume you. It just remained there, nameless: a sad, dark thing that weighed you down only some of the time. When the memory became too faint, too abstract, it would transform itself into an old rotator cuff injury, a pain so thin yet so sharp that he could trace the line of it all the way across his shoulder blade and down his back.

"So then," Control said, Whitby beginning to be crushed by their tandem attention and Cheney gone, having orchestrated a subtle jailbreak right under Control's nose. "So then, the boyfriend has it on tape that some stranger was talking to his girlfriend, which would probably be enough for a beating. But then he has a comrade follow this stranger to a café about twenty minutes away by car. The operative doesn't notice—he's forgotten to take the steps to see if he was being tailed, because he's so thrilled with himself and so confident in his abilities." Because he was part of a dynasty. Because he knew so much. "And guess who the operative is talking to? His supervisor. Only, members of this militia had a run-in with the supervisor a few years back, which, it turns out, is why it's me in the field rather than him in the first place. So now they know the person talking to his girlfriend is comparing notes with a known government agent."

Here he deviated from the script long enough to remind Grace of what he had endured just that morning: "It was like I was floating above it all, above everyone, looking down, gliding through the air. Able to do anything I wanted to." Saw the connection register with her, but not the guilt.

"Now they know that a member of their militia has had contact with the government—and on top of that, the boyfriend, as noted, is the possessive, controlling, jealous type. And that boyfriend works himself into a rage, watching the operative come back the next day, not doing much more than nodding at McCarthy, but for all he knows they've got a secret method of communication. It's enough that the operative has come back. The boyfriend gets it into his head that his girlfriend might be part of it, that maybe McCarthy is spying on them. So what do you think they do?"

Whitby took the opportunity to give an answer to a different question: He slid out from behind the table and ran away down the curve of the wall, headed for the science division without even a hurried goodbye.

Leaving Control with Grace.

"Are you going to guess?" Control asked Grace, turning the full weight of his anger and self-loathing on the assistant director, not caring that all eyes in the cafeteria were on them.

To reanimate the emotions of a dead script, he had started thinking of things like *topographical anomalies* and *video of the first expedition* and *hypnotic conditioning*—inverse to the extreme where ritual decreed he hold words in his head like *horrible goiter* and *math homework* to stop from coming too soon during sex.

"Are you going to fucking guess?" he hissed in a kind of mega-whisper, wanting to confess not to anyone in the audience, but to the biologist.

"They shoot Rachel McCarthy," she said.

"Yes, that's right!" Control shouted, knowing that even the people serving the food at the far-distant buffet could hear him, were looking at him. Maybe fifteen people remained there, in the cafeteria, most trying to pretend none of this was happening.

"They shoot Rachel McCarthy," Control said. "Although by the time they're searching for me, I'm already safe at home. After, what? Two or three conversations? A standard surveillance operation from my perspective. I'm being pulled in for a debriefing while other, more seasoned, agents are brought in to follow up on the lead. Except by then the militia has beaten McCarthy half senseless and driven her to the top of an abandoned quarry. And they want her to tell the truth, to just tell the truth about the person in the bar. Which she can't do, because she's innocent and didn't know I was an operative. But that's the wrong answer—any answer is the wrong answer by then." Will always be the wrong answer. And around the time that he's excited he helped crack the case wide open, and a judge is issuing warrants, the boyfriend has shot McCarthy in the head, twice, and let her fall, dead, into the shallow water below. To be found three days later by the local police.

Anyone else might have been finished, although he'd been too green to know that. He hadn't known until years later that his mother had rescued him, for better or worse. Called in favors. Pulled strings. Greased palms. All the usual clichés that masked every unique collusion. Because—she told him when she finally confessed, when it no longer mattered one way or the other—she believed in him and knew that he had much more to offer.

Control had spent a year on suspension, going to therapy that couldn't repair the breach, endured a retraining program that cast a broad net to catch a tiny mistake that kept escaping anyway over and over in his mind. Then he had been given an administrative desk job, from which he'd worked his way up through the ranks again, to the exalted non-position of "fixer," with the clear understanding that he'd never be deployed in the field again.

So that one day he could be called upon to run a peculiar backwater agency. So that what he couldn't bring himself to confess to any of his girlfriends he could shout out loudly in a cafeteria, in front of a woman who appeared to hate him.

The little bird he'd seen flying darkly against the high windows of the cafeteria flew there still, but the way it flitted reminded him now more of a bat. The rain clouds gathered yet again.

Grace still sat in front of him, guarded from on high by cohorts from the past. Control still sat there, too, Grace now going through his lesser sins, one by one, in no particular order, with no one else left to hear. She had read his file and gotten her hands on more besides. As she reeled it off, she told him other things—about his mother, his father, the litany a lurching parade or procession that, curiously, no longer hurt about halfway through. A kind of numb relief, instead, began to flood Control. She was telling him something, all right. She saw him clearly and she saw him well, from his skills right down to his weaknesses, from his short relationships to his nomadic lifestyle to his father's cancer and ambivalence about his mother. The ease with which he had embraced his mother's substitution of her job for family, for religion. And all of the rest of it, all of it, her tone of voice managing the neat trick of mixing grudging respect with compassionate exasperation at his refusal to retreat.

"Have you never made a mistake?" he asked, but she ignored him.

Instead she gave him the gift of a motive: "This time, your contact tried to cut me off from Central. For good." The Voice, continuing to help him in the same way as a runaway bull.

"I didn't ask for that." Well, if he had, he didn't want it anymore.

"You went into my office again."

"I didn't." But he couldn't be sure.

"I'm trying to keep things the way they are for the *director*, not for me."

"The director's dead. The director's not coming back."

She looked away from him, out through the windows at the courtyard and the swamp beyond. A fierce look that shut him out.

Maybe the director was flying free over Area X, or scrabbling with root-broken fingernails into the dirt, the reeds, trying to get away . . . from something. But she wasn't here.

"Think about how much worse it could get, Grace, if they replace me with someone else. Because they're never going to make you director." Truth for truth.

"You know I did you a favor just now," she said, pivoting away from what he'd said.

"A favor? Sure you did."

But he did know. That which was uncomfortable or unflattering she had now off-loaded pointlessly, ordnance wasted, a gun shot into the air. She had let out the rest of the items in her jewelry box of condemnation, and by not hoarding told him she would not be using it in the future.

"You're a lot like us," she said. "Someone who has made

a lot of mistakes. Someone just trying to do better. To be better."

Subtext: *You can't solve what hasn't been solved in thirty years. I won't let you get out ahead of the director.* And what misdirection in that? What was she pushing him toward or away from?

Control just nodded, not because he agreed or disagreed but because he was exhausted. Then he excused himself, locked the cafeteria bathroom, and vomited up his breakfast. He wondered if he was coming down with something or if his body was rejecting, as viciously as possible, everything in the Southern Reach.

018: RECOVERY

Cheney came back to prowl around outside the bathroom—concerned, whispering "Do you think you're all right, man?" as if they'd become best buddies. But eventually Cheney went away, and a little while later Control's cell phone rang just as he'd propped himself up on the toilet seat. He pulled the phone out of his pocket. The Voice. The bathroom seemed like the perfect place to take this call. Cold porcelain after having slammed the bathroom door shut was a relief. So were the tiny cool blue tiles of the floor. Even the faint whiff of piss. All of it. Any of it.

Why were there no mirrors in the men's room?

"Next time, take my call *when* I call," the Voice warned,

with the implication that s/he was a busy wo/man, just as Control noticed the flashing light that meant he had a message.

"I was in a meeting." I was watching videotape. I was talking to the biologist. I was getting my ass handed to me by the assistant director because of you.

"Is your house in order?" the Voice asked. "Is it in order?"

Two thousand white rabbits herded toward an invisible door. A plant that didn't want to die. Impossible video footage. More theories than there were fish in the sea. Was his house in order? An odd way for the Voice to phrase it, as if they spoke using a code to which Control did not have the key. Yet it made him feel secure even though that was counterintuitive.

"Are you there?" the Voice asked brusquely.

"Yes. Yes, my house is in order."

"Then what do you have for me?"

Control gave the Voice a brief summary.

The Voice considered that for a moment, then asked, "So do you have an answer now?"

"To what?"

"To the mystery behind Area X." The Voice laughed an oddly tinny metallic laugh. Haw haw haw. Haw.

Enough of this. "Stop trying to cut Grace off from her contacts at Central. It isn't working and it's making it harder," Control said. Remembering her care with setting up the videos of the first expedition, too wrung out by lunch to process it yet. Twinned to Control's disgust at the Voice's clearly inadequate and extreme tactics was the sudden conviction, admittedly irrational, that somehow the Voice was responsible for sticking him in the middle of the Southern

Reach. If the Voice actually was his mother, then he'd be correct about that.

"Listen, John," the Voice growled, "I don't report to you. You report to me, and don't forget that." Meant to be delivered with conviction, and yet somehow failing.

"Stop trying," Control repeated. "You're doing harm to me—she knows you're trying. Just stop."

"Again, I don't report to you, Control. Don't tell me what to do. You asked me to fix it, and I'm trying to fix it." Feedback made Control take the phone away from his ear.

"You know I saw the video of the first expedition this morning," he said. "It threw me." By way of halfhearted apology. Grandpa had taught him that: Redirect while seeming to address the other party's grievance. It'd been done enough to him in the past.

But for some reason that set the Voice off. "You think that's a fucking excuse for not doing your goddamn job. Seeing a video? Get your head out of your asshole and give me a real report next time—and then maybe I'll be a lot more willing to do your bidding the way you want me to do your bidding. Got it, fuckface?"

The swear words were delivered in a peculiar, halting way, as if the Voice were completing a Mad Lib where the only scripted parts were the words *fucking, goddamn, asshole,* and *fuckface.* But Control got it. The Voice was a shithead. He'd had shithead bosses before. Unless the real Voice was taking a break and this was the sub's attempt at improv. Megalodon mad. Megalodon not happy. Megalodon have tantrum.

So he gave in and made some conciliatory sounds. Then he elaborated and told the tale of his "progress," the story structured and strung together not as the plaintive, halting start-stop of what-the-hell that it was, but instead as an analytical and nuanced "journey" that could only be interpreted as having a beginning and a middle pushing out toward a satisfying end.

"Enough!" the Voice said at some point.

Later: "That's better," the Voice said. Control couldn't really tell if the severity of that rushed cheese-grater-on-cheese-grater tone had lightened. "For now, continue to collect data and continue to question the biologist, but press her harder." Had already done that, and it had gone poorly. Uncovering useful intel was often a long-term project, a matter of listening for what didn't matter to fall away for just a moment.

After another pause, the Voice said, "I have that information you asked for."

"Which information?" Plant, mouse, or . . . ?

"I can confirm that the director did cross the border."

Control sat up straight on the toilet seat. Someone was knocking timidly at the door. They'd have to wait.

"When? Right before the last eleventh expedition?"

"Yes. Completely unauthorized and without anyone's knowledge or permission."

"And she got away with it."

"What do you mean?"

"She wasn't fired."

A pause, then the Voice said, "No doubt she should have been terminated. But, no, she got probation. The assistant director took her place for six months." Impatient, as if it didn't matter.

What was he supposed to do with that? Probably a question for his mother. Because surely someone higher up must have known the director was going across the border and then someone had protected her when she came back.

"Do you know how long she was gone? Is there a report of what she found?"

"Three weeks. No report."

Three weeks!

"She must have been debriefed. There must be a record."

A much longer pause. Was the Voice consulting with another Voice or Voices?

Finally the Voice conceded the point: "There is a debriefing statement. I can have a copy sent to you."

"Did you know that the director thought the border was advancing?" Control asked.

"I am aware of that theory," the Voice said. "But it is no concern of yours."

How was that no concern of his? How did someone go from calling him a fuckface to using a phrase like "no concern of yours"? The Voice was a bad actor, Control concluded, or had a bad script, or it was deliberate.

At the end of their conversation, for no good reason, he told a joke. "What's brown and sticky?"

"I know that one," the Voice said. "A stick."

"A turd."

Click.

"Go ahead and check the seats for change, John." Control, back in his office, exhausted, ambushed by odd flashes of memory. A colleague at his last position coming up to him after a presentation and saying in an accusing tone, "You contradicted me." No, I *disagreed* with you. A woman in college, a brunette with a broad face and beautiful brown eyes that made him ache, whom he'd fallen for in Fundamentals of Math but when he'd given her a poem had said to him, "Yes, but do you dance?" No, I write poetry. I'm going to be some kind of spy. One of his college professors in political science had made them write poetry to "get your juices flowing." Most of the time, though, he'd been studying, going to the shooting range, working out, using parties to get in practice for a lifetime of short-term relationships.

"Go ahead and check the seats for change, John," said Grandpa Jack. Control had been twelve, visiting his mother up north for a rare trip that didn't include going to the cabin or fishing. They were still getting the balance right; the divorce was still being finalized.

On a weekend afternoon, in the freezing cold, Jack had rolled up in what he called a "muscle car." He'd taken it out of hibernation because he had hatched a secret plan to drive Control to a lingerie show at a local department store. Control only had a vague idea of what that meant, but it sounded embarrassing. Mostly he didn't want to go because the next-door neighbor's daughter was his age and he'd had a crush on her since the summer. But it was hard to say no to Grandpa. Especially when Grandpa had never taken him anywhere without his mother there.

So Control checked the seats for change while Grandpa fired up the bright blue muscle car, which had sat cold for two hours while Grandpa talked to his mother inside. But Control also thought Grandpa was reacquainting himself with the mysteries of its workings, too. The heat was blasting away and Control was sweating in his coat. He checked the seats eagerly, wondering if Grandpa had left some money there on purpose. With money, he could buy the neighbor girl an ice cream. He was still in summer mode.

No money, just lint, paper clips, a scrap of paper or two, and something cold, smooth, sticky, and shaped like a tiny brain from which he recoiled: old bubble gum. Disappointed, he broadened his search from the long backseat to the dark cavern under the front passenger side. He extended his arm awkwardly forward so his hand could curl around to search, came up against something bulky yet soft taped there. No, not soft—whatever it was had been wrapped in cloth. With a bit of coaxing, he managed to pull it free, the awkward weight a muffled thud on the car floor. There was a dull metal-and-oil smell. He picked it up, unwrapped it from the cloth, and sat back, the rough coldness of it cupped in both hands . . . only to find his grandpa staring at him intently.

"What've you got there?" the old man asked. "Where'd you find that?" Which Control thought were dumb questions and then, later, disingenuous questions. The eager look on Grandpa Jack's face as he turned to stare, one arm still on the steering wheel.

"A gun," Control said, although Grandpa could see that. He remembered later mostly the darkness of it, the darkness of its shape and the stillness it seemed to bring with it.

"A Colt .45, it looks like. It's heavy, isn't it?"

Control nodded, a little afraid now. He was sweating from the heat. He'd already found the gun, but his grandpa's expression was that of someone waiting for the gift they'd given to be unwrapped and held high—and him too young to sense the danger. But he'd already made the wrong decision: He should never have gotten in the car.

What kind of psycho gave a kid a gun, even unloaded? This was the thought that occurred now. Perhaps the kind of psycho who wouldn't mind coming out of retirement at his remote cabin to work for Central again as the Voice, to run his own grandson.

⌒

Midafternoon. *Try. Try again.*

Control and the biologist stood together, leaning on the sturdy wooden fence that separated them from the holding pond. The Southern Reach building lay at their backs, a gravel path like a rough black river leading across the lawn. Just the two of them . . . and the three members of security who had brought her. They had spread out at a distance of about thirty feet and chosen angles that took into account all escape routes.

"Do they think I'll run away?" Ghost Bird asked him.

"No," Control said. If she did, Control would put the blame on them.

The holding pond was long and roughly rectangular. Inside the fence, on the far shore, a rotting shed lay on the side nearest the swamp. A scrawny pine tree half-throttled by rusted Christmas lights stood beside the shed. The water was choked with duckweed and hydrangea and water lilies. Dragonflies patrolled ceaselessly over the gray, sometimes black water. The frogs made such raucous forecasts of rain that they drowned out the crickets and, from the fringe of grass and bushes on the opposite side of the pond, came the chatter and bustle of wrens and warblers.

A lone great blue heron stood solemn and silent in the

middle of the pond. Thunderclouds continued to gather, its feathers dull in the fading light.

"Should I thank you for this?" Ghost Bird asked. They were leaning on the top of the fence. Her left arm was too close to his right arm; he moved a little farther away.

"Don't thank anyone for what you should already have," he said, which brought a half turn of her head toward him and the view of one upraised eyebrow above a thoughtful eye and a noncommittal mouth. It was something his grandfather on his father's side had said, back when he was selling clothespins door-to-door. "I didn't make the wood storks disappear," he added, because he had not meant to say the first thing.

"Raccoons are the worst predators of their nests," she said. "Did you know that they pre-date the last ice age? Farther south, they roost in colonies, but in this region they're endangered, so they're more solitary."

Control had looked it up and the wood storks should have returned by now if they were going to. They tended to be creatures of habit.

"I can only give you thirty or forty minutes," he said. Bringing her here felt now like a terrible indulgence, possibly even a kind of danger, although he did not know to whom. But he also knew he couldn't have left things as they were after the morning session.

"I hate it when they mow it and try to take out the duckweed," she said, ignoring him.

He wasn't sure what to say to that. It was just a holding pond, like thousands of others. It wasn't meant to be a habitat. But, then, they'd found her in an empty lot.

"Look—there are still some tadpoles," she said, pointing,

something approaching contentment on her face. He was beginning to understand that keeping her inside had been cruel. Perhaps now she wouldn't see the conversation between them solely as an interrogation.

"It is nice out here," he said, just to say something, but it was nice. It felt even better than he'd thought to get out of the building. He'd had some idea of questioning her, but the strong smell of rain and the way that the distant sky formed dark curtains of downpours fast approaching had de-feated that impulse.

"Ask her about the director," the Voice said. "Ask her if the director mentioned having been across the border before." Pushed that away. You're a hologram. You're a con-struct. I'm going to throw chum overboard until you're so blood-enraged you can't swim properly.

Ghost Bird nudged a large black beetle with her shoe. It was frantic, ceaselessly caroming through the links of the fence and back over. "You know why they do that?"

"No, I don't," Control said. Over the past four days, he had realized there were many things he didn't know.

"They just sprayed insecticide here. I can smell it. You can see the hint of foam on its carapace. It disorients them as it kills them; they can't breathe because of it. They become what you might call panicked. They keep searching for a way to get away from what's already inside of them. Toward the end, they settle down, but that's only because they don't have enough oxygen to move anymore."

She waited until the beetle was over a piece of flat ground and then brought her shoe down, hard and fast. There was a crunch. Control looked away. Forgiving a friend who had done something to upset him, his father had once said that she heard a different kind of music.

"Ask her about the empty lot," the Voice said.

"Why do you think you ended up at the empty lot?" Control asked, mostly to placate the audience. Any one of the three might report back to Grace.

"I ended up here, at the Southern Reach." A guarded note had entered her voice.

"What does it mean to you, that place?" The same as this place, or more?

"I don't think it was where I was meant to be," she said after a pause. "Just a feeling. I remember waking up and not recognizing it for a moment and then when I did, being disappointed."

"Disappointed how?"

Ghost Bird shrugged.

Lines of lightning created fantastical countries in the sky. Thunder came on like an accusing voice.

Ask her if she left anything in the empty lot. Was it his question or the Voice's?

"Did you leave anything there?"

"Not that I remember," she said.

Control said something he had rehearsed beforehand. "Soon you'll need to be candid about what you remember and what you don't remember. They'll take you away from here if I don't get results. And I'll have no say in where they send you if that happens. It might be worse than here, a lot worse."

"Didn't I tell you I wasn't the biologist?" She said it quietly, but with bite.

Ask her what she really is.

He couldn't suppress a wince, even though he had meant it when he had said she didn't owe him anything for bringing her out to the pond.

"I'm trying to be honest. I'm not her . . . and there's something inside of me I don't understand. There's a kind of . . . brightness . . . inside."

Nothing in the medical updates, except an elevated temperature.

"That's called life," Control said.

She didn't laugh at that, but said, quietly, "I don't think so."

If she had a "brightness" inside of her, there was a corresponding darkness inside of him. The rain approached. The humidity was driven away by a wild breeze. Ripples spread across the pond, and the shed wheezed as the wind pushed against it. The little Christmas pine whipped back and forth.

"You're all alone out here, aren't you, John?"

He didn't have to answer because it had started to rain— hard. He wanted to hurry back in so they wouldn't get soaked, but Ghost Bird wouldn't cooperate. She insisted on taking slow, deliberate steps, let the water needle her face, run down her neck, and soak her shirt.

The blue heron moved not at all, intent on some prey beneath the surface.

HAUNTINGS

000

In his dreams now, the sky is deep blue with just a twinge of light. He stares from the water up at the cliff far above him. He can see the silhouette of someone peering down at him from the top . . . can see the way the person leans far over the edge to stare—farther than any human could, yet keeps leaning at a more severe angle, pebbles dislodged and peppering the water around him. While he lies in wait, there, at the bottom of the cliff, swimming vast and unknowable among the other monsters. Waiting in the darkness for the soundless fall, without splash or ripple.

020: SECOND RECOVERY

Sunday. An ice pick lodged in a brain already suffused with the corona of a dull but persistent headache that radiated forward from a throbbing bolus at the back of his skull. A kind of pulsing satellite defense shield protecting against anything more hostile that might sag into its decaying orbit.

A cup of coffee. A crumb-strewn Formica countertop with a view of the grimy street through a clean window. A wobbly wooden stool to go with shaky hands trying to hold it steady. The faint memory of a cheap disinfectant rising from the floor, tightening his throat. A woman repeated orders behind him, while he tried to spread out across the counter so none of the customers in line could join him. From the look of the coatrack to his left, some people had come in during the winter and never left.

The Voice, a weak but persistent drumbeat, from centuries ago: "Is your house in order? Is your house in order? Tell me, please, is your house in order?"

Was his house in order?

Control hadn't changed his clothes or showered in two days. He could smell his own rich stink like the musk rising off some animal prized by trappers. The sweat was being drawn through his pores onto his forehead again, reaching out in supplication to the ever-hotter Hedley sun through the window, the fans inside the coffee shop not strong enough. It had rained from the previous afternoon until the middle of the night, left large puddles full of tiny brown shrimp-like things that curled up and died in rust-colored agonies as the water evaporated.

Control had come to a halt there at the end of Empire Street, where it crossed the far end of Main Street. When he was a teenager, the coffee shop had been a retro soda joint, which he missed. He'd sit at the air-conditioned window counter with a couple of friends and be grateful for ice cream and root beer, while they talked a lot of crap about girls and sports. It had been nice then, a kind of refuge. But over time the straightlaced bohemian leanings of the so-called railroad district had been usurped by hustlers, con artists, drug addicts, and homeless people with nowhere else to go.

Through the window, waiting for the phone call he knew would come, Control dissected the daily terroir playing out across the street, in front of the discount liquor store. Two skateboarders, so preternaturally lean they reminded him of malnourished greyhounds, stood on that opposite corner in T-shirts and ragged jeans with five-year-old sneakers on their feet but no socks. One of them had a brown mutt on a hemp leash meant for a much larger dog. He'd seen two skateboarders while out jogging Tuesday night, hadn't he? It had been dark, couldn't be sure this was them. But possibly.

Within minutes of Control watching, they'd been joined by a woman he definitely hadn't seen before. Tall, she wore a blue military cap over dyed-red short hair, and a long-sleeved blue jacket with gold fringe at the shoulders and cuffs. The white tank top under the jacket didn't cover her bare midriff. The blue dress pants with a more muted gold stripe on the side ended halfway down her calves and then in bare, dirty feet, with the bright red dots of nail polish visible. It reminded Control of something a rock star might have worn in the late 1980s. Or, idle strange thought: She was some decommissioned officer of the S&S Brigade, missing, forgotten, memory shot, doomed to play out the end-game far from anywhere conducive to either science or superstition.

She had a flushed, ruddy aspect to her face, and talked

in an animated way to the skateboarders, a bit too manic, and at the same time pointing down the street, but then breaking off to approach any pedestrian who walked by, hands expressive as she delivered some complex tale of hardship or the logic behind a need. Or perhaps even suggesting more. She shrugged off the first two who ignored her, but the skateboarders got on her about it and the third she yelled after, as if he'd been rude. Roused to action by this, a fat black man in a gray plastic-bag trench coat too hot for Hedley in any season popped up like a stage prop from behind a large garbage can at the far end of the liquor store's frontage. He harangued the man who had shunned the redheaded woman; Control could hear the obscenities through the glass. Then the fat man collapsed back into his former post, evaporating as fast as he'd been conjured up.

The woman could be wearing a wig. The man in the trench coat might have nothing to do with their little charade. He could be utterly out of practice in surveillance, too.

The redheaded woman, shrugging off the affront, walked around the corner to stand facing the traffic on Empire in the shade of the liquor store's side wall. She was joined by one of the skateboarders, who offered her a cigarette, both of them leaning against the brick and continuing to talk in an animated fashion. The second skateboarder now came out of the liquor store with an opened can of wet dog food—Control had missed something vital about that store—and banged it with a scrap and clatter out of the can and into a left-leaning can-shaped pile on the sidewalk right in front of the store. He then pushed the tower into pieces using the can, and for some reason threw the empty can at the fat black man half-hidden from Control's view by the garbage. There was no response to that, nor did the mutt seem enthusiastic about the food.

Although they'd accosted a few customers from the coffee shop, even come up close to the glass on his side of the street, they seemed oblivious to his presence. Which made Control wonder if he had become a wraith or if they were enacting a ritual, meant for an audience of one. Which implied a deeper significance to it all, even though Control knew that might be a false thought, and a dangerous one. Central rarely employed amateurs, but that didn't mean it wasn't possible. Nothing much seemed impossible now. "Is there something in the corner of your eye that you cannot get out?" Another thing the Voice had said to him, which he had taken as a kind of oblique taunt.

If the scene in front of him was innocent, could he disappear into it, transition from one side of the glass to the other? Or were there conspiracies even in buying dog food, begging money for a drink? Intricacies that might escape him.

First thing Saturday morning, Control had called the Voice, from his house. He had placed an electronic bullhorn rigged with a timer on one side of his desk, set the timer. He had placed a neon orange sheet of paper with his reminders on it to the right, along with a pen. He drank a shot of whiskey. He smashed his fists down on the desk, once, twice, three times. He took a deep breath. Then he made the call, putting the Voice on speakerphone.

Sounds of creaking and shuffling before the Voice debuted. No doubt downstairs in the study of his/her mansion. Or in the basement of a flophouse. Or the barn of a farm, undercover with the chickens.

"Is your house in order?" the Voice asked. A sluggish quality to the Voice, as if the megalodon had been roused from slumber in icy waters. The Voice's tone felt like an insult; it made Control even colder, began to leach away the trepidation in favor of a form of disgust shot through with stubbornness.

Deep breath. Then, preempting anything the Voice might say, Control launched into a shouted string of obscenities of the most vile kind, contorting his throat, hurting it. After a surprised pause, the Voice shouted "Enough!" then muttered something long and quivery and curling. Control lost the thread. The bullhorn went off. Control shook himself out of it, read the words on the orange sheet of paper. Checked off the first line. Launched again into a string of obscenities. "Enough!" Again, persistent, stubborn, the Voice muttered something, this time moist and short and darting. Control floated and floated and forgot. The bullhorn went off. Control saw the words on the orange sheet of paper. Checked off the second line. Obscenities. Mutters. Floating. Bullhorn ripping through. Control saw the words on the orange sheet of paper. Check mark. Repeat. Rinse. Repeat. Fifth time. Sixth time. The seventh time the script changed. He fed back to the Voice all the muttering glottal, moist, soft words he'd gleaned from the director's cheat sheet. Heard the wet gasp and shriek of hitting the target, then an awkward lunge of words toward him, but feeble, disconnected, unintelligible.

That had left a scar. He doubted his incantation had had the full effect, but the point was that the Voice knew and had had a very unpleasant experience.

The bullhorn went off. Control saw the words on the orange sheet of paper. He was done. The Voice was done. They'd have to get another handler, one not quite so manipulative.

"Here's a joke for you," Control said. "What's the difference between a magician and a spy?" Then he hung up.

He had reviewed the surveillance of his Wednesday and Thursday conversations with the Voice on Friday night after a vigorous jog. He'd been suspicious, hadn't trusted the way he seemed to fade in and out during those conversations, or how the Voice had infiltrated his thoughts. With Chorizo on his lap, and the feed piped in from his phone to the television, Control had seen the Voice execute hypnotic commands, seen himself become unfocused, head floating a bit on his neck, eyelids fluttering, while the Voice, never dropping the metallic, guttural disguise, gave him orders and suggestions. The Voice told him not to worry about Whitby, to put his concern aside, minimize it, because "Whitby's never mattered." But then later backtracked and expressed interest in him finding Whitby's strange room. Had he been drawn to that hidey-hole because of some subliminal intel? A reference to Grace, along with an order to go back to her office, then some dithering about "too risky" when the Voice learned about the new locks. A lot of exasperation about the director's notes and the slow progress in sorting through them. That this was mostly due to the director's disorganized process made him wonder if that had been the point of the chaos. Had the Voice even *told* Control to go by "Control" at the agency? Resisted the madness of such thoughts.

The Voice, while Control languished under hypnosis, had a sharpness and focus not as present otherwise, and a kind of casual perversity, telling Control s/he wanted a joke to end their next phone call, "one with a punch line." As far as he could tell, he also had been serving as a living tape recorder for the Voice. The Voice had pulled out of Control verbatim conversations, which explained why he had been so late getting home Wednesday even though the conversation had seemed short.

He'd been on an expedition sent into the Southern Reach and just like the expeditions into Area X, not told the truth. He had been right to feel that he was getting information coming in with an extra stutter-step. What else had he done that he might never know?

So he'd written on the neon orange sheet that he could not possibly miss:

CONTROL, YOU ARE BEING SUBJECTED TO HYPNOTIC SUGGESTION BY THE VOICE
___ Check this line and scream obscenities. Move down one line.
___ Check this line and scream obscenities. Move down one line.

Rinse, repeat, brought out of it by the bullhorn, pulled back into it. Until, finally, he reached the end: "Check this line and repeat these phrases"—all of the phrases he'd found in the director's desk. Shout them, actually.

Are you excited, too? . . . The possibility of significant variation . . . Paralysis is not a cogent analysis . . . Consolidation of authority . . . There's no reward in the risk . . . Floating and floating, like nothing human but something free and floating . . .

Overload the system as the scientists with the white rabbits had been unable to. Push the Voice into some kind of collapse.

He had been betrayed, would not now have a moment when he would not be looking over his shoulder. Saw the biologist by the holding pond, the two of them looking at the shed. Leading her back into the Southern Reach, as it swallowed them. His mother leading him by the hand up the path to the summer cottage, Grandpa waiting for them, an enigmatic smile making a mystery of his face.

The cure for his discoveries, for not having to think about them, had been a kind of self-annihilation as he trekked undaunted from Saturday afternoon to Sunday morning, through the small but plump underbelly of Hedley—which as far as he could tell had forgotten there was a Southern Reach. He recalled a pool hall—the crack of ball against ball, the *thud* and *thack*, the comfort of the felt-lined pockets, the darkness, the smell of chalk and cigarettes. Hitting the cue ball with the eight ball as a joke, and a handprint slapped in chalk on the ass of a woman's jeans—or as he thought of it later, although she'd placed it there, a hand too far. He had withdrawn soon after, not as interested as he'd thought in the banality of a grainy morning sun seen through the windows of a cheap motel, an imprint of a body on the sheets, a used condom in the wastebasket. These were visions for others, at least in that moment—because it just seemed like too much work. He'd still be in the same place. He'd still be hearing Lowry from the videos. He'd still be seeing, in slow motion no less, Grace offering him the contents of her box of complaints. His mind would still be whirring as it contracted and expanded, grappling with Area X.

He took in a late-night movie at a run-down theater with gum and soaked-in cola on the stained blue carpet. He was the only one there. Against the odds, the theater had survived from his teenage years to now. The movie was terrible, the kind of science-fiction film where the plot holes almost seemed like alien interference imposed from some higher dimension. But the quiet coolness of the place soothed his jangled nerves. Until it was time to get up again and lurch his way to the next bar, his path taking him along the waterfront in an epic pub crawl. Was that Cheney knocking, asking if he was okay?

He had three shots of cheap whiskey in a place so run down it didn't have a name. He had a gulp of some local moonshine at a party not far from the pier where ages ago he'd looked out across the river. Told himself over and over that the hypnosis was a small thing, not a large thing, and that it meant nothing. Nothing at all. Too big a deal. Too little. He thought about calling his mother. Couldn't. Wanted to call his father. Impossible.

He went into another bar already drunk, found himself

confronted by a ghost. Earlier that night he had glimpsed hints of them—in the curl of a lip that sparked a memory, a flicker of an eyelid, the way someone's hand lingered on a tabletop. Those shoes. That dress. But when you encountered a real ghost—the Thing Entire—it was a shock . . . it took your breath. Not away. It didn't take your breath away—your breath wasn't *going* anywhere. Your breath was still in you, locked up, not of use to you. Took your pulse only to mutter dire predictions for the future. So when you came back into the moment, you doubted at first who you were, because the Ghost Entire trapped Control somewhere between the person he had been and the person he had become. And yet it was still just a wraith. Just a woman he had known in high school. Intensely. For the first time. Close enough that Control felt somehow like he was being disrespectful to the biologist, that the overlay of the ghost was disrupting his impression of Ghost Bird. Even if that was ridiculous. And all of it taking him farther and farther from the Southern Reach.

Trying to escape the residue of that, at another point on the carousel compass of his adventures—utterly shitfaced and giddy—he had spun onto a stool in a biker bar, winding up next to the assistant director. The whole place was still raucous and ill-behaved at two in the morning. It stank of piss, as thick as if cats had been marking their territory. Control gave her a leaky lantern of a grin, to go with an emphatic nod. She gave him a look of blank neutrality.

"The file is empty. There's nothing on her." On who? Who was he talking about? "If you could put me in your own special hell, it'd be working at the old S.R. anyway—for a lifetime, right?"

Halfway through, he realized that it couldn't really be

Grace and that the words might not even be coming out of his mouth.

She unnerved him with the candor of her unblinking gaze.

"You don't have to look like that," he added. Must've said it this time.

"Like what?" she said, her head turned a little to the side. "Like a man's fucked up outta his mind and in my bar? Go to hell."

He'd reared back on his stool at that suggestion, trying to assemble his wits like pieces on a game board. A weight on his chest, in the dark and the light. He'd thought he was smarter. He'd thought she'd gotten mired in old ways of thinking. But it turned out new ways of thinking didn't help, either. Time for another drink, somewhere else. A kind of oblivion. Then regroup.

Control met her doubtful stare as he left with a bleary smile. He was making progress. She receded from him, pushed back by a waft of wind from the bar door opening and the judgmental stare of the streetlamps.

Control rubbed his face, didn't like the feel of stubble. He tried to wipe the fuzziness from his mind, the sourness from his tongue, the soreness from his joints. He was convinced the Voice had said to him, at one point, "Is there something in the corner of your eye that you cannot get out? I can help you get it out." Easy, if you'd put it there in the first place.

The woman in the uniform was probably a drug addict and definitely homeless or a squatter. You used amateurs for surveillance when the target was "in the family," when you wanted to use the natural landscape—the natural terroir—to its best advantage or when your faction was dead broke or incompetent. It occurred to him that she didn't notice him because she'd been paid to pretend not to notice him.

The skateboarder with the dog had clearly staked out the corner as his territory, sharing it with the fat drunk man. There was something about both of them that seemed more natural, perhaps because an element of theater—smashing out dog food on the curb—didn't fit with the idea of not drawing attention. The other skateboarder had left and come back several times, but Control hadn't seen him pass drugs or money or food to the other two. Maybe he was slumming it for a day, or served as a lookout for some larger con, or he was Mother's watcher, part of the tableau but not. Or perhaps there was nothing going on except three people who knew one another and helped one another out, and just happened to be down on their luck.

The thing about staying in one place for so long was that you began to get a sense, while watching, of being watched, so it didn't startle him when the cell phone rang. It was the call he'd been expecting.

"I understand you've been behaving badly," she said.

"Hello to you, too, Mother."

"Are you rough right now? You sound rough."

"I'm fine. I have complete control of my faculties."

"Then why do you seem to have lost your mind." This said in the brisk, professional tone she used to disguise emotional tells. A sense that she was as "on" with him as with any other agent she ran.

"I've already thrown the phone away, Mother. So don't

think about reinstating the Voice." If she had called yesterday, he would have been yelling at her by now.

"We can always get you another one."

"Quick question, Ma." She hated *ma* or *mom*, barely tolerated *mother*, would have preferred the severe Severance even though he was her precious only child. That he knew of. "If you were to send someone on an expedition into somewhere dangerous—let's say, into the Southern Reach—how would you keep them calm and on track? What kinds of tools might you use?"

"The usual things, really, John. Although I'm not sure I like your tone."

"The usual things? Like hypnosis, maybe, backed up by conditioning beforehand at Central." He was keeping his voice low, much as he wanted to lash out. He liked the coffee shop counter. He didn't want to be asked to leave.

A pause. "It might have come into play, yes, but only with strict rules and safeguards—and only in the subject's absolute best interests."

"The subject might have preferred to have had the choice. The subject might've preferred not to be a drone." The subject might prefer to know that his hopes and desires and impulses were all definitely his *own* hopes, desires, impulses.

"The subject might not have had the intel or perspective to be involved in that decision. The subject might have needed an inoculation, a vaccine."

"Against what?"

"Against any number of things. Although at the first sign of something serious happening, we would pull you out and send a team in."

"Like what? What would you consider serious?"

"Whatever might happen."

Infuriatingly opaque, as always. Making decisions for him, as always. He was channeling his father's irritation now as much as his own, the specters of so many arguments at the dinner table or in the living room. He decided to take the conversation onto the street after all, stood in the mouth of the alley just to the left of the coffee shop. Not many people were out walking around—most of them were probably still in church, or scoring drugs.

"Jack used to say that if you don't give an operative all the information they need, you might as well cut your own leg off," he said. "Your operation is screwed."

"But your operation isn't screwed, John," she said, with some force. "You're still there. You're still in touch with us. Me. We're not going anywhere."

"Good point, except I don't think that 'we' means Central. I think you mean some faction within Central, and not an effective one. Your Voice made a mess trying to take the assistant director out of the mix. Give her another week and I'll be Grace's administrative assistant." Or was the point to waste a lot of Grace's time and attention?

"There are no factions, just Central. The Voice is under a lot of stress, John. Even more now. We all are."

"The hell there aren't factions." Now he was Jack, hard to throw off topic. "The hell there aren't." "The hell there isn't." "The hell you say."

"You won't believe me, John, but I've done you a favor placing you at the Southern Reach."

Everyone had forgotten the definition of *favor*. First Whitby, then Grace, now his mother. He didn't trust himself to respond, so he didn't.

"A lot of people would've killed for that position," she said.

He had no answer for that, either. While they'd been talking, the woman had disappeared, and the storefront was deserted. Back in the day the liquor store had been a department store. Long before Hedley was built, there had been an indigenous settlement here, along the river—something his father had told him—and the remains of that, too, lay beneath the facade of the liquor store.

Down below the store, too, a labyrinth of limestone cradling the aquifer, narrow caves and blind albino crawfish and luminescent freshwater fish. Surrounded by the crushed remains of so many creatures, loamed into the soil, pushed down by the foundations of the buildings. Would that be the biologist's understanding of the street—what she would see? Perhaps she would see, too, one possible future of that space, the liquor store crumbling under an onslaught of vines and weather damage, becoming akin to the sunken, moss-covered hills near Area X. A loss she might not mourn. Or would she?

"Are you there, John?"

Where else would he be?

For a long time now, Control had suspected his mother had taken someone else under her wing as a protégé—it seemed almost inevitable. Someone sculpted, trained, and deployed to correct the kinds of mistakes made by Control. The thought reoccurred whenever he was feeling particularly insecure or vulnerable, or sometimes just because it could be a useful mental exercise. Now he was trying to visualize the perfectly groomed protégé walking in and taking over the Southern Reach from him. What would this person have done differently? What would this person do *right now*?

While his mother continued to talk, plunging ahead with what seemed like a lie.

"But I was mostly calling for an update, to see if you think you're making progress"—this his mother's attempt to subvert his silence with an apology. Slight emphasis on *progress*.

"You know exactly how it's going." The Voice would have told her everything It knew up to the point he had derailed It.

"True, but I haven't heard your side."

"My side? My side is that I've been dropped into a pit of snakes with a blindfold on and my hands tied behind my back."

"That's just a bit dramatic, don't you think?" said the streak of light.

"Not as dramatic as whatever you did to me at Central. I've got missing hours, maybe a missing day."

"Nothing much," she said in a bland tone that let him know she was bored with the topic. "Nothing much. Prepared you, stiffened your resolve, that's all. Made you see some things more clearly and others less so."

"Like introduce fake memories or—"

"No. That kind of thing would make you such an expensive model that no one here could *afford* you. Or afford to send you to the Southern Reach."

Because everyone would kill for this position.

"Are you lying to me?"

"You'd better hope not," she said with an in-rushing verve, "because I'm all you've got now—by your own actions. Besides, you'll never really know for sure. You've always been the kind of person who peels away the layers, even when there are no layers left. So just take it at face value, from your poor long-suffering mother."

"I can see you, Mother. I can see your reflection in the glass. You're right around the corner, watching, aren't you? It's not just your proxies. You're in town, too."

"Yes, John. That's why there's that kind of tinny echo. That's why my words seem to be falling on deaf ears, because you're hearing them twice. I'm interrupting myself, apparently."

A kind of rippling effect spread through him. He felt elongated and stretched, and his throat was dry. "Can I trust you?" he asked, sick of the sparring.

Something sincere and open in his voice must have reached her, because she dropped the distant tone and said, "Of course you can, John. You can't trust *how* I'll get somewhere, but you have to trust I know where I'm going. I always know where I'm going."

That didn't help him at all. "You want me to trust you? Then tell me, Mother. Tell me who the Voice was." If she wouldn't, the impulse in him to just disappear into the underbelly of Hedley, to fade into that landscape and not come back, might return. Might be too strong to suppress.

She hesitated, and her hesitation scared him. It felt real, not staged.

Then: "Lowry. God's honest truth, John. Lowry was the Voice."

Not thirty years distant at all. But breathing in Control's ear.

"Son of a bitch."

Banished and yet returned via the videos that would play forever in his head. Haunting him still.

Lowry.

"Go ahead and check the seats for change, John." Grandpa Jack staring at him as he held the gun.

There had come a sharp rapping at the window. It was his mother, leaning over to look in the window. Even through the condensation, Control could tell when she saw the gun on his lap. The door was wrenched open. The gun suddenly vanished, and Jack, on the other side, was out on his ear, Mother standing over him while he sat on the curb in front of the car. Control took the risk of lowering the left rear window a bit, then leaned forward so he could observe them better through the front windshield. She was talking quietly to Grandpa while she stood in front of him, arms folded and her gaze straight ahead, as if he stood at eye level. Control couldn't see where the gun had gone.

A sense of menace radiated out from his mother that he had never seen in such a concentrated form before. Her voice might be low, and he couldn't hear most of what she was saying, but the tone and quickness of it was like a sharp-ened butcher knife slicing, effortless, through raw meat. His grandpa gave a peculiar nod in response, one that was almost more like he was being pushed back by some invisible force or like she was shoving him.

She unfolded her arms and lowered her head to look at Grandpa, and Control heard, "Not this way! Not this way.

You can't force him into it." For some reason, he wondered if she was talking about the gun or Grandpa's secret plan to take him to the lingerie show.

Then she walked back to the car to collect him, and Grandpa got in and drove off slowly. Relief swept over Control as they went back inside the house. He didn't have to go to the lingerie show. He might be able to go next door later.

Mother only talked about the incident once, when they got back in the house. They took off their coats, went into the living room. She took out a pack of cigarettes and lit one. With her big, wavy hair and her slight features and her white blouse, red scarf, crisp black pants, and high heels she looked like a magazine model, smoking. An agitated model. Now he had experienced another unknown thing beyond the fact that she could fight fiercely for him: He hadn't known she was a smoker.

Except, she'd turned it back on him, as if he had been responsible. "What the hell were you thinking, John? What the hell were you thinking?"

But he hadn't been. He'd seen his grandpa's wink when he mentioned the department-store show, had liked that the man who could be stern or even disapproving was confiding in him, trusting him to keep a secret from his mother.

"Don't touch guns, John," she said, pacing back and forth. "And don't do every stupid thing your grandpa tells you to do." Later he decided to abide by the second commandment but to ignore the first, which he doubted she had meant—even nicknamed his various guns "Gramps" or "Grandpa." He used guns, but he didn't like them and didn't like relying on them. They smelled like their perspective.

Control never told his father about the incident, for fear it would be used against his mother. Nor did he recognize until later that the whole trip had actually been about the gun, or about finding the gun. That, perhaps, it had been evolving into a kind of test.

Sitting there in the coffee shop after his mother hung up the thought crept in that perhaps his mother's anger about the gun had itself been a tableau, a terroir, with Jack and Jackie complicit, actors in a scene meant already, at that young age, to somehow influence him or correct his course. To begin a kind of indoctrination in the family empire.

He wasn't sure he knew the difference anymore between what he was meant to find and what he'd dug up on his own. A tower could become a pit. Questioning a biologist could become a trap. An expedition member might even return thirty years later in the form of a voice whispering strange nothings in his ear.

When he got home Sunday night, he checked his recording of the conversation with his mother, felt an overload of relief when there were no gaps, no evidence that his mother, too, was deceiving him.

He believed that Central was in disarray, and that he'd been run by a faction, under hypnotic control. Now the ceiling was no doubt falling in on the clandestine basement, and the megalodon was feeling nervous within the cracked glass of its tank. Grace had bloodied It. Him. And then Control had delivered a follow-up punch.

"Only Lowry had enough experience of the Southern

Reach and Area X to be of use," his mother had told him, but fear leaked out of her words, too, and she went on and on about Lowry while Control felt as if a historical figure had popped out from a portrait alive to announce itself. A broken, erratic, rehabilitated historical figure who claimed to remember little not already captured by the videos. Someone who had leveraged a promotion, received due to a tangled knot of pity and remorse or some other reason than competence.

"Lowry is an asshole." To stop her talking about him. Just because you survived, just because you were labeled a hero, didn't mean you couldn't also be an asshole. She must have been desperate, had no choice. Rearing up behind that, whispers he remembered now that might have come from Lowry's direction: of shadow facilities, of things allied with the hypnosis and conditioning efforts but more hideous still.

"I knew there might be things you'd tell him you wouldn't tell me. We knew it might be better if you didn't know . . . some of the things we needed you to do."

Anger had warred with satisfaction that he'd smoked them out, that at least one variable had been removed. A need to know more balanced against already feeling overwhelmed. While trying to ignore an unsettling new thought: that his mother's power had boundaries.

"Is there anything you're hiding from me?"

"No," she said. "No. The mission is still the same: Focus on the biologist and the missing director. Dig through the notes. Stabilize the Southern Reach. Find out what has been going on that we don't know about."

Had that been the mission? That fragmented focus? Maybe the Voice's mission, which was his now, he supposed.

He chose to take the lie that she had told him everything at face value, thought perhaps the worst of it was now behind him. He'd shaken off the chains. He'd taken everything Grace could throw at him. He'd seen the videos.

Control went into the kitchen and poured a whiskey, his only one of the day, and downed it in one gulp, magical thinking behind the idea that it would help him sleep. As he put the empty glass back on the counter, he noticed the director's cell phone by the landline. In its case, it still looked like a large black beetle.

A premonition came to him, and a memory of the scuttling on the roof earlier in the week. He got a dish towel, picked up the phone, opened the back door with Chorry at his heels, and tossed the phone deep into the gloom of the backyard. It hit a tree, caromed off into the darkness of the long grass at the edge of the property. Fuck you, phone. Don't come back. It could join the Voice/Lowry phone in some phone afterlife. He would rather feel paranoid or stupid than be compromised. He felt vindicated when Chorry-Chorrykins refused to follow the phone, wanted to stay inside. A good choice.

021: REPEATING

When Monday morning arrived, Control didn't go into the Southern Reach right away. Instead he took a trip to the director's house—grabbed the driving instructions from the Internet and holstered his gun and got on the highway. It had been on his list to do once the notes in his office were categorized, just to make sure Grace's people had cleaned out the house as thoroughly as she claimed. The confirmation of the Voice's/Lowry's manipulation, and by extension his mother's, remained a listless feeling, something buzzing around in the background. As answers went, Lowry got him no further, gave him no real leverage—he'd been manipulated by someone untouchable and ethereal. Lowry, shadowing himself as the Voice, haunting the Southern Reach from afar. Control now trying to merge them into one person, one intent.

There was also an impulse, once he was on his way, not to return to the Southern Reach at all—to bypass the director's house, too—and detour onto a rural road, take it over to his father's house, some fifty miles west.

But he resisted it. New owners, and no sculptures left in the backyard. After his dad's death, they'd gone to good homes with aunts and uncles, nieces and nephews, even if he'd felt as if the landscape of his formative years was being dismantled, piece by piece. So no solace there. No real history. Some of his relatives still lived in the area, but his father had been the bond between them, and he'd last known most of them as a teenager.

Bleakersville had a population of about twenty thousand—just big enough to have a few decent restaurants, a small arts center, and the three blocks of historic district. The director lived in a neighborhood with few white faces in evidence. Lots of overhanging pines, oaks, and magnolia trees, hung heavy with moss, sodden branches from the storms lying broken on the potholed road. Solid cedar or cement houses, some with brick accents, mostly brown and blue or gray, with one or two cars in gravel or pine-needle driveways. He drove past a couple of communal basketball hoops and some black and Latino kids on bicycles, who stopped and stared until he was gone. School had been out for a couple of weeks.

The director's house lay at the end of a street named Standiford, at the top of a hill. Choosing caution, Control parked a block away, on the street below, then walked into the backyard, which slanted up the hill toward her house. The backyard was overgrown with untrimmed azalea bushes and massive wisteria vines, some of them wrapped tight around the pine trees. A couple of halfhearted compost islands languished behind circles of staked chicken wire. Much of the grass had yellowed and died over time, exposing tree roots.

Three cement semicircles served in lieu of a deck, covered over with leaves and what looked like rotted birdseed alongside a pie pan filled to the top with dirty water. The white French doors stained green with mold beyond them would be his entry point. One problem—he would have to pick the lock, since he hadn't put in a formal request to visit. Except he wanted to pick the lock, he realized. Didn't want to have a key. As he worked on it with the tools he'd brought, the rain began to fall. Thick drops that clacked and thunked against last winter's fallen magnolia leaves.

He sensed he was being watched—some hint of movement from the corner of his eye, perhaps—just as he'd managed to open the door. He stood up and turned to his left.

In the neighbor's yard, well back from the chain-link fence, a black girl, maybe nine or ten, with beaded cornrows, stared warily at him. She wore a sunflower dress and white plastic sandals with Velcro straps.

Control smiled and waved. In some other universe, Control fled, abandoning his mission, but not in this one.

The girl didn't wave back, but she didn't run away, either.

He took that as a sign and went inside.

No one had been here in months, but there was a kind of swirling movement to the air that he wanted to attribute to a fan he couldn't see, or an air-conditioning unit that had just cut out. Except that Grace had had the electricity turned off until the director returned, "to save money for her." The rain was coming down hard enough now that it added to the gloom, so he turned on his flashlight. No one would notice—he was too far away from the windows, and the glass doors had a long dark curtain across them. Most people would be at work anyway.

The director's neighbors would have known her as a psychologist in private practice, if they had known her at all. Was the photo in Grace's office an anomaly, or did the director often eat barbecue with a beer in her hand? Had Lowry, back in the day, come over in a baseball cap, T-shirt, and torn jeans for hot dogs and fireworks on the Fourth of July? People could double or triple themselves to become different in different situations, but somehow he thought the director probably had been solitary. And it was here, in her home, that the director, over time, against protocol, and in some cases illegally, had brought Area X evidence and files, erasing the divide between her personal and professional lives.

Seen through the tunnel of the flashlight beam, the

small living room soon gave up its secrets: a couch, three lounge chairs, a fireplace. What looked like a library lay beyond it, behind a dividing wall and through worn saloon-style doors. The kitchen was to the left and then a hallway; a massive refrigerator festooned with magnet-fixed photos and old calendars guarded the corner. To the right of the living room was a door leading to the garage, and beyond that probably the master bedroom. The entire house was about 1,700 square feet.

Why had the director lived here? With her pay grade, she could have done much better; Grace and Cheney both lived in Hedley in upper-middle-class subdivisions. Perhaps there was debt he didn't know about. He needed better intel. Somehow the lack of information about the director seemed connected to her clandestine trip across the border, her ability to keep her position for so long.

No one had lived here for over a year. No one except Central had come in. No one was here now. And yet the emptiness made him uneasy. His breath came shallow, his heartbeat elevated. Perhaps it was just the reliance on the flashlight, the unsettling way it reduced anything not under its bright gaze to a pack of shadows. Maybe it was some part of him acknowledging that this was as close to a field assignment as he'd had in years.

A half-empty water glass stood by the sink, reflecting his light as a circle of fire. A few dishes lay in the sink, along with forks and knives. The director had left this clutter the day she'd gotten in her car and driven to the Southern Reach to lead the twelfth expedition. Central apparently had not been instructed to clean up after the director—nor after themselves. The living-room carpet showed signs of boot prints as well as tracked-in leaves and dirt. It was like a diorama from a museum devoted to the secret history of the Southern Reach.

Grace might have had Central come here and retrieve anything classified, but in terms of the director's property theirs had been a light touch. Nothing *looked* disturbed even though Control knew they had removed five or six boxes of material. It just looked cluttered, which was no doubt the way they'd found it, if the office he'd inherited was any indication. Paintings and prints covered the walls above a few crowded CD stands, a dusty flat-screen television, and a cheap-looking stereo system on which had been stacked dozens of rare old-timey records. None of the paintings or photographs seemed personal in nature.

An elegant gold-and-blue couch stood against the wall dividing the living room from the library, a pile of magazines taking up one cushion, while the antique rosewood coffee table in front of the couch looked as if it had been requisitioned as another desk: books and magazines covered its entire surface—same as the beautifully refinished kitchen table to the left. Had she done most of her work in these rooms? It was homier than he'd thought it would be, with good furniture, and he couldn't quite figure out why that bothered him. Did it come with the house, or was it an inheritance? Did she have a connection to Bleakersville? A theory was forming in his head, like a musical composition he could hum from vague memories but not quite yet name or play.

He walked through the hallway beside the kitchen, encountered another fact that seemed odd for no particular reason. Every door had been closed. He had to keep opening them as if going through a series of air locks. Each time, even though there was no prickle of threat, Control prepared to jump back. He discovered an office, a room with some filing cabinets and an exercise bike and free weights, and a guest bedroom with a bathroom opposite it. There were a lot of doors for such a small house, as if the director or Central had been trying to contain something, or almost as if he were traveling between different compartments of the director's brain. Any and all of these thoughts spooked him, and after the third door, he just said the hell with it and entered each with a hand on Grandpa in its holster.

He circled around into the library area and looked out one of the front windows. Saw a branch-strewn overgrown lawn, a battered green mailbox at the end of a cement walkway, and nothing suspicious. No one lurking in a black sedan with tinted windows, for example.

Then back through the living room, through the other hallway, past the garage door, and into the master bedroom on the left.

At first, he thought the bedroom had been flooded and all of the furniture had washed up against the nearest walls. Chairs were stacked atop the dressers and armoire. The bed had come to rest against the dressers. About seven pairs of shoes—from heels to trainers—had been tossed as flotsam on top of the bed. The covers were pulled up, but sloppily. On the far side of the room, in the flashlight's gleam, a mirror shone crazily from beyond a bathroom door.

He took out Grandpa, released the safety, aimed wherever his flashlight roved. From the dressers now over the bed, now to the wall against which the bed had previously rested, which was covered in thick purple curtains. Cautious, he pulled them back, revealing all-too-familiar words beneath a high horizontal window that let in a stagnant light.

Where lies the strangling fruit that came from the hand of the sinner I shall bring forth the seeds of the dead.

Written in thick dark marker, the same wall of text, with the same map beside it that he had painted over in his office. As if the moment he had rid himself of it, it had appeared in the director's bedroom. Irrational sight. Irrational thought. Now a hundred Controls were running from the room and back to the car in a hundred pocket universes.

But it had been here for a while. It had to have been. Sloppy of Grace's people not to remove it. Too sloppy.

He turned toward the bathroom. "If anyone's there, come out," he said. "I have a gun." Now his heart was beating so fast and his hand was so tight on the flashlight he didn't think it could be pried loose.

But no one came out.

No one was there, as he confirmed by forcing himself to breathe more slowly. By forcing himself to check every corner, including a small closet that seemed more cavernous the farther he progressed into it. In the bathroom, he found the usual things—shampoo, soap, a prescription for blood pressure drugs, a few magazines. Brown hair dye and a hairbrush with gray strands snarled in it. So the director had felt self-conscious about reaching middle age. The brush gleamed when his flashlight struck it, seemed to want to communicate, akin to the scribbled-on receipts and torn magazine pages that had laid bare parts of her life to him, more meaningful to him than his own.

He returned to the bedroom and played the flashlight beam over the wall again. No, not the exact same tableau. The same words, the exact same words. But no height marks. And the map—it was different, too. This version showed the island and its ruined lighthouse, along with the topographical anomaly and the lighthouse on the coast. This version also showed the Southern Reach. A line had been drawn between the ruined and functional lighthouses and the topographical anomaly. That line had then been extended to the Southern Reach. They looked very much like outposts on a border, like on ancient maps of empires.

Control backed away and then down the hall into the living room, feeling cold, feeling distant. He could not think of a scenario in which Central had seen those words, that map, and not removed it.

Which meant that it had been created after they had searched the house. Which meant . . . which probably meant . . .

He didn't allow himself the thought. Instead, he went to the front door to confirm a sudden suspicion.

The knob turned easily in his hand. Unlocked.

Which meant nothing.

Yet now his foremost idea, his only real idea, was to get out of the house. But he still had the presence of mind to lock the front door and return to the back.

Pushed open the French doors, out into the rain.

Walked-ran back to the car.

Not until he was parked well away, on Bleakersville's main street, did he call his mother, tell her what he had found, and ask her to send a team in to investigate. If he'd done it from the site, they'd have kept him there for far too long. As they talked, Control tried to convince himself of benign interpretations, almost as much as his mother did. "Don't make leaps, John, and *don't tell Grace* because she'll overreact," which was correct. Anyone from the Southern Reach could have drawn that on the wall—Whitby as prime suspect other than the former director. Pushing against that relative comfort: A disturbing vision of the director wandering through neighborhoods and parks, across fields, into forests. Revisiting old haunts.

"But, John, there *is* something I need to tell you."

"Tell me, then." Had she given up Lowry's identity as the Voice so she could hide something else?

"You know the places where we picked up the anthropologist and the surveyor?"

"A front porch, the back of a medical practice."

"We've noticed some . . . inconsistencies in those places. The readings are different."

"How? How are they different?"

"We're still sorting through the data, but we've quarantined the areas, even though it's difficult."

"But not in the empty lot? Not where the biologist was?"

"No."

022: GAMBIT

Late morning. An attempt to regain . . . control. The old familiar debriefing room whose deficiencies he had become oblivious to, expecting a call from his mother with a report about the director's house that couldn't possibly come until hours from now.

He had told Grace he was about to interview the biologist and wanted her there, in the room, this time. A few minutes later, Grace came in wearing a bright yellow dress in a flower pattern, black belt at the waist—some kind of Sunday best—not peering around the doorway, not looking like he might lob a grenade at her. He was immediately suspicious.

"Where's the biologist?" Grace asked, in a kind of conspiratorial way. Control was sitting by himself.

Control pushed out the chair opposite with his foot by way of reply, pretending to busy himself looking over some notes.

"I'm sorry," he said. "You just missed the biologist. But she had some very interesting things to say. Do you want to know what she said about you, for example?"

Somehow Control had expected Grace would see it as a trap, get up and try to leave, and he'd have to convince her to stay. But she remained sitting there, appraising him.

"Before I tell you, you should know that all recording devices have been turned off. This is just between the two of us."

Grace folded her arms. "That is fine with me. Continue."

Control felt wrong-footed. He had expected she would go check, make sure he wasn't lying. Maybe she had checked before coming into the room. Grandpa Jack's advice had been that for this kind of work you needed "a second guy, always." Well, he didn't have a second guy or gal. He plunged on anyway.

"Let me get to the point. Before the final eleventh expedition, the director crossed over the border secretly, by herself. Did you know about this in advance? And did you provide material aid? Did you provide command-and-control decision-making? Were you, in fact, *complicit* in making sure she got back across the border? Because this is what the biologist says the director told her." None of this was in the official report on the incident, which the Voice had sent via e-mail before their abrupt leave-taking over the phone. There, in the report, the director had claimed to have acted on her own.

"Interesting. What else did the biologist tell you?" No heat behind the words.

"That the director gave you instructions to wait at the border every night for a week on very specific dates about three weeks after she snuck across. To help her with her return." According to security records, each of those days Grace had left the Southern Reach early, although there was no record of her at the border checkpoints.

"This is all in the past," Grace said. "What are you trying to prove? Exactly."

Control had begun to feel like a chess player who thinks he has a great move, but the opponent is either brilliant or bluffing or has something untouchable four moves ahead.

"Really? That's your reaction? Because both of those accusations would be enough to file an addendum to the report with Central. That you colluded with the director to violate regulations and security protocols. That you provided material support. She was put on probation. What do you think you'd get for lying?"

Smiling, Grace asked, "What do you want?"

Not exactly an admission, but it allowed him to continue on with the script in his head, muffled the alarm bells. "Not what you think, Grace. I'm not pushing for you to resign, and I don't want to report this information to Central. I'm not out to get the director. I want to understand her, that's all. She went over the border. I need to know exactly why and how, and what she found. The report on file is vague." Wondered now if Grace had written the report, or overseen its writing.

The report had mostly focused on the director's punishment and the steps taken to once again tighten border security. There was a brief statement from the director that appeared to have been written by a lawyer: "Although I meant to act in the best interests of the Southern Reach and the requirements of my position, I deeply apologize for my actions and recognize that they were reckless, endangering, and not in keeping with the agency's mission statement. If allowed to return, I will endeavor to adhere to the standard of conduct expected of me, and of this position." "Measurements and samples" were also mentioned in the report, but Control had as yet been unable to track them down. They had not been placed in the storage cathedral, that much he knew. Unless that boiled down to a plant and a mouse and an old cell phone.

"The director did not share her every thought with me," Grace said in an irritated tone, as if this fact bothered her, but with a strange half-smile on her face.

"I find it hard to believe that you don't know more than you're telling me."

This did not move Grace to respond, so he prodded her with "I'm not here to destroy the director's legacy, or yours. I brought you here not just because of what the biologist said but also because I think we could *both* have autonomy here. That we could run the agency in a way that means your position remains unchanged." Because as far as he was concerned, the agency was fucked and he was now an undercover agent in the field, entering hostile territory. So use whatever you don't care about as a bargaining chip. Maybe before he found a way out he'd even give Whitby that transfer he'd once wanted. Maybe he'd return to Central and have a beer with Lowry.

"How gracious of you," Grace said. "The schoolboy is offering to share the power with the teacher."

"That's not the analogy I would have made. I would have—"

"Anything the director did, she did because she believed it was important."

"Yes, but what did she do? What was she up to?"

"Up to?" Grace said, with a little snort of disbelief.

He chose his words very carefully. "Grace, I am already here. I am already in the middle of this. You should just tell me what's going on." What was the look that could convey without the reinforcement of words that he had already seen some very strange shit? "Remember, none of this is on the record."

Grace considered that for a second with what seemed like amusement. Then she began to talk.

"You have to understand the director's position," Grace said. "The first expedition had set the tone within the organization. Even though the original director, by the time Cynthia got here, was trying to change that." Cynthia? For a moment, Control wondered who Cynthia was because he'd thought of her as "the director" for so long. "The personnel here felt that the first expedition failed because the Southern Reach did not know what it was doing. That we had sent them in, and they had died because we did not know what we were doing, and we could never really make up for that." The first expedition: a sacrifice to a lack of context. A lament unrecognized as such until it was too late. "And Lowry's presence here at the agency"—was she reading his mind, did she somehow know?—"from my understanding, only made that worse. He was a living ghost, a reminder held up as a hero when he had just been a survivor. So his advice was given more weight, even when it was wrong. The director only really had a chance to pursue her own agenda after Lowry had been promoted to Central, even though that, too, was a problem. Lowry pushed for more expeditions even though the director wanted fewer, and whereas before she could control Lowry, now he was beyond her control. So we kept sending people in, throwing them up against a complete unknown. This did not sit well with the director, although she followed orders because she had to."

He found himself being swept along by her narrative. "How did the director get her own agenda through? In what ways?"

"She became obsessed with metrics, with changing the context. If she could have her metrics, then Lowry could, grudgingly, have his expeditions, the conditioning and hypnosis he championed, although over time she came to understand why Lowry pushed the hypnosis."

Control kept seeing Lowry in the context of the camera flying through the air: Lowry crawling, the camera soaring, and the truth perhaps somewhere in the middle. And then Lowry making Control crawl and soar.

None of this really spoke to the director's secret mission across the border, though. Was Grace just tossing information at him to avoid talking about it? It was more than she'd ever said to him before.

"What else?" he asked. "What else did she do?"

She spread her hands as if for emphasis and the smile on her face was almost beatific. "She became obsessed with making it react."

"Area X?"

"Yes. She felt that if she could make Area X react, then she would somehow throw it off course. Even though we didn't know what course it was on."

"But it *had* reacted: It killed a lot of people."

"She believed that nothing we had done had *pushed* whatever is behind Area X. That it had handled anything we did too easily. Almost without thought. If thought could be said to be involved."

"So she went across the border to make Area X react."

"I will not confirm that I knew about her trip or helped in any way," Grace said. "I will tell you my belief, based on what she said to me after she came back."

"It wasn't the reaction she wanted," Control said.

"No. No, it was not. And she blamed herself. The director can be very harsh, but never harsher than with herself. When Central decided to go ahead with the last eleventh expedition, I am sure the director hoped that she had made a difference. And maybe she had. Instead of the usual, what came back were cancer-ridden ciphers."

"Which is why she forced herself onto the twelfth expedition."

"Yes."

"Which is why her methods had become suspect."

"I would not agree with that assessment. But, yes, others would say that."

"Why did Central let her go on the twelfth expedition?"

"For the same reason they reprimanded her after she went across by herself but did not fire her."

"Which was?"

Grace smiled, triumphant. At knowing something he should have known? For some other reason?

"Ask your mother. Your mother had a hand in both things, I believe."

"They had lost confidence in her anyway," Grace said next, bitterness bleeding into her voice. "What did they care if she never came back? Maybe some of them at Central even thought it solved a problem." Like Lowry.

But Control was still stuck on Jackie Miranda Severance, Severance for short, Grandpa always "Jack." His mother had placed him in the Southern Reach, in the middle of it all. She had worked for the Southern Reach briefly, when he was a teenager, to be close to him, she had said. Now, as he questioned Grace, he was trying to make the dates synch up, to get a sense of who had been at the Southern Reach and who had not, who had left by then and who was still incoming. The director—no. Grace—no. Whitby—yes. Lowry—yes, no? Where had his mother gone when she left? Had she kept ties? Clearly she had, if he were to believe Grace. And did her sudden appearance to him with a job offer correspond to knowing she had some kind of emergency on her hands? Or was it part of a more intricate plan? It could make you weary, untangling the lines. At least Grandpa had been more straightforward. Oh, look. There's a gun. What a surprise. I want you to learn how to use a gun. Make everything do more than one thing. Sometimes you had to take shortcuts after all. Wink wink. But his mother never gave you the wink. Why should she? She didn't want to be your friend, and if she couldn't convince you in some more subtle way, she'd find someone she could convince. He might never know how much other residue he'd already encountered from her passage through Southern Reach.

But the idea that the director might have reached out to others in the agency, and at Central, comforted Control. It made the director less an eccentric, less a "single-celled plot" as his mother put it, than someone genuinely trying to solve a problem.

"What happened on her trip across the border?" Control, pressing again.

"She never told me. She said it was for my own protection, in case the investigators subpoenaed me." He made a note to return to that later.

"Nothing at all?"

"Not a single thing."

"Did she give you any special instructions before she went on leave or after she came back?" From what Control could intuit from the files he'd read, Grace was more constrained by rules and regulations than the director, and the director might have felt slightly undermined by her assistant director's adherence to them. Or perhaps that was the point: that Grace had kept her grounded. In which case, Grace would almost certainly have been in charge of operational details.

Grace hesitated, and Control didn't know if that meant she was debating telling him more or was about to feed him a line of bullshit.

"Cynthia asked me to reopen an investigation into the

so-called S&S Brigade, and to assign someone to report in more detail on the lighthouse."

"And who did the research?"

"Whitby." Whitby the loon. It figured.

"What happened to this research?" He couldn't recall seeing this information in the files he had been given before he'd come to the Southern Reach.

"Cynthia held on to it, asked for a hard copy and for the electronic copies not to be entered into the record . . . Are you planning to go down the same rabbit holes?"

"So you thought it was a waste of time?"

"For us, not necessarily for Cynthia. It seemed irrelevant to me, but nothing we gathered would make much sense without knowing what was in the director's mind. And we did not always know what was in the director's mind."

"Is there anything else you want to tell me?" Being bold now that Grace was finally opening up to him.

A sympathetic expression, guided or pushed his way. "Do you smoke?"

"Sometimes." This past weekend. Banishing demons and voices.

"Then let's go out to the courtyard and have a smoke."

It sounded like a good idea. If he was completely honest with himself, it sounded like bliss.

They reconvened out at the edge of the courtyard, nearest the swamp. The short jaunt from room to open air had not been without revelation: He'd finally seen the janitor, a wizened little white guy with huge glasses who wore light green overalls and held a mop. He couldn't have been more than five feet tall. Control resisted the urge to break ranks with Grace to tell him to switch cleaners.

Grace in the courtyard seemed even more relaxed than inside, despite the humidity and the annoying chorus of insect voices rising from the undergrowth. He was already sweating.

She offered him a cigarette. "Take one."

Yes, he would take one, had been missing them ever since his weekend binge. The harsh, sharp taste of her unfiltered menthols as he lit up was like a spike through the eyeball to cure a headache.

"Do you like the swamp?" he asked.

She shrugged. "I like the quiet out here, sometimes. It can be peaceful." She gave him a wry smile. "If I stand with my back to the building, I can pretend it isn't there."

He nodded, was silent for a moment, then said, "What would you do if the director came back and she was like the anthropologist or the surveyor?" Just adding to the light conversation. Just a gaffe, he realized as soon as he'd said it.

Grace remained unfazed. "She won't."

"How can you be so sure?" He almost broke his promise to his mother then and told Grace about the writing on the wall in the director's house.

"I have to tell you something," Grace said, changing direction on him. "It will be a shock, but I don't mean it to be that way."

Somehow, even though it was too late, he could see the hit coming before the impact, almost as if it were in slow-motion. It still knocked him off his feet.

"Here's what you should know: Central took the biologist away late Friday evening. She's been gone the whole weekend. So you must have been talking to a ghost, because I know you would not lie to me, John. You wouldn't lie to me, would you?" Her look was serious, as if there were a bond between them.

Control wondered if the woman in the military jacket was back in front of the liquor store. He wondered if the skateboarder was in the process of dumping another can of dog food on the sidewalk, the plastic-bag man about to pop up to shout at passersby. He wondered if he should go join them. There was within him a generous affection for all of them, matched by a wide and growing sadness. A shed out back. Christmas lights wound around a pine. Wood storks.

No, he had not talked to the biologist that morning. Yes, he had thought she was still at the Southern Reach, had depended on that fact. He had already planned his next session in detail. It would be back in the interrogation room, not outside. She would sit there, maybe in a different mood from the other times but perhaps not, waiting for his now-familiar questions. But he wouldn't ask any questions. Time to change the paradigm, the hell with procedures.

He would have pushed her file over to her, said, "This is everything we know about you. About your husband. About your past jobs and relationships. Including a transcript of your initial interview sessions with the psychologist." This wouldn't be an easy thing for him to do: Afterward, she might become a different person than he knew; he might be letting Area X farther into the world, in some odd way. He might be betraying his mother.

She would make some remark about having outlasted him already, and he would reply that he didn't want to play games anymore, that Lowry's games had already made him weary. She would repeat the same line he had said to her out by the holding pond: "Don't thank people for giving you what you should already have." "I'm not looking for thanks," he would reply. "Of course you are," she would say, without reproach. "It's the way human beings are built."

"You had her sent away?" Said so quietly that Grace asked him to repeat it.

"You had formed too much of an attachment. You were losing your perspective."

"That wasn't your call!"

"I am not the one who sent her away."

"What do you mean?"

"Ask your supervisor, Control. Ask your cabal at Central."

"It's not my cabal," he said. Cabal versus faction. Which was worse? This was a record for not-fixing. A record for being sent in only to be shut out. He wondered what kind of bloodbath had to be occurring at Central right now.

He took a long drag on the cigarette, stared out at the god-awful swamp, heard from a distance Grace asking him if he was all right, his reply of "Give me a second."

Was he all right? In the long line of things he could legitimately be not all right about, this ranked right up there. He felt as if something had been severed far too prematurely, that there had been much more to say. He tamped down the impulse to walk back inside and call his mother, because, of course, she must already know and would just give him an amplified echo of what Grace had said, no matter how much this could be seen as Lowry punishing him: "You were getting too close to her in too short a time. You went from an interrogation scenario to having conversations with her in her cell to chewing on sedge weeds while you gave her a guided tour of the outside of the building—*in just four days.* What would have come next, John? A birthday party? A conga line? Her own private suite at the Hilton? Perhaps a little voice inside starts to say, 'Give her her files,' hmm?"

Then he would have lied and said that wasn't true or fair and she'd have fallen back on Grandpa Jack's offensive old-school line about fair being "for losers and pussies," and he wouldn't be talking about Chorry. Control would claim she was interfering with his ability to do the job she had sent him to do and she'd counter with the idea of getting him transcripts of any subsequent interviews, which would be "just as good." After which he might say, lamely, that's not the point. That he needed the support, and then he'd trail off awkwardly because he was on thin ice talking about sup-port, and she wouldn't help him out, and he'd be stuck. They never spoke about Rachel McCarthy, but it was always there.

"So we should talk about division of duties," Grace said.

"Yes, we should." Because they both knew she now had the upper hand.

But his mind was elsewhere the whole time that Grace was massacring his troops, before she left the courtyard. Grace would run most things going forward, with John Rodriguez abdicating responsibility for all but figurehead duties at the most important status meetings. He would resubmit his recommendations through Grace, leaving out the point-less ones, and she would decide which to implement and which not to implement. They would coordinate so that eventually his working hours and Grace's working hours overlapped as little as possible. Grace would assist him in making sense of the director's notes, and as he acclimated himself to the new arrangements, that would be his major responsibility, although in no way did Grace acknowledge that the director might be dead or have gone completely off the tracks and hurtled through the underbrush over a cliff in her last days at the Southern Reach. Even as she did acknowledge that mouse-and-plant were eccentric, and also accepted the ex post facto reality that he had already painted over the director's wall beyond the door.

None of which in this rout—this retreat that had no vanguard or rearguard, but was just a group of desperate men hacking at the muck and mire of a swamp with outdated swords while Cossacks waited for them on the plain—went completely against Control's true wishes anyway, but this was not how he had seen it coming, with Grace dictating the terms of his surrender. And none of which saved him from a kind of grieving not at the power he was losing but at the person he had lost.

Still out there, smoking, after Grace had left, with a pat on his shoulder that was meant as sympathy but felt like failure. Even as he now counted her a colleague if not quite a friend. Trying to resurrect the idea of the biologist, the image of her, the sound of her voice.

"What should I do now?"

"I'm the prisoner," the biologist said to him from her cot, facing the wall. "Why should I tell you anything?"

"Because I'm trying to help you."

"Are you? Or are you just trying to help yourself?"

He had no answer to that.

"A normal person might give up. That would be very normal."

"Would you?" he asked.

"No. But I'm not normal."

"Neither am I."

"Where does that leave us?"

"Where we've always been."

But it didn't. Something had occurred to him, finally seeing the janitor. Something about a ladder and a lightbulb.

023: BREAK DOWN

Control found a flashlight, tested it out. Then he walked past the cafeteria that had by now become an irritating repetition, as if he had navigated across the same airport terminal for several days while chewing the same piece of gum. At the door to the storage room, he made sure the corridor was clear then quickly ducked inside.

It was dark. He fumbled for the lightbulb cord, pulled it. The light came on but didn't help much. As he'd remembered, the metal shade above the bulb and its low position, just an inch or so above his head, meant all you could see were the lower shelves. The only shelves the janitor could reach anyway. The only shelves that weren't empty, as the shadows revealed as his eyes adjusted.

He had a feeling that Whitby had been lying. That this *was* the special room Whitby had offered to show him. If he could solve no other mystery, he would solve this one. A puzzle. A diversion. Had Lowry's magical interference hastened this moment or postponed it?

Slowly the beam of his flashlight panned across the top of the shelves, then onto the ceiling, maybe nine feet above him. It had an unfinished feeling, that ceiling. Irregular and exposed, of different shades, the wooden planks were crossed by an X of two beams, and appeared to have been built around the shelves. The shelves continued to rise, empty, all the way up to the ceiling and then beyond. He could just see the gap where the next row of shelves continued, beyond the ceiling. After a moment more of inspection, Control noticed a thin, nearly invisible cut along the two beams that formed a square. A trapdoor? In the ceiling.

Control considered that. It could just lead to an air duct or more storage space, but in trying to imagine where this room existed in the layout of the building, he had to take into account that it lay just opposite Whitby's favorite spot in the cafeteria, and that this meant, if the stairs to the third level lay between them, that there could be considerable space up above, tucked in under the stairs.

He went to work looking for the ladder, found it, retractable, hidden in a back corner, under a tarp. He hit the bulb as he moved the ladder into position, dislodging dust, and the space came alive with a wild and flickering light.

At the top of the ladder, he turned on his flashlight again and, awkwardly, with his other hand, pushed against the ceiling at the center of the half-hidden square. This high, he could see that the "ceiling" was clearly a platform fitted around the shelves.

The door gave with a creak. He exhaled deeply, felt

apprehensive, the ladder rungs a little slippery. He opened the door. It fell back on its coil hinges smoothly, without a sound, as if just oiled. Control shone his flashlight across the floor, then up to the shelves that rose another eight feet to either side. No one was there. He returned to the central space: the far wall and then the slant of a true ceiling.

Faces stared back at him, along with the impression of vast shapes and some kind of writing.

Control almost dropped the flashlight.

He looked again.

Along the wall and part of the ceiling, someone had painted a vast phantasmagoria of grotesque monsters with human faces. More specifically, oils splotched and splashed in a primitive style, in rich, deep reds and blues and greens and yellows, to form approximations of bodies. The pixelated faces were blown-up security head shots of Southern Reach staff.

One image dominated, extending up the wall and with the head peering down with a peculiar three-dimensional quality from the slanted ceiling. The others formed constellations around this image, and then much-worried sentences and phrases existing in a rich patina of cross-outs and paint-overs and other markings, as if someone had been creating a compost of words. There was a border, too: a ring of red fire that transformed at the ends into a two-headed monster, and Area X in its belly.

Reluctantly Control pulled himself up into the space, keeping low to distribute his weight until he was sure the platform could hold him. But it seemed sturdy. He stood next to the shelves on the left side of the room and considered the art in front of him.

The body that dominated the murals or paintings or whatever word applied depicted a creature that had the form of a giant hog and a slug commingled, pale painted skin mottled with what was meant to be a kind of mangy light green moss. The swift, broad strokes of arms and legs suggested the limbs of a pig, but with three thick fingers at their ends. More appendages were positioned along the midsection.

The head, atop a too-small neck rendered in a kind of gauzy pink-white, was misshapen but anchored by the face pasted onto it, the glue glistening in the flashlight beam. The face Control recognized from the files: the psychologist from the final eleventh expedition, a man who, before his death from cancer, had said in the transcripts, "It was quite beautiful, quite peaceful in Area X." And smiled in a vague way.

But here he had been portrayed as anything but peaceful. Using a pen, someone—Whitby? Whitby—had given the man a mask of utter, uncomprehending anguish, the mouth open in a perpetual O.

Arrayed to the right and left were more creatures—some private pantheon, some private significance—with more faces he recognized. The director had been rendered as a full-on boar, stuffed with vegetation; the assistant director as a kind of stout or ferret; Cheney as a jellyfish.

Then he found himself. Incomplete. His face taken from his recent serious-looking mug shot, and the vague body of not a white rabbit but a wild hare, the fur matted, curling, half penciled in. Around which Whitby had created the outlines of a gray-blue sea monster, a whalelike leviathan, with purple waves pushing out from it, and a huge circle of an eye that tunneled out from his face, making of him a cyclops. Radiating from the monster-body were not just the waves but also flurries of unreadable words in a cramped, crabby scrawl. As surprising and disturbing walls went, it beat the director's office by quite a lot. It made his skin prickle with sudden chills. It made him realize that he still had been half relying on Whitby's analysis to provide him with answers. But there were no answers here. Only proof that in Whitby's head was something akin to a sedimentary layer of papers bound by a plant, a dead mouse, and an ancient cell phone.

On the floor opposite him, near the right-hand shelves, a trowel, a selection of paints, a stand that allowed Whitby to reach the ceiling. A few books. A portable stove. A sleeping bag, bundled up. Had Whitby been *living* here? Without anyone knowing about it? Or guessing but not wanting to really know? Instead, just foist off Whitby on the new director. Disinformation and obfuscation. Whitby had put this together over a fairly long period of time. He had patiently been working at it, adding to it, subtracting from it. Terroir.

Control had been standing there with his back to the shelves for only about a minute.

He had been standing there recognizing that there was a draft in the loft. He had been standing there without realizing that it wasn't a draft.

Someone was breathing, behind him.

Someone was *breathing* on his neck. The knowledge froze him, froze the cry of "Jesus fuck!" in his throat.

He turned with incredible slowness, wishing he could seem like a statue in his turning. Then saw with alarm a large, pale, watery-blue eye that existed against a backdrop of darkness or dark rags shot through with pale flesh, and which resolved into Whitby.

Whitby, who had been there the entire time, crammed into the shelf right behind Control, at eye level, bent at the knees, on his side.

Breathing in shallow sharp bursts. Staring out.

Like something incubating. There, on the shelf.

At first, Control thought that Whitby must be sleeping with his eyes open. A waxwork corpse. A tailor's dummy. Then he realized that Whitby was wide awake and staring at him, Whitby's body shaking ever so slightly like a pile of leaves with something underneath it. Looking like something boneless, shoved into a too-small space.

So close that Control could have leaned over and bit his nose or kissed it.

Whitby continued to say nothing, and Control, terrified, somehow knew that there was a danger in speaking. That if he said anything that Whitby might lunge out of his hiding place, that the stiff shifting of the man's jaw hid something more premeditated and deadly.

Their eyes locked, and there was no way around the fact that each had seen the other, but still Whitby did not speak, as if he too wanted to preserve the illusion.

Slowly Control managed to direct his flashlight away from Whitby, stifling a shudder, and with a gritting of teeth overrode his every instinct not to turn his back on the man. He could feel Whitby's breath pluming out.

Then there was a slight movement and Whitby's hand came to rest on the back of his head. Just resting there, palm flat against Control's hair. The fingers spread like a starfish and slowly moved back and forth. Two strokes. Three. Petting Control's head. Caressing it in a gentle, tentative way.

Control remained still. It took an effort.

After a time, the hand withdrew, with a kind of reluctance. Control took two steps forward, then another. Another. Whitby did not erupt out of his space. Whitby did not make some inhuman sound. Whitby did not try to pull him back into the shelves.

He reached the trapdoor without succumbing to a shudder, lowered himself legs-first into that space, found the ladder with his feet. Slowly pulled the door closed, not looking toward the shelves, even in the dark. Felt such relief with it closed, then scrambled down the ladder. Hesitated, then took the time to lower and fold away the ladder. Forced himself to listen at the door before he left the room, leaving the flashlight in there. Then walked out into the bright, bright corridor, squinting, and took in a huge breath that had him seeing dark spots, a convulsion he could not control and wanted no one to see.

After about fifty steps, Control realized that Whitby had been up in the space without using the ladder. Imagined Whitby crawling through the air ducts. His white face. His white hands. Reaching out.

In the parking lot, Control bumped into a jovial apparition who said, "You look like you've seen a ghost!" He asked this apparition if he had heard anything strange in the building over the years, or seen anything out of the ordinary. Inserted it as small talk, as breathing space, in what he hoped was just a curious or joking way. But Cheney flunked the question, said, "Well, it's the high ceilings, isn't it? Makes you see things that aren't there. Makes the things you do see look like other things. A bird can be a bat. A bat can be a piece of floating plastic bag. Way of the world. To see things as other things. Bird-leafs. Bat-birds. Shadows made of lights. Sounds that are incidental but seem more significant. Never going to seem any different wherever you go."

A *bird can be a bat. A bat can be a piece of floating plastic bag.* But could it?

It struck Control—hard—that he might not have Cheney any more sussed out than Whitby—a hastily prepared facade that was receding across the parking lot, walking backward to speak a few more words at him, none of which Control really heard.

Then, starting the engine and released past the security gate, almost without a memory of the drive, or of parking along the river walk, Control was mercifully free of the Southern Reach and found himself down by the Hedley pier. He explored the river walk for a while, so far inside his head he didn't really see the shops or people or the water beyond.

His trance, his bubble of no-thought, was punctured by a little girl shouting, "You're getting here too late!" Relief when he realized she wasn't talking to him, her father walking past him then to claim her.

Where he wound up was little better than a dive bar, but dark and spacious, with pool tables in the back. Somewhere nearby was the pontoon dock from his Tuesday jog. Up a hill lay his house, but he wasn't ready to go back yet. Control ordered a whiskey neat, once the bartender had finished being hit on by a good old boy who looked a little like an aging version of the first-string quarterback from high school.

"He was a smooth talker, but way too many neck folds,"

Control said, and she laughed, although he'd said it with venom.

"I couldn't hear what he was saying—the wattles were too loud," she said.

He chuckled, drawn out of his thoughts for a moment. "What're you doin' tonight, honey? Am I right that you're doin' it with me?" Imitating the man's terrible pickup line.

"I'm sleeping tonight. Falling asleep now."

"Me, too," he said, still chuckling. But he could feel her gaze on him, curious, as she turned back to washing glasses. Their conversation hadn't been any longer than the ones he'd had with Rachel McCarthy, so many years ago. Or about anything more substantial.

The TV was on low, showing the aftermath of massive floods and a school massacre in between commercials for a big basketball series. Behind him he could hear a group of women talking. "I'm going to believe you for now . . . because I don't have any better theories." "What do we do now?" "I'm not ready to go back. Not yet." "You prefer this place, you really do, don't you?" He couldn't have said why their chatter bothered him, but he moved farther down the bar. The divide between their understanding of the world and his, perhaps already wide, had grown exponentially in the last week.

He knew if he went home, he'd start thinking about Whitby the Deranged, except he couldn't stop thinking about Whitby anyway, because he had to do something about Whitby tomorrow. It was just a matter of how to handle it.

Whitby had been at the Southern Reach for so long. Whitby had not hurt anyone at any point during his service for the Southern Reach. *Service* preamble to thinking about how to say "Thank you for your service, for your many years. Now take your weird art and get the fuck out."

Even as he had so many other things to do, and still no call from his mother about the director's house. Even as he nursed the wound of losing the biologist. The Voice had said Whitby was unimportant, and remembering, that Control felt that Lowry had said it with a kind of familiarity, like how you'd dismiss someone you'd worked with for a length of time.

Before leaving the Southern Reach for Hedley, he had taken a closer look at Whitby's document on terroir. Found that when you did that—trained an eye that did not skim—it began to fall apart. That the normal-sounding subsection titles and the preambles that cited other sources hid a core where the imagination became unhinged, unconcerned with the words that had tried to fence it in, to guide it along. Monsters peered out with a regularity that seemed earned given the video from the first expedition, but perhaps not earned in the right direction. He stopped reading at a certain point. It was at a section where Whitby described the border as "invisible skin," and those who tried to pass through it without using the door trapped forever in a vast stretch of *otherwhere* hundreds of miles wide. Even though the steps by which Whitby had gotten to this point had seemed, for a time, sobering and deliberate.

And then there was Lowry. He'd asked Cheney about Lowry in the parking lot, too, Cheney giving Control a rare frown. "Lowry? Come back here? Not now. Not ever, I would think." Why? A pause, like questing static on the line. "Well, he's damaged. Saw things that none of us will hopefully ever see. Can't get close to it, can't escape it. He's found his appropriate distance, you could say." Lowry, creating a web of incantations, spells, whatever, could create more of a shield between himself and Area X, because he couldn't ever forget, either. Needing to see, but too afraid to look, passing his fear on to others. Whitby's distance much closer, his spells of a more visceral nature.

By contrast, all of the ceaseless, restless notes from the director were staid, practical, stolid, and yet in the end— ordering a boilermaker after his shot, to make his next shot go down easy—they were probably meaningless, as useless as Whitby's terroir that would never explain a goddamn thing, that amounted to a kind of religion, because even with all of her additional context, the director still had not found the answer as far as he could tell.

He rasped out a request for another drink.

That would probably be his fate: to catalogue the notes of others and create his own, ceaselessly and without effect. He would develop a paunch and marry some local woman who had already been married once. They would raise a family in Hedley, a son and a daughter, and on weekends he would be fully present with his family, work a distant memory that lay across the border known as Monday. They would grow old in Hedley, while he worked at the Southern Reach, putting in his hours and counting the years, the months, the days until retirement. They would give him a gold watch and a few pats on the back and by then his knees would be shot from all the jogging so he would be sitting down, and he'd be balding a little.

And he still wouldn't know what to do about Whitby. And he would still miss the biologist. And he might still not know what was going on in Area X.

The drunk man came up and shook him out of his thoughts with a slap on his back. "You look like I know you. You look kinda familiar. What's your name, pardner?"

"Rat Poison," Control said.

The truth was, if the man who looked like the high school quarterback had responded by turning into something monstrous and torn him out into the night, part of Control wouldn't have minded because he would have been closer to the truth about Area X, and even if the truth was a fucking maw, a fanged maw that stank like a cave full of putrefying corpses, that was still closer than he was now.

OOX

When Control left the house on Tuesday morning, the director's beetle-phone lay on his welcome mat. It had returned to him. Looking down at it, hand on the half-open front door, he could not help seeing it as a sign . . . but a sign of what?

Chorry jumped past him and into the bushes while Control squatted down to get a closer look. Days and nights out in the yard hadn't helped it much. The grotesquery of the thing . . . some animal had gnawed at the casing and it was smeared with dirt and grass stains. Now it looked more like something alive than it had before. It looked like something that had gone exploring or burrowing and come back to report in.

Under the phone, thankfully, was a note from the landlord. In a quivering scrawl she had written, "The lawn man found this yesterday. Please dispose of phones in the garbage if you are done with them."

He tossed it into the bushes.

In the morning light, during that ever-longer walk through the doors and down the corridor to his office, Control's recollection of Whitby on the rack, stuffed into a shelf, the disturbing art on the wall, took on a slightly changed, more forgivable texture: a long-term disintegration whose discovery had urgency to him personally but for the Southern Reach was just one symptom of many seeking ways to take Whitby out of the "sinister" file and place him under "needs our help."

Still, in his office, he wrestled with what to do about Whitby—did the man fall under his jurisdiction or Grace's? Would she be resistant, slough it off, say something like "Oh, that Whitby"? Maybe together, he and Grace would go up into Whitby's secret room and have a good laugh about the grotesqueries to be found there, and then jointly paint it all white again. Then they'd go have lunch with Cheney and Hsyu and play board games and share their mutual love of water polo. Hsyu would say, as if he'd already disagreed with her, "We shouldn't take the meaning of words for granted!" and he would shout back, "You mean a word like *border*?" and she would reply, "Yes, that's exactly what I mean! You get it! You understand!" Followed by an impromptu square dance, dissolving into a chaos of thousands of glowing green ferns and black glittering mayflies gusting across their path.

Or not.

With a snarl of frustration, Control put aside the question of Whitby and buried himself again in the director's notes, kept Grace's intel about the director's focus in mind while trying to divine from those dried entrails more than they might actually contain. From Whitby, he wanted for the moment only distance and time so that there would be no hand reaching out to him.

He returned to the lighthouse, based on what Grace had told him. What was the purpose of a lighthouse? To warn of danger, to guide coastal vessels, and to provide landfall for ships. What did it mean to the Southern Reach, to the director?

Among the layers in the locked drawer, the most prominent concerned the lighthouse, and that included pages he had confirmed with Grace came from an investigation that was inextricably tied to the history of the island to the north. That island had had numerous names, as if none would stick, until now it was simply known as Island X at the Southern Reach, although some called it "Island Y," as in "Why are we bothering to research this?"

What did fascinate—even resonate—was the fact that the beacon in the lighthouse on the coast had originally been placed in a lighthouse built on Island X. But shipping lanes had shifted and no one needed a lighthouse that helped ships navigate the shallows. The old lighthouse fell into ruin, but its eye had been removed long before.

As Grace had noted, the beacon interested the director the most: a first-order lens that constituted not just a remarkable engineering feat but also a work of art. More than two thousand separate lenses and prisms had been mounted inside a brass framework. The light from at first a lamp and then a lightbulb was reflected and refracted by the lenses and prisms to be cast seaward.

The entire apparatus could be disassembled and shipped in sections. The "light characteristics" could be manipulated in almost every conceivable way. Bent, straightened, sent bouncing off surfaces in a recursive loop so that it never reached the outside. Sent sideways. Sent down onto the spiraling steps leading up to the top. Beamed into outer space. Slanted past the open trapdoor, where lay so many journal accounts from so many expeditions.

An alarming note that Control dismissed because he had no room left in his brain for harmful speculation, x-ed out and crumpled on the back of a ticket for a local Bleakersville production of some atrocity called *Hamlet Unbound*: "More journals exist than accounted for by expedition members." He hadn't seen anywhere a report on the number of journals, no count on that.

The Séance & Science Brigade, which had operated along that coast since the fifties, had been obsessed with the twin lighthouses. And as if the S&SB had shared something personally with her, the director had zeroed in on the beacon's history, even though the Southern Reach as an institution had already ruled it out as "evidence pertaining to the creation of Area X." The number of ripped-out pages and circled passages in a book entitled *Famous Lighthouses* noted that the beacon had been shipped over just prior to the states dissolving into civil war, from a manufacturer whose name had been lost along the way. The "mysterious history" included the beacon being buried in the sand to keep it away from one side or another, then sent up north, then appearing down south, and eventually popping up at Island X on the forgotten coast. Control didn't find the history mysterious so much as hectic, overbusy, thinking of the amount of effort that had gone into carting and dragging this beacon, even in its constituent pieces, all over the country. The number of miles the beacon had traveled before finding a permanent home—that was really the only mystery, along with why anyone had thought to describe the fog signal as sounding like "two large bulls hung up by their tails."

Yet this had captivated the director, or seemed to have, roughly around the time of the planning for the twelfth expedition, if he could trust the dates on the article excerpts. Which did not interest Control as much as the fact that the director kept annotating, amending, adding data and fragments of accounts from sources she did not accredit—these sources maddeningly not in Grace's DMP archive and not alluded to in any of the notes he had looked through. This frustrated him. The banality of it, too, as if ceaselessly reviewing what she already knew for something she felt she had missed. Was the message coming down to Control from the director that he should resurrect old lines of inquiry, or that the Southern Reach had run out of ideas, had begun to endlessly recycle, feeding on itself?

How Control hated his own imagination, wished it would just shrivel up and turn brown and fall out of him. He was more willing to believe that something was staring out at him from the notes, something hidden looking at him, than to accept that the director had been pursuing dead ends. And yet he couldn't see it; he could still only see her searching, and wonder why she was searching so hard.

On impulse, he took down all of the framed images on the far wall and searched them for anything hidden—took off the back mats, disassembled them entirely. But he found nothing. Just the reeds, the lighthouse, the lighthouse keeper, his assistant, and the girl staring out at him from more than thirty years ago.

In the afternoon, he turned to Grace's DMP file, cross-checking it against the piles of notes. Which, because it was a proprietary program, meant that he was clicking Ctrl to go from page to page. Ctrl was beginning to seem the only control he actually had. Ctrl only had one role, and it performed that role stoically and without complaint. He hit Ctrl with ever more malice and force, even though every hour that he looked at the notes rather than dealt with Whitby seemed a kind of blessing. Every hour that Whitby didn't show his face, even though his car remained in the parking lot. Did Whitby want help? Did he know he needed help? Someone needed to tell Whitby what he had become. Could Grace tell him? Could Cheney? No. They had not told him yet.

Ctrl Ctrl Ctrl. Always too many pages. Ctrl this. Ctrl that. Ctrl crescendos and arias. Ctrl always clicking past information, because the information he found on the screen seemed to lead nowhere anyway, while the vast expanse of clutter that spread out in waves from his desk to the far wall contained too much.

His office began to close in on him. Listless pushing around of files and pretend efforts to straighten bookshelves had given way to further Internet searches on the places the biologist had worked before joining the twelfth expedition. This activity had proven more calming, each vista of wilderness more beautiful than the last. But eventually the parallels to the pristine landscape of Area X had begun to encroach and the bird's-eye view of some of the photographs reminded him of that final video clip.

He took a break around five, then went back to his office for a while, after short, friendly conversations with Hsyu and Cheney in the corridor. Although Hsyu seemed flushed, talking a bit too fast for some reason, her aspect ratio skewed. Cheney's big catcher's mitt of a hand had rested on Control's shoulder for an uncomfortable second or two, as the man said, "A second week! Which is a good sign, surely? We hope you find it all to your liking. We're open to change. We're open to changes, if you know what I mean, once you've heard what we have to say. And how we say it." The words almost made sense, but somehow Cheney was off today, too. Control had had days like that.

That left only the problem of Whitby; he hadn't seen him the whole afternoon, and Whitby hadn't responded to e-mails, either. It felt important to get it over with, not to let it slide into Wednesday. The *how* had become clear to him, along with what was fair and what wasn't fair. He would do it in front of Cheney in the science division, and leave Grace out of it. This had become his responsibility, his mess, and Cheney would just have to go along with his decision. Whitby would be forced to accept a leave of absence and psychiatric counseling, and with any luck the strange little man would never return.

It was late, already after six. He had lost track of time, or it had lost track of him. The office was still a mess corresponding to the contours of the director's brain, Grace's DMP files not changing those contours in any useful way.

He took Whitby's terroir manuscript with him, feeling that perhaps selective readings from it would convince Whitby of the problem. He again crossed the wide expanse of the cafeteria. The huge cafeteria windows gathered up the gray of the sky and pushed it down onto the tables, the chairs; it would rain again before long. The tables were empty. The little dark bird or bat had stopped flying and sat perched high up on a steel beam near the windows. "There's something on the floor." "Have you ever seen anything like that?" Fragments of conversation as he passed by the door to the kitchen, and then a kind of sharp but faint weeping sound. For a moment, it puzzled Control. Then he realized it must come from some machine being operated by the cafeteria staff.

Something else had been gnawing at Control for much longer, as if he'd forgotten his wallet or other essential item when he'd left the house. But it now resolved, the weeping sound pushing it into his conscious mind. An absence. The rotting honey smell was gone. In fact, he realized he hadn't smelled rotting honey the entire day, no matter where he had been. Had Grace at least passed on that recommendation?

He turned the corner into the corridor leading to the science division, kept walking under the fluorescent lights, immersed in a rehearsal of what he would say to Whitby, anticipating what Whitby might say back, or not say, feeling the weight of the man's insane manuscript.

Control reached out for the large double doors. Reached for the handle, missed it, tried again.

But there were no doors where there had always been doors before. Only wall.

And the wall was soft and breathing under the touch of his hand.

He was screaming, he thought, but from somewhere deep beneath the sea.

AFTERLIFE

Control, at the heart of a different tragedy, could see nothing but Rachel McCarthy with a bullet in her head, falling endlessly into the quarry. The sense of nothing being real during that time. That the room they had put him in, and the investigator assigned to him, were both constructs, and if he just kept holding on to that thought eventually the investigator would dissolve into nothing and the walls of his cell would fall away, and he would walk out into a world that was real. Then and only then would he wake up to continue with his life, which would follow the path it had followed to that point.

Even though the chair for the long hours of questioning cut into the back of his thigh and left a mark. Even though he smelled the bitter cigarette smoke on the investigator's jacket, and heard the hiccupping whir of the tape in the recorder the man had brought in as a backup for the room's video recording.

Even though the texture of the wall felt like a manta ray from the aquarium: firm and smooth, with a serrated roughness but with more give, and behind it the sense of something vast, breathing in and out. A rupture into the world of the rotted honey smell, fading fast but hard to forget. Like the swirling flourish of a line of balsamic on a chef's plate. The line of dark blood leading to a corpse on a cop show.

His parents had read "Tiger, Tiger, burning bright" to him as a child. They had collaborated on a social studies project with him, his mother on research and his father on cut-and-paste. They had taught him how to ride a bike. The pathetic little Christmas tree next to the shed linked forever now to the first holiday season he could remember. Standing on the pier in Hedley, looking across the river led to the lake by the cottage where he would fish with his grandpa. Naming the sculptures in his father's backyard became a chess set on the mantel. The wall was still breathing, though, no matter what he did. The impact of a long-ago linebacker's helmet to the chest during a scrimmage, surfacing only now so that he had trouble breathing, all the air knocked out of his lungs.

Control didn't remember leaving the corridor but had recovered himself in mid-sprint toward the cafeteria. Whitby's terroir manuscript clenched in a viselike grip. He meant to retrieve some other things from his office. He meant to go into his office and retrieve some other things. His office. His other things.

He was pulling every fire alarm he passed. He was shouting over the klaxon at people who weren't there to leave. Disbelief. Shock. Trapped inside his head the way some were trapped in the science division.

But in the cafeteria he was running so fast he slipped and fell. When he got up, he saw Grace, holding open the door leading to the courtyard. Someone to tell. Someone to tell. There was only wall. There was only wall.

He shouted her name, but Grace did not turn, and as he came up on her, he saw that she stared at someone slowly walking up from the edge of the courtyard through a thick rain, against the burnt umber of the singed edges of the swamp beyond. A tall, dark outline lit by the late-afternoon sun, shining through the downpour. He would recognize her anywhere by now. Still in her expedition clothes. So close to a gnarled tree behind her that at first she had merged with it in the gray of the rain. And she was still making her way to Grace. And Grace, in three-quarter profile there in front of her, smiling, body taut with anticipation. This false return, this corrupted reunion. This end of everything.

For the director trailed plumes of emerald dust and behind her the nature of the world was changing, filling with a brightness, the rain losing its depth, its darkness. The thickness of the layers of the rain getting lost, taken away, no longer there.

The border was coming to the Southern Reach.

In the parking lot, shoving the key into the ignition, office forgotten, not wanting to look back. Not wanting to see if an invisible wave was about to overtake him. Still cars in the parking lot, still people inside, but he didn't care. He was leaving. He was done. A scrabbling, broken-nail panic at the thought of being trapped there. Forever. Shouting at the car to start after it had already started.

He raced for the gates—open, no security, no sound from

behind him at all. Just a vast silence, snuffing out thought. His hands were curled, clawlike, fingernails dragging into his palms as he clutched the wheel.

Speeding, not caring about anything but making it to Hedley, even though he knew that might not be any kind of choice at all. Pulling out his phone, dropping it, but not stopping, groping for it as he reached the highway, screeched onto the on-ramp, relieved to see normal traffic. He stifled a dozen impulses—to stop the car and use it to block off the exit, to roll down his window in the rain and shout out a warning to the other motorists. Stifled any impulse that impeded the deep and impervious instinct to get away.

Two fighter jets roared overhead, but he couldn't see them.

He kept changing the radio channels to current news reports. Not sure what would be reported, but wanting something to be reported even though it was still happening, hadn't finished yet. Nothing. No one. Kept trying to get the feel of the wall off his hand, wiping it against the seats, the steering wheel, his pants. Would have plunged it into dog shit to get the feeling off.

When he'd turned away from Grace, he'd seen that Whitby occupied his usual seat in the back of the cafeteria, under the photograph of the old days. But Whitby came in only intermittently now, the transmission garbled. Some of the words in tone and texture still recalled human speech. Others recalled the video from the first expedition. Whitby had failed some fundamental test, had crossed some Rubicon and now sat there, jaw oddly elongated as he tried to get words out, alone, beyond Control's help. He realized then, or at some point later, that maybe Whitby wasn't just crazy. That Whitby had become a breach, a leak, a door into Area X, expressed as an elongated equation over time . . . and if the director had now come back to the Southern Reach, it wasn't because of or for Grace, it was because Whitby had been calling out to her like a human beacon. This version of her that had returned.

Trapped by his thoughts. That the Southern Reach hadn't been a redoubt but instead some kind of slow incubator. That finding Whitby's shrine might have triggered something. That placing trust in a word like *border* had been a mistake, a trap. A slow unraveling of terms unrecognized until too late.

Whitby's gaze had followed him in his flight toward the front entrance, and Control had run almost sideways to make sure Whitby never left his view until the corner took him. He could see the leviathans from his dream clearly now, staring at him, seeing him with an awful clarity. He had not escaped their attention.

Calling his mother. Hypnotize me. Hypnotize this out of me. Unable to reach her. Leaving messages shouted out, half-coherent.

The corridor leading into Hedley in the banality of rush-hour traffic. The mundane quality of the rain coming down, feeling the pressure behind him. Tried to control his breathing. Every bit of advice his mother had ever given him had gotten knocked out of his head.

Had it stopped? Had the director stopped? Or was it still onrushing?

Was an invisible blot now seeping out across the world?

Already reviewing in his mind, as he began to recover,

began to function, what he could have done differently. What, if anything, might have made a difference, or if it was always going to happen like this. In this universe. On this day.

"I'm sorry," he said inside the car—to no one, to Grace, to Cheney, even to Whitby. "I'm sorry." But for what? What was his role in this?

As he reached the bottom of the hill, leading up to his house, the radio reports began to reflect his reality in slivers and glints of light. Something had occurred at the military base, perhaps related to the "continuing environmental clean-up efforts." There had been an odd glow and odd sounds and gunfire. But no one knew anything. Not for sure.

Except that Control now knew the thing that had been eluding him, hiding in the deeper waters for him to recognize it. Revealed now, too late to do any good. For, in the stooped shoulders and the tilt of the director's head—there, approaching, in the flesh—Control had finally realized that the girl in the photograph with the lighthouse keeper was the director as a child. There was a kind of slouch or lurch to the shoulders that, despite the different perspectives and the difference in years, was unmistakable if you were looking for it. Now that he could see it, he couldn't unsee it. There, hiding in plain sight in the photograph from the director's wall, was a photograph of the director as a child, taken by the S&S Brigade, standing side by side with Saul Evans, whose words decorated the wall of the topographical anomaly in living tissue. She had looked at that photo every day in her office. She had chosen to place that photograph there. She had chosen to live in Bleakersville, in a house full of heirlooms probably owned by someone on her mother's side of the family. Who at the Southern Reach had known?

Or had this been another conspiracy of one, and the director had hidden that connection all on her own?

Assuming he was right, she had been at the lighthouse right before the Event. She had gotten out before the border came down. She knew the forgotten coast like she knew herself. There were things that she'd never had to put down on paper, just because of who she was, where she came from.

For all Control knew, the director had been one of the last people to see Saul Evans alive.

He pulled up in front of the house, sat there a moment, feeling beat-up, drained, unable to process what was happening. Sweat dripped off him, his shirt drenched, his blazer lost, back at the Southern Reach. He got out of the car, searched the hidden horizon beyond the river. Was that a faint flare-up of light? Was that the muffled echo of explosions, or his imagination?

When he turned to the porch, a woman was standing on the steps next to the cat. He felt relief more than surprise.

"Hello, Mother."

She looked almost the same as always, but the high fashion had a slight bulk to it, which meant under the chic dark red jacket she probably had on some sort of light body armor. She'd also be carrying. Her hair was pulled back in a ponytail, which made the lines of her face more severe. Her features bore the stress of an ongoing puzzlement and pain of some kind.

"Hello, Son," she said, as he brushed by her.

Control let her talk at him as he opened the front door, then went into the bedroom and began to pack. Most of his clothes were still clean and folded in the drawers. It was easy to fit some of them quickly and neatly into his suitcase. To pack his toiletries from the adjoining bathroom, to get out the briefcase full of money, passports, guns, and credit cards. Wondering what to bring with him from the living room, in terms of personal effects. Definitely a piece from the chess-board. He wasn't hearing much of what his mother was saying, stayed focused on the task in front of him. In doing it perfectly.

Grace had stood there waiting to receive the director and he had pleaded with her to leave, pleaded with her to turn from the door and to run like hell for some kind of safety. But she wouldn't do it, wouldn't let him pull her away, had summoned a reserve of strength that was too much against his panic. But let him see the gun concealed in a shoulder holster, as if that might be a comfort. "I have my orders and they are no concern of yours." As he fell out of her orbit, fell free of everything at the Southern Reach.

His mother forced him to stop packing, closed the suit-case, which he had piled too high anyway, and took his hand, put something in it.

"Take this," she said.

A pill. A little white pill.

"What is it?"

"Just take it."

"Why not just hypnotize me?"

She ignored him, guided him to a chair in the corner. He sat there, heavy and cold in his own sweat. "We will talk after you take the pill. After you take a shower." Said in a sharp tone, the one she used with him to cut off discussion or debate.

"I don't have time for a shower," he said. Staring at the wallpaper, which began to blur. Now he would inhabit the very center of corridors. He would put no hand to any surface. He would behave like a ghost that knew if it made contact with anyone or anything its touch would slide through and that creature would then know that it existed in a state of purgatory.

Severance slapped him hard across the face, and he could hear right again.

"You've had a shock. I can see that you've had a shock, Son. I've had a few myself the last few hours. But I need you to start thinking again. I need you *present.*"

He looked up at her, so like and unlike his mother.

"Okay," he said. "Okay." He took the pill, lurched to his feet while he had the will, headed for the bathroom. There had been nothing recognizable in the director's eyes. Nothing at all.

In the shower, he started to cry because he still couldn't get the feel of the wall off his hand, no matter how hard he tried. Couldn't shake the thinning of the rain, the look on Whitby's face, Grace's rigid stance, or the fact it had all happened only an hour ago and he was still trying to piece it together.

But when he stumbled out, dried himself off, and put on a T-shirt and jeans, he felt calmer, almost normal. There was still a slight wobble, but the pill must have kicked in.

He used hand sanitizer, but the texture remained on his hand like an unshakable phantom.

His mother was making coffee in the kitchen, but he went past her without a word, through the sudden cold of the air-conditioning vent, and opened the front door, letting in a blast of humidity and heat.

It had stopped raining. He could see down to the river, to a horizon that held, somewhere, the Southern Reach. Everything was quiet and still, but there were vague coronas of green light, of purple light, that shouldn't be there. A vision of whatever was in Area X spilling out over the land, spreading out across the river to Hedley.

"You won't see much from here," his mother said from behind him. "They're still attempting containment."

"How far has it spread?" he asked, shaking a bit as he closed the door and entered the kitchen. He took a sip of the coffee she had set in front of him. It was bitter but it took his mind off his hand.

"I won't lie, John. It's bad. The Southern Reach is lost. The new border isn't far beyond the gates. They're all trapped in there." The suggestion of the rain *thinning* behind the director. Grace, Whitby, who knew who else, caught up in a true nightmare now. "It might stop there, for a very long time."

"You're full of shit," he said. "You don't know what it will do."

"Or it might speed up. You're right—we can't know."

"That's right—we can't. I was there, right in the middle of it. I saw it coming." Because *you put me there*. A howl inside of betrayal, and then a thought that struck him when he saw the tired, worried look on her face. "But there's more, isn't there? Something more you haven't told me." There always was.

Even now she hesitated, didn't want to divulge a secret classified in a country that might not exist in a week. Then said in a flat voice, "The contamination at the sites from which we extracted the surveyor and the anthropologist has broken through quarantine and continued to grow, despite our best efforts."

"Jesus Christ," he said.

Even through the dulling effects of the pill, he wanted to be rid of his itching brain, his ignited skin, the flesh beneath, to in some way become so ethereal and unbound to the earth that he could unsee, disavow, disavow.

"What kind of contamination?" Although he thought he knew.

"The kind that cleanses everything. The kind you can't see until it's too late."

"There's nothing you can do?"

A rasping laugh escaped her, like she was trying to cough something up. "What are we going to do, John? Are we going to combat it by starting a mining operation there? Pollute those places to hell and back? Put traces of heavy metals in the water supply?"

He just stared at her, unbelieving. "Why the *fuck* did you station me at the Southern Reach if you knew this could happen?"

"I wanted you close to it. I wanted you to know, because that protects you."

"That *protects* me? Against the end of the world?"

"Maybe. Maybe it does. *And* we needed fresh eyes," she said, leaning beside him against the kitchen counter. He always forgot how slight she was, how thin. "I needed *your* fresh eyes. I couldn't know that things would change this fast."

"But you had a clue it might."

She kept letting drop bits of information. Was he meant to pick them up, like the gun under the seat, just because she was unraveling?

"Yes, I had a clue, John. It's why we sent you. Why a few of us thought we needed to do something."

"Like Lowry."

"Yes, like Lowry." Lowry, hiding back at Central, unable to face what had happened, as if the videos were now spilling into real life.

"You let him hypnotize me. You let them *condition* me." Unable to suppress his resentment at that, even now. He might never know the extent of it.

"I'm sorry, but that was the trade-off, John," she said, resolute, sticking to her story. "That was the trade-off. I got the person I want for the job, Lowry got some kind of . . . control. And you got protection, in a way."

Derisive, thinking he knew the answer: "How many others are there at Central, Mother? In this faction?"

"Mostly just us, John—Lowry and me—but Lowry has allies, many," she said in a small voice.

Just them. A cabal of two against a cabal of one, the director. And none of them seeming to have it right. And now all of it in ruins.

"What else?" Pushing to punish her, because he didn't want to think about the idea of localized Area Xs.

A bitter laugh. "We back-checked the extraction locations of the members of the last eleventh expedition to see if they exhibit a similar effect. We found nothing. So now we think they probably had a different purpose. And that purpose was to contaminate the Southern Reach itself. We had clues before. We just didn't interpret them the right way, couldn't agree on what it all meant. We just needed a little more time, a little more data." Bodies that had decomposed "a little faster" as Grace had put it, when the director had ordered them exhumed.

There was in his mother's fragmentation the admission that Central's was a soul-crushing failure. That they had been unable to conceive of a scenario in which Area X was smarter, more insidious, more resourceful.

None of this could obliterate the look on Grace's face, in the rain, as the director approached—the elation, the vindication, the abstract idea, viscerally expressed across her features, that sacrifice, that loyalty, that diligence would now be rewarded. As if the physical manifestation of a friend and colleague long thought dead could erase the recent past. The director, followed by that unnatural silence. Were her eyes closed, or did she not have eyes anymore? The emerald dust splashed off her into the air, onto the ground, with each step. This person who should not have been there, this shell of a soul of whom he had uncovered only fragments.

His mother started over, and he let her because he had no choice, needed time to acclimate, to adjust. "Imagine a situation, John, in which you are trying to contain something dangerous. But you suspect that containment is a losing game. That what you want to contain is escaping slowly, inexorably. That what seems impermeable is, in fact, over time becoming very permeable. That the divide is more perforated than unperforated. And that whatever this thing is seems to want to destroy you but has no leader to negotiate with, no stated goals of any kind." It was almost a speech he could imagine the director giving.

"You mean the Southern Reach, the place you sent me into. With the wrong tools."

"I mean that the group I've been part of has believed for a while now that the Southern Reach might be compromised, but the majority have believed, until today, that this wasn't just wrong but laughably ridiculous."

"How did you get involved?"

"Because of you, John. Long ago. Because of needing an assignment to a place near where you and your father lived." Volunteered: "It was a side project. Something to watch, to keep an eye on. That became the main course."

"But why did it have to be me?"

"I told you." Pleading for him to understand: "I know you, John. I know who you are. I'd know if you . . . changed."

"Like the biologist changed." Burning now, that she'd put him in harm's way without telling him, without giving him the choice. Except, he'd had a choice: He could have stayed where he was, continued to believe he lived beyond the border when that was a lie.

"Something like that."

"Or just changed as in became more cynical, jaded, paranoid, or burned-out."

"Stop it."

"Why should I?"

"I did the best I could."

"Yeah."

"Growing up, I mean, John. I did the best I could, considering. But you're still angry. Even now, you're still angry. It's too much. It's too much." Talking around the edge of a catastrophe. But wasn't that what people did, if you were still alive?

He put his coffee down. There was a knot in his shoulders that might never come out. "I'm not thinking about that. That doesn't matter. It doesn't matter now."

"It matters most of all now," she said, "because I may never see you again." Her voice, for the only time he could remember, breaking up.

The weight of that hit him hard, and he knew it was true, and he felt for a moment as if he were falling. The enormity, the impossibility of it, was too much. How it had come to this point, he barely knew, even though he had been there every step of the way.

He brought her close, held her, as she whispered in his ear: *"I took my eye off things. I thought the director agreed with us. I thought I could handle Lowry. I thought we would work through it. I thought we had more time."* That the problem was smaller. That somehow it was containable. That somehow she wouldn't be hurting him.

His mother. His handler. But after a moment he had to let her go. No way to fully cross that divide, to heal everything that needed to be healed. Not now.

She told him one more thing, then, delivered to him like a penance.

"John, you should know that the biologist escaped our custody over the weekend. She's been AWOL for the past three days."

An elation, a surge of an unwarranted, selfish euphoria that came in part from having banished her from his thoughts as the nightmare at the Southern Reach played out—and now his reward, that she had, in a way, been returned to him.

All of the rest of the answers to his questions rose up later, long after his mother had left in his car, after he had packed, reluctantly abandoned the cat, took her car, as she had suggested. But he stopped on a quiet street a few blocks away and hot-wired another car because he didn't trust Central. Soon he was outside of Hedley, in the middle of nowhere. He felt the absence of his father terribly as he passed where they had lived. Because his father might have been a comfort now. Because now it didn't matter what secrets he told or didn't tell.

At the airport about ninety miles away, in a city big enough to have international connections, he left his vehicle in the parking lot along with his guns and booked two tickets. One was to Honduras, with a layover on the west coast. The other had two layovers and wound up about two hundred miles from the coast. The second he bought under an alias. He checked in for Honduras, then sat in the airport bar, nursing a whiskey, waiting for the puddle jumper. Apocalyptic visions of what Area X would absorb if it moved forward came to him. Buildings, roads, lakes, valleys, airports. Everything. He scanned the closed-caption televisions for any news, trying to outthink the people from Central who might be on her trail, might already have picked up her trail. If he was the biologist, he would have train-hopped to start, which meant he might easily catch up with her. From where she'd escaped, she had just as far to travel as he did.

A blond woman at the bar asked him what he did and he said, recklessly, without thought, "A marine biologist." "Oh, with the government." "No, freelance," which sounded absurd after he'd said it. Then spent long minutes putting distance between himself and the subject. Because he wanted to stay there, at the bar, around people but not involved with them.

"How'd she escape?" he'd asked his mother.

"Let's just say she's stronger than she looks, and very resourceful." Had his mother given her the resources? The time? The opportunity? He hadn't wanted to ask. "Central suspects she will return to the empty lot because of the lack of contamination at that site."

But he knew that wasn't where she would go.

"Is that what you think?" his mother asked.

"Yes," he said.

No, she would go north, she would go to the wilderness above the town of Rock Bay, even if she didn't believe she was the biologist. She would go somewhere personal to her. Because she felt the urge, not because Area X wanted her to. If she had been right, if she'd been their true soldier, she would have been as mind-wiped as the others.

At least, that's what he chose to believe. To have a reason for his packing, and a place to think of as a sanctuary. Or a hiding place.

They announced boarding for his flight. He was headed west, yes, but he'd step out at the first connecting flight, rent a car from there, take that rental to another, then perhaps steal a car, always the arc going south, south, suggesting a slow descent. But then he'd go dark completely and head north.

He'd actually pulled at Grace to get her away, had taken her hand and pulled her off-balance, would have dragged her if he'd been able. Shouted at her. Given her all the reasons, the primal, visceral reasons. But Grace couldn't see any of it, wrenched away from him with a stare that made him give up. Because it was self-aware. Because she was going to see it through to the end, and he couldn't do that. Because he really wasn't the director. So he let Grace fade away into the rain as the director came up toward the door and he retreated in mindless panic to the cafeteria and then out to his car. And he didn't feel guilty about any of it.

A beep from his phone told him that, coming in over some unimaginable distance, he had received the last, useless videos from the Southern Reach, from the chicken and the goat.

The footage told him nothing, gave him no closure, no sense of what might have happened to Grace. The quality was grainy, indistinct. Each clip was about six seconds in duration and each cut off at the same time. In the first, his chair sat empty until the very end, when something blurred appeared to sit down. It might have been the director but the outline was ill-defined. The other video showed a slumped Whitby in the chair opposite, doing something peculiar with his hands that made his fingers look like soft coral swaying in a sea current. A wordless droning in the background. Was Whitby now in the world of the first expedition? And if so, did he know it?

Control watched both video clips twice, thrice, and then deleted them. This act did not delete the subjects, but it made him more distant from them, and that would have to be good enough.

The usual influx of heat and then frigid cold on the airplane. The grappling with frayed seat belts. As they rose,

Control kept waiting for something to swat the plane out of the sky, wondered if Central would be there to greet him when he touched down, or something odder still. He wondered why the stewardesses were looking at him funny by mid-flight, and realized he'd been responding to their rote kindness with the intensity of someone who has never experienced courtesy, or never expects to experience it again.

The couple in the seats next to him were of the annoying yet ordinary type who said almost everything for their audience, or to affirm their own couple-hood. Yet even them he wanted to warn, in a sudden, unexpected outpouring of raw and almost uncontainable emotion. To somehow articulate what was happening, what was going to happen, without sounding crazy, without scaring them or him. But, ultimately, he popped another calm pill and leaned back in his seat and tried to banish the world.

"How do I know that going after the biologist isn't an idea you've put in my head?"

"The biologist was the director's weapon, I believe. You said in your reports she doesn't act like the others. Whatever she knows, she represents a kind of chance. Some kind of chance." Control hadn't shared with his mother the full experience of his last moments at the Southern Reach. Not everything he had seen, or that whatever the director was now or wherever she'd grown up, she was less herself than at any point in the past. That whatever plan she'd had was probably irrelevant.

"And you are my weapon, John. You're the one I chose to *know everything.*"

The comfort of the scratched metal armrests with the fat, torn padding on top. The compartmentalized scoops of sky captured by the oval windows. The captain's unnecessary progress reports, interspersed with the stupid but comforting jokes over the intercom. He wondered where the Voice was, if Lowry was having flashbacks or freaking out in a more general way. Lowry, his buddy. Lowry, the pathetic megalodon. This is your last chance, Control. But it wasn't. It was, instead, an immolation. If he was remembered at all, it would be as the harbinger of disaster.

He ordered a whiskey with ice, to see it gleam, to keep the ice in his mouth and experience the smooth cold with the hint of bite. It helped him fall into a lull, a trough of self-induced tiredness, trying to slow the wheels of his mind. Trying to wreck those wheels.

"What will Central do now?" he'd asked his mother.

"They'll come after you because of your association with me." Would have come after him anyway, for not reporting in and for going after the biologist.

"What else will they do?"

"Try to send in a thirteenth expedition, if a door still exists."

"And what about you?"

"I'll keep making the case for the course I think is right," she said, which she had to know was a huge risk. Did that mean she'd go back, or keep some distance from Central until the situation stabilized? Because Control knew that she would keep fighting until the world disappeared around her. Or Central got rid of her. Or Lowry used her as a scapegoat. Did she think Central wouldn't try to blame the messenger? He could have asked why she didn't just liquidate her savings and head for the most remote place possible . . .

and wait. But if he had, she would have asked him the same thing.

At the end of the flight, a woman in the aisle seat opposite told him and his two seatmates to open their window for landing. "You gotta open the window for landing. You gotta open it. For landing."

Or what? Or what? He just ignored her, did not pass the message on, closed his eyes.

When he opened them, the plane had landed. No one waited for him as he disembarked. No one called out his name. He rented a car without incident.

It was as if a different person put the key in the ignition and drove away from everything that was familiar. There was no going back now. There was no going forward, either. He was going in sideways, sort of, and as frightening as that was, there was the thrill of excitement, too. You couldn't feel dead this way, or as if you were just waiting for the next thing to happen to you.

Rock Bay. The end of the world. If she wasn't there, it was a better place than most to wait for whatever happened next.

Dusk of the next day. In a crappy motel on the coast with the word *Beach* in its name, Control obsessively stripped and cleaned his Glock, bought off a dealer using a fake name not thirty minutes after he'd cleared the airport, in the back lot of a car dealership. Then reassembled it. Having to focus on a repetitive and detailed task kept his mind off the void looming outside.

The television was on, but nothing made sense. The

television, except for the vaguest of footnotes about a possible problem at the "Southern Reach environmental recovery site," did not tell the truth about what was going on. But it hadn't made sense for a very long time, even if no one knew that, and he knew his contempt would mirror that of the biologist, if she had been sitting where he was sitting. And the light from the curtains was just a stray truck barreling by in the dark. And the smell was of rot, but he thought perhaps he'd brought that with him. Even though he was far away from it now, the invisible border was close—the checkpoints, the swirling light of the door. The way that light seemed almost beveled, almost formed an image in that space between the curtains, and then fell away again into nothing.

On the bed: Whitby's terroir manuscript, which he hadn't looked at since leaving Hedley. All he'd done was put it in a sturdy waterproof plastic case. He kept realizing, with a kind of resigned surprise, a kind of slow registering or reimagining meant to cushion the blow, that the invasion had been under way for quite some time, had been manifesting for much longer than anyone could have guessed, even his mother. And that perhaps Whitby had figured something out, even if no one had believed him, even if figuring it out had exposed him to something that had then figured *him* out.

When he was finished with the Glock, he sat in a chair facing the door, clenching the grip tight even though it made his fingers throb. It was another way to keep from being overwhelmed by it. Pain as distraction. All of his familiar guides had gone silent. His mother, his grandparents, his father— none of them had anything to say to him. Even the carving in his pocket seemed inert, useless now.

And the whole time, sitting in the chair then lying in the bed with its worn blanket and yellowing sheets with cigarette burns in them, Control could not get the image of the biologist out of his head. The look on her face in the empty lot—that blankness—and then, later, in the sessions, the warring of contempt, wildness, casual vulnerability, and vehemence, strength. That had laid him low. That had expanded until it hooked into the whole of him, no part of him not committed. Even though she might never know, could give two shits about him. Even though he would be content should he never meet her again, just so long as he could believe she was still out there, alive and on her own. The yearnings in him now went in all directions and no direction at all. It was an odd kind of affection that needed no subject, that emanated from him like invisible rays meant for everyone and everything. He supposed they were normal feelings once you'd pushed on past a certain point.

North is where the biologist had fled, and he knew where she would end up: It was right there in her field notes. A precipice she knew better than almost anyone, where the land fell away into the sea, and the sea rushed up onto the rocks. He just had to be prepared. Central might catch up to him before he got there. But lurking behind them might be something even darker and more vast, and that was the killing joke. That the thing catching up with all of them would be even less merciful—and would question them until, like a towel wrung dry and then left out in the sun, they were nothing but brittle husks and hollows.

Unless he made it north in time. If she was there. If she knew anything.

He left the motel early, just as the sun appeared, grabbed breakfast at a café, and continued north. Here it was all cliffs and sharp curves and the sense that you might dive off into the sky around each upward bend. That the little thought you always overrode—to stop turning the wheel to match the road—might not be stifled this time and you'd gun the engine and push on into the air, and snuff out every secret thing you knew and didn't want to know. The temperature rarely rose above seventy-five, and the landscape soon became lush—the greens more intense than in the south, the rain when it came a kind of mist so unlike the hellish downpours he'd become used to.

At a general store in a tiny town called Selk that had a gas station whose antiquated pumps didn't take credit cards, he bought a large knapsack, filled it with about thirty pounds of supplies. He bought a hunting knife, plenty of batteries, an ax, lighters, and a lot more. He didn't know what he'd need or how much she'd need, how long he might be out there in the wilderness, searching for her. Would her reaction be what he wanted it to be—and what reaction was that? Assuming she was even there. He imagined himself years from now, bearded, living off the land, making carvings like his father, alone, slowly fading into the backdrop from the weight of solitude.

The cashier asked him his name, as part of a sales pitch for a local charity, and he said "John," and from that point on, he used his real name again. Not Control, not any of the aliases that had gotten him this far. It was a common name. It didn't stand out. It didn't mean anything.

He continued the tactics he'd been using, though. Domestic terrorism had made him familiar with a lot of rural areas. For his second assignment out of training, he had spent time in the Midwest on the road between county health departments, under the guise of helping update immunization software. But he'd really been tracking down data on members of a militia. He knew back roads from that other life and took to them as if he'd never left, used all the tricks with no effort although it had been a long time since he'd used them. There was even a kind of stressful freedom to it, an exhilaration and simplicity he hadn't known for a long time. Then, like now, he'd doubted every pickup truck, especially if it had a mud-obscured license plate, every slow driver, every hitchhiker. Then, as now, he'd picked local roads with dirt side roads that allowed him to double back. He used detailed printed maps, no GPS. He had almost wavered on his cell phone, but had thrown it into the ocean, hadn't bought a temporary to replace it. He knew he could have bought something that couldn't be traced, but anyone he called would no doubt be bugged by now. The urge to call any of his relatives, to try his mother one last time, had faded with the miles. If he'd had something to say, he should have picked up the phone a long time ago.

Sometimes he thought of the director as he drove. Along the banks of a glistening, shallow lake in a valley surrounded by mountains, ripping off pieces of sausage bought at a farmers' market. The color of the sky so light a blue yet so untroubled by clouds that it didn't seem real. The girl in the old black-and-white photo. The way she had fixated on the lighthouse but never referred to the lighthouse keeper. Because she had been there. Because she had been there until almost the end. What had she seen? What had she known? Who had known about her? Had Grace known? The hard work to find the levers and means to eventually be hired by the Southern Reach. Had anyone along the way known her secret and thought it was a good idea, as opposed to a compromising of the agency? Why was she hiding what she knew about the lighthouse keeper? These questions worried at him— missed opportunities, being behind, too much focus on plant-and-mouse, on the Voice, on Whitby, or maybe he would have seen it earlier. The files he still had with him didn't help, having the photograph there in the passenger seat didn't help.

Driving through the night now, he came back to the coast again and again, his headlights reflecting orange dashes and white reflectors and, sometimes, the silver-gray of a railing. He had stopped listening to the news on the radio. He didn't know if the subtle hints of impending catastrophe he gleaned existed only in his imagination. He wanted more and more to pretend that he existed in a bubble without context. That the drive would last forever. That the journey was the point.

When he grew too tired, he stopped in a town whose name he forgot as soon as he left, having coffee and eggs at a twenty-four-hour diner. The waitress asked him where he was headed, and he just said, "North." She nodded, didn't ask him anything else, must have seen something in his face that discouraged it.

He didn't linger, cut his meal short, nervous about the black sedan with the tinted windows in the parking lot, the battered old Volvo with the rain forest stickers on it whose owner had been slouched out there smoking a cigarette for a little too long.

The rain from off the sea thickened into fog, brought him to a twenty-mile-an-hour crawl in the dark never sure what would come out of the haze at him. Once a truck rattled his frame to the core, once a deer danced briefly past the headlights like a moving canvas, then was gone.

He came to the conclusion in the early dawn that it didn't matter if his mother had lied to him. It was a tactical detail, not strategic. He was always going to pursue this course, convinced himself that once he had gone to the Southern Reach that he was always going to be on this road in the middle of nowhere, headed north. The gnarled, wind-torn trees became a dark haphazard smoke in the mist, self-immolating into ash, as if he were seeing some version of the future.

The night before he would reach the town of Rock Bay, John let himself have a last meal. He pulled into a fancy restaurant in a town that lay in the shadow of the coastal mountains, cupped by the curve of a river that looked anemic next to the waves and striations of different-colored sand radiating out from the water. Scattered piles of driftwood and dead trees looked as if they'd been placed there to hold it all down.

He sat at the bar, ordered a bottle of good red wine, a petite filet with garlic mashed potatoes and mushroom gravy. He listened to the humble-brag of Jan, the experienced bartender, with a deliberately naïve enthusiasm—entertaining stories from stints working overseas in cities John had never visited. The man stared furtively at John at times, from a craggy Nordic face bordered by long yellow hair. Wondering, perhaps, if John would ask him what he was doing among the driftwood here at the butt end of the world.

A family came in—rich, white, in Polo shirts and sweaters and khaki pants as if from a clothing catalogue. Oblivious of him. Oblivious of the bartender, ordering burgers and fries, the father sitting directly to John's left, shielding his kids from the stranger. Exactly how strange, they could not know. They existed in their own bubble: They had just about everything and knew almost nothing. Their conversation was all about sitting up straight and chewing what they ate and a football game they'd watched and some tourist shop down in the village. He didn't envy them. He didn't hate them. He felt a curious nothing about them. All of the history here, everything encoded, rendered meaningless. None of it could mean anything next to the secret knowledge he carried with him.

The bartender shot John a roll of the eyes as he patiently put up with the kids' changing orders and the subtle condescension in the way the father talked to him. While the woman in the military uniform and her two skateboarder friends from Empire Street gathered ethereal to either side of John, staring at the family's meal with unabashed hunger. How many operatives went unremarked upon, never registered, were never heard from, never sustained. Snuffed out in darkness and crappy safe houses and dank motels. Made invisible. Made irrelevant. And how many could have been him. Were still him, laboring here, unbeknownst to this family or even the bartender, still trying, even though it wasn't just the border to Area X that negated people but everyone in the world beyond.

When the family had left, and along with them his companions, he asked the bartender, "Where can I get a boat?" in an agreeably conspiratorial way. A fellow world-weary traveler, his tone implied. A fellow adventurer who sometimes ignored legality in the same way as the bartender did in his stories. You're the man. You can hook me up.

"You know boats?" Jan asked.

"Yes." On lakes. Close to shore. Anything more and he'd be the punch line of one of Jack's jokes.

"Maybe I can help," the bartender said, with a grin. "Maybe I could arrange that." The fractured light from a chandelier composed of glass globes lit up his face as he leaned in to whisper, "How soon do you need it?"

Now. Immediately. By the morning.

Because he wasn't going to drive into Rock Bay.

The *Living with Salt* was a modified flat-bottom skiff, with a shallow bow and a stubborn reluctance to turn starboard with any kind of grace. It had a tiny shed of a cabin that would give him some relief from the strong ocean winds and a powerful if seasoned motor. It was ancient and the white paint had flaked, exposing the wood beneath. It almost looked like a tugboat to John, but had been used as a fishing vessel by the grizzled, barrel-bellied, bowlegged walking cliché of a fisherman who sold it to him for twice what it was worth. He almost thought the man had some illegal side business, must also be playing a part. He bought enough gasoline to either blow him sky high or last until the end of the world and loaded in the rest of his supplies.

It came with oars "for if the motor should give out" and nautical maps "though God help you if you don't seek

shelter, there's a storm" and a flare gun. After a little per-
suading that involved more money, it also came with the
skipper's old raincoat, hat, pipe, galoshes, and a fishing net
with a hole in it. The pipe felt weird in his mouth, and the
galoshes were a bit too big, but it made him believe that
from a distance his disguise might hold.

The motor had a ragged hiccupping mutter he didn't
like, but he had little choice—and he believed the boat
might be as fast as the car on the treacherous roads that lay
ahead, and harder to trace. As he lurched downriver toward
the sea, he had a sense of impending apocalypse, the beached
and blackened driftwood evidence not of bonfires and storms
but of some more radical catastrophe.

Old houses lay among the rocks of the coast and the few
crude beaches as he chugged along through choppy waters
and calm waters, struggling to learn the jump and list of the
boat, slowly adjusting to the current. Most of the houses were
falling apart, and even those awake with lights at dusk seemed
only temporarily resurrected. Smoke from grills. People on
piers below. They all looked like they'd be gone by winter.

He passed an abandoned lighthouse, a low, squat white
tower with a black crown. It slid past in silence, the fitted
stones showing through the ruined paint, the beacon dark,
and he had a startled sense of doubling, as if he were somehow traveling up the coast of an alternative Area X. The sense
that he had passed beyond some boundary.

Somewhere in the fog, if he looked closely, he'd see Lowry
and Whitby, wandering lost. Somewhere, too, the Séance &
Science Brigade taking their measurements, and Saul Evans
walking up the spiral steps of the lighthouse, with a girl,

oblivious, playing on the rocks below. Perhaps even Grace, gathering the remnants of the Southern Reach around her.

By midafternoon, he had reached the part of the coast where the land curved sharply, an inlet that led to the town of Rock Bay. What the biologist called "Rock Bay" was actually the tidal pools and reefs that lay about twenty miles north of town. But her former cottage had been right outside of the town. Or village, if you wanted to be specific. Because it only had about five hundred residents.

The *Living with Salt* wasn't the kind of boat that John could pull up onto the shore and hide under branches. But he wanted to do a recon of Rock Bay before moving on. He chanced going a little ways up the wide inlet, half-hidden by rock islands that jutted out from the water. Soon he spotted a rotten old pier where he could tie up. According to the maps it was close enough to the local wildlife refuge that he could walk from there and intersect a hiking trail, following it close to the town. He left behind his hat and pipe and, taking his raincoat, binoculars, and gun, made his way inland through scrubland and then forest. The smell of fresh cedar invigorated him. Soon enough, he was looking down from a bluff at the wooden bridge leading into town and the tiny main street beyond. He'd come across a roadblock manned by local police well before the bridge, but he'd seen nothing suspicious on the trails—just a jogger and a couple of teenagers clearly looking for a place to smoke pot. From his vantage now, looking down with his binoculars through the intense tree cover, though, he could see half a dozen black sedans and SUVs with tinted windows parked on the main street. The vehicles reeked of Central, as did the too-coiffed would-be lumberjacks who stood near the vehicles in bright plaid shirts and jeans and boots that looked too new to have yet been through a slog.

If they had come in such small numbers, then either this location was one of many being searched or the biologist was by now only part of a much larger problem, Central fully occupied elsewhere. Somewhere in the south, perhaps.

Depending on how well they knew the biologist's habits, they might believe that she'd prefer to hide somewhere farther north, along the coastline. But they'd have to rule out the town and its environs first. All around was dense coastal scrubland or even denser rain forest, none of it easy to traverse. The kind of terroir even experienced locals could get lost in, once you went beyond the town, especially during the rainy season.

On a hunch, he abandoned his position on the bluff and took a trail down and across the stream straddled by the wooden bridge, then up the opposite side back onto a rise that eventually led him over a series of moss-covered, cedar-rich hills, into a position near the water. Opposite him, across the narrow inlet, lay the cottage where the biologist had lived. He crept in hunched-over zigzag fashion through the breaks in the sharp bramble, lay among twisted black trees with thorny leaves at a good vantage point.

The cottage was only a little larger than his boat, and just enough forest had been cleared for a tiny lawn in front and to let a dirt road curl up the rise to the left. Beyond that rise, hidden, lay a larger settlement: a main house, from which he could see a tendril of white smoke rising via an obscured chimney.

But no smoke rose from the cottage. Nothing stirred around the cottage, either, in a way that he found unnatural. He kept scanning the woods to either side until after about an hour, after about fifty sweeps of the area, he realized that a patch of ground had moved: camouflage. Which, after a few moments, resolved into a man with a rifle and scope stretched out beneath a military-style blind, covering the cottage. Once he'd spotted one operative, others came clear to him: in trees, behind logs, even staring out in one uncareful moment from the cottage itself. He knew the biologist would not now come anywhere near the cottage, if she'd ever wanted to.

So he retreated into the wilderness and made his way back to his boat by a circuitous and tiring route. He didn't think he had been spotted, but he didn't want to leave it to chance. Thankful, too, to be back at the boat. He'd exhausted his small store of rusty woodcraft and felt he had been lucky. Lucky, too, that his boat was still there and the area still seemed deserted.

He ate a can of cold beans and cast off, hugging the coast until the last moment—and then making a calm and steady run across the mouth of the inlet, certain that somehow he would be uncovered from afar and Central would swoop down on him.

Yet despite how wide the expanse seemed in those moments, there were only the seagulls and the pelicans, the cormorants and, high above, what he thought might be an albatross. Only the choppy waves and a distant foghorn and the dim shapes of boats closer in and farther out. Nothing that didn't look local, no fishermen who looked newly minted.

Easier, better, to go farther away from all of this. She would be in the most desolate, isolated place she could find, daring anyone to follow her.

Either there or not. If not, it was all useless anyway.

Pursuit felt like an intermittent pulse. It died away and then picked up again. Through binoculars he saw a speedboat far off curving fast toward him. He heard a helicopter, although he couldn't see it, and spent a nervous twenty minutes in pointless fishing with his ripped, useless net, his formless hat pulled down over his forehead. Pretending with everything he had to be a fisherman. Then the sounds faded, the speedboat looped back down the coast. Everything was as before, for a very long time.

This new landscape above the Rock Bay inlet was even more foreign to him, and colder—and a relief, as if Area X were just a climate, a type of vegetation, a simple terroir, even if he knew this wasn't true. So many shades and tones of gray—the gray that shone down from the sky, a ceaseless and endless gray that was so still. The mottled matte gray of the water, before the rain, broken by the curls of wavelets, the gray of the rain itself, prickles and ripples against the ocean's surface. The silver gray of the real waves farther out, which came in and hit the bow as he guided the boat into them, rocking and the engine whining. The gray of something large and ponderous passing underneath him and making the boat rise as he tried to keep it still and motorless for those moments, holding his breath, life too close to dream for him to exhale.

He understood why the biologist liked this part of the

world, how you could lose yourself here in a hundred ways. How you could even become someone very different from who you thought you were. His thoughts became still for hours of his search. The frenetic need to analyze, to atomize the day or the week fell away from him—and with it the weight and buzz of human interaction and interference, which could no longer dwell inside his skull.

He thought about the silence of fishing on the lake as a child, the long pauses, what his grandpa might say to him in a hushed tone, as if they were in a kind of church. He wondered what he would do if he couldn't find her. Would he go back, or would he melt into this landscape, become part of what he found here, try to forget what had happened before and become no more or less than the spray against the bow, the foam against the shore, the wind against his face? There was a comfort to this idea almost as strong as the urge to find her, a comfort he had not known for a very long time, and many things receded into the distance behind him, seemed ridiculous or fantastical, or both. Were, at their core, unimportant.

During the nights of his journey farther north, tied up as best he could where the coastline allowed it—the lee of a rock island large enough to shield him, the bottom able to hold the anchor despite slippery kelp—he began to see strange lights far behind him. They rose and fell and glided across the sea and the sky, some white and some green or purple-tinged. He could not tell if they were searching or defined a purpose less purposeful. But the lights broke the spell and he turned on the radio that night, holding it to his ear to keep the volume down as he huddled in his sleeping bag. But he only heard a few unintelligible words until static set in, and he did not know if this was because of some catastrophe or the remoteness of his location.

The stars above were large and fixed. They existed against a fabric of night as vast and deep as his sleep, his dream. He was tired now, and hungry for something beyond cans and protein bars. He was sick of the sound of the waves and the sound of his boat's engine. It had been three days since leaving Rock Bay, and he had caught no sign of her along the coast, would soon come to the most remote part of the area. He had long since passed the point where anything inland could be reached by road, but only by hiking trail or helicopter or boat. The very edge of anything that could be called Rock Bay.

If he kept conserving food and water, he had enough to last another week before he had to turn back.

The morning of another day. In a lull, drifting, he rowed into an inlet surrounded by black rocks as sharp as shark fins, as craggy as any mountainside. He'd decided to get close because it looked similar to the coastline sketched in the biologist's field entries.

The rocks were covered in limpets and starfish, and in the shallows the hundred bristling dark shapes of sea urchins like miniature submerged mines. He had seen no one for two days. His arms were sore and aching from rowing. He wanted a hot meal, a bath, some landmark to tell him for certain where he was. The boat had begun to take on water; he spent some time now bailing, his fear of moving even a little ways from shore greater than that of running aground on something jagged.

The rocks formed a rough line or ridge all the way back to shore, and it was hard to navigate around them. A swell carried him too close, and he rammed up against them, felt the jarring in his bones. He put out an oar to push off; it slid off smoothly at first, and he had to try again, then frantically rowed until he was a safe distance from the suck and roll.

It took him a moment to realize why his oar had slid, why there had been no usual grinding crunch. Someone had been eating the limpets and mussels. The rock had been almost bare except for some kelp. He looked through his binoculars, saw that rocks a little farther in were bare, too, and closer to shore, a few showed pale circular marks where the limpets had resisted their picking.

No sign of a fire or of habitation nearby, but someone or something had been grazing on them. If a person, he knew it could have been anyone. Yet it was more than he'd had to go on yesterday. Trepidation and relief and a certain indecisiveness warred within him. If a person, whoever it was might have already seen the boat. He thought to make landfall there, then reversed himself and rowed back the way he'd come, back down the coast by just one cove, hidden by another of the huge rocks that rose from the ocean to form an inhospitable island.

By then, the boat had taken on more water and he realized that he was going to spend most of his time bailing, not rowing, or worrying about sinking, not rowing. So he brought the boat up close to shore, dropped anchor, and waded to a little black sand beach sheltered by overhanging trees, sat there gasping for long minutes. This was his last chance. He could try to fix the boat. He could try to turn back, limp back down the coast to Rock Bay. Be done with this, be done with the idea of this forever. Leave the vision of the biologist in his head, never manifesting in front of him, and then just face whatever had been growing there, behind him. He wondered what his mother was doing in that moment, where she was. Then a flash of Whitby reaching out a hand from the shelf struck him sideways, and of Grace at the door, waiting for the director.

He went back out to the boat, took everything useful he could fit into the backpack, including Whitby's terroir manuscript. Staggering a little under the weight of that, he began to make his way back toward the line of black rocks, trying to stay concealed by the tree line. Soon the boat was just a memory, something that had once existed but not any longer.

That night, he noticed lights in the sky, again distant but coming nearer. He imagined he could hear the sound of a ship's engine, but the lights faded, the sound faded, and he went to sleep to the hush and whisper of the surf.

At dusk of the next day, John saw a movement on the rocks, and he trained his binoculars on it. He wanted to believe that the figure was the biologist, that he knew her outline against the worn sky, the way that she moved, but he had only seen her captive. Inert. Deactivated. Different.

The first time, he lost her almost immediately from his

vantage some distance from the rocks, couldn't tell if she was coming back in or going farther out. Rocks and form merged and blurred, and then it was night. He waited for the appearance of a light or a fire, but saw neither. If it was the biologist, she was in full survivalist mode.

Another day passed, and he saw nothing except seagulls and a gray fox that came to an abrupt halt when it saw him and then evaporated into the mist that coated everything for far too long. He worried that whoever he had seen had passed on, that this wasn't an outpost but just another marker on a longer journey. He ate another can of beans, drank sparingly from the water canteen. Huddled, shivering, beneath deep cover. He was reaching the edge of his woodcraft again, was made more for back roads and small-town surveillance than for living out in the wild. He thought he'd probably lost about five pounds. He kept taking in deep breaths of cedar and every green, living thing as a temporary antidote.

The figure came out at dusk again, crawling and hopping across the sheets of black rock with an expertise John knew would be beyond him. As he identified her as the biologist through the binoculars, his heart leapt and his blood stirred and the little hairs on his arms rose. A flood of emotion came over him, and he stifled tears—of relief or of something deeper? He had been existing inside himself for long enough now that he wasn't sure. But he righted himself immediately. He knew that if she got back to shore, she'd disappear into the rain forest. He did not like his odds of tracking her there.

If she saw him clambering after her, though, and he didn't get a chance to confront her, she'd slip through his fingers and he'd never see her again. This, too, he knew.

The tide had begun to come in. The light was dull and flat and gray. Again. The wind had become harsh. Out at sea, there was nothing to indicate human beings existed except for the rising and falling figure of the biologist, and a deep vein of black smoke opening up into the sky from some vessel so far out at sea that it wasn't visible even with the binoculars.

He waited until she was more than halfway out, wondering if she'd lost some natural caution because it was still easier to cut her off than it should have been. Then he snuck along the other side of the ridge of rock, hunched over, trying to keep his silhouette off her horizon, although he'd be framed by forest, not the fading light. He had brought the knapsack with him out of paranoia that she or someone else might steal it while he was gone. Although he had stripped it down somewhat, it threw off his balance, made it harder to hold his gun and climb the rocks. He could have left Whitby's manuscript behind, but this had seemed more and more important to keep in view at all times.

He tried to keep his steps short and to bend his knees, but even so slipped many times on the uneven rocks, slick with seaweed and rough and sharp from the edges of the shells of limpets and clams and mussels. Had to reach out to keep his balance and cut himself despite the cloth he'd tied over his palms. Very soon his ankles and knees felt weak.

By the time he was halfway out, the ridge of rocks had narrowed, and he had no choice but to clamber atop them. When he looked up from that vantage for the first time, the biologist was nowhere to be seen. Which meant she had either found some miraculous way back to shore, or she was hidden somewhere ahead of him.

No matter how he hunched and bent, she was going to have a clear line of sight at him. He didn't know what options she had—rock, knife, homemade spear?—if she wasn't glad to see him. He took off his hat, shoved it in the pocket of his raincoat, hoping that if she was watching she would at least recognize that it was him. That this recognition might mean more to her than "interrogator" or "captor." That it might make her hesitate should she be lying in wait.

Three-quarters of the way and he wondered if he should just head back. His legs were rubbery, matched the feel of the rocks where the kelp swelled over them. The waves to either side struck with more force, and although he could still see now—the sun a quiver of red against the far horizon, illuminating the distant smoke—he'd have to use his flashlight going back. Which would alert anyone on the shore to his presence; he hadn't come all this way just to betray her to others. So he continued on with a sense of fatalism. He'd sacrificed all his pawns, his knights, bishops, and rooks. Abuela and Abuelo were facing an onslaught from the other side of the board.

In the tiring, repetitious work of climbing on, of continuing on and not going back, a grim satisfaction spread in a last surge of energy through his body. He had pursued this line of inquiry to the end. He had come very far, this thought mixed with sadness for what lay behind, so many people with whom he'd forged such slight connections. So many people that, as he neared the end of the rocks, he wished he had known better, tried to know better. His caring for his father now seemed not like a selfless effort but something that had been for him, too, to show him what it meant to be close to someone.

At the end of the ridge, he came upon a deep lagoon of ever-rippling encircled water, roughly cradled by the rocks. Lagoon was perhaps too gentle a word for it—a gurgling deep hole, whose sharp and irregular sides could cut hand or head easily. The bottom could not be seen.

Beyond, just the endless ocean, frothing to get in, smashing against the closed fist of the rocks so that spray flecked his face and the force of the wind buffeted him. But in the lagoon, all was calm, if unknowable in its dark reflection.

She appeared so close, from concealment on his left, that he almost jumped back, caught himself in time by bending and putting out a hand.

In that moment, he was helpless and in steadying himself he found that she had a gun trained on him. It looked like a Glock, like his own, standard-issue. He hadn't expected that. Somehow, somewhere, she had found a gun. She was thinner, her cheekbones as cutting as the rocks. Her hair had begun to grow out, a dark fuzz. She wore thick jeans and a sweater too big for her but heavy, and high-quality brown hiking boots. There was a defiance on her face that warred with curiosity and some other emotion. Her lips were chapped. In this, her natural environment, she seemed so sure of herself that he felt awkward, ungainly. Something had clicked into place. Something had sharpened her, and he thought it might be memory.

"Throw your gun into the sea," she said, motioning to his holster. She had to raise her voice for him to hear her, even this close—close enough that with a few steps he could have reached out and touched her shoulder.

"We might need it later," he said.

"We?"

"Yes," he said. "More are coming. I've seen the lights." He did not want to share what had happened to the Southern Reach. Not yet.

"Toss it, now, unless you want to get shot." He believed her. He'd seen the reports from her training. She said she wasn't good with guns, but the targets hadn't agreed.

So there went Grandpa version 4.9 or 5.1. He hadn't kept track of the expeditions. The sea made it disappear with a smack that sounded like one last comment from Jack.

John looked over at her, standing across from him while the waves blasted the rocks and despite the gray and despite the wet and the cold, despite the fact he might die sometime in the next few minutes, he started to laugh. It surprised him, thought at first someone else was laughing.

Her grip tightened on the gun. "Is the idea of me shooting you funny?"

"Yes," he said. "It's very, very funny." He was laughing hard enough now that he had to bend to his knees to keep his balance on the rocks. A fierce joy or hysteria had risen inside of him, and he wondered in an idle, distant way if perhaps he should have sought out this feeling more often. The look of her, against the backdrop of the swell and the fall of the sea, was almost too much for him. But for the first time he knew he had done the right thing in coming here.

"It's funny because there have been many other times . . . so many other times when I would've understood why someone wanted to shoot me." That was only part of it, the other part being that he had felt almost as if Area X was about to shoot him, and that Area X had been trying to shoot him for a very long time.

"You followed me," she said, "even though I clearly don't want to be followed. You've come to what most people consider the butt end of the world and you've cornered me here. You probably want to ask more questions, although it should be clear that I'm done with questions. What did you think would happen?"

The truth was, he didn't know what he had thought would happen, had perhaps unconsciously fallen back on an idea of their relationship at the Southern Reach. But that didn't apply here. He sobered up, hands held high now as if surrendering.

"What if I said *I* had answers," he said. But all he had to show her that was tangible was Whitby's manuscript.

"I'd say you're lying and I'd be right."

"What if I said you still hold some of the answers, too." He was as serious as he had been giddy just moments before. He tried to hold her with his gaze, even through the murk, but he couldn't. God, but the coast here was painfully beautiful, the dark lush greens of the fir trees piercing his brain, the half-raging sky and sea, the surge of salt water against the rocks twinned to the urgent wash of blood through his arteries as he waited for her to kill him or hear him out. Seditious thought: There would be nothing too terrible about dying out here, about becoming part of all of this.

"I'm not the biologist," she said. "I don't care about my past as the biologist, if that's what you mean."

"I know," he said. He'd figured it out on the boat, even if he hadn't articulated it yet. "I know you're not. You're some version, though. You have her memories, to some extent, and somewhere back in Area X, the biologist may still be alive. You're a replica, but you're your own person."

Not an answer she had expected. She lowered the gun. A little. "You believe me."

"Yes." It had been right there. In front of him, in the video, in the very mimicry of cells, the difference in personality. Except she'd broken the mold. Something had been different in her creation.

"I've been trying to remember this place," she said, almost plaintively. "I love it here, but the entire time I've felt like it was the one remembering me."

A silence that John didn't know if he wanted to break, so he just stood there.

"Are you here to take me back?" she said. "Because I'm not going back."

"No, I'm not," he said, and realized it was true. Whatever impulse in that regard that might have lived within him had been snuffed out. "The Southern Reach doesn't exist anymore," he admitted. "There may not be anything we'd recognize out there very soon."

There in the twilight, no birds now overhead, the smoke fading into the dusk, the raucous surf the only thing that seemed alive besides the two of them.

"How did you know I'd be here?" she asked, deep in thought. "I was so careful."

"I didn't. I guessed." Somehow his face must have given something of his thoughts away, because she looked a little startled, a little wrong-footed.

"Why would you do that if you don't want to take me back?"

"I don't know." To try to save the world? To save her? To

save himself? But he did know. Nothing had changed since the interrogation room. Not really.

When he looked up again, she was saying, "I thought I could just stay here. Build the life she didn't build, that she messed up. But I can't. It's clear I can't. Someone will be after me no matter what I do."

Now that the sun had truly set there was a glimmer of a light dimly familiar to him coming from deep in the lagoon below.

"What's down there?" he asked.

"Nothing." Said too quickly.

"Nothing? It's too late to lie—there's no point." It was never too late to lie, to obscure, to delay. Control knew this too well.

But she didn't. She hesitated, then said, "I was sick when I got here. One night I came out here and I had a dizzy spell and I was unconscious for a while. I woke up with the tide rising and I wasn't sick anymore. The brightness was done with me. But there was something at the bottom of that hole."

"What?" Although he thought he already knew. The swirling light was too familiar, despite being broken by ripples and the thickness of the water.

"It's a way into Area X, I think," she said, and now she looked scared. "I think I brought it with me." He didn't know how she knew this. He thought it might be true, remembered what Cheney had said about how difficult and enervating that travel could be. Whitby's horrible description of the border.

Now that the darkness was complete and she was just a

shadow standing in front of him, they could both see the lights farther down the coast. Bobbing. Floating. Trudging. Dozens of them. And so far down below, that glimmer, that hint of an impossible light.

"I don't think we have much longer," he said. "I don't even know if we have the night. We'll have to find a place to hide." Not wanting to think about the other possibility. Not wanting even a hint of it in his thoughts to invade her thoughts.

"It will be high tide soon," she said. "You have to get off the rocks." But not her? Even though he could not see her face, he knew the expression that must be etched there.

"We *both* have to get off the rocks." He wasn't sure he meant it. He could hear the helicopter now, could hear boats again, too. But if she was unhinged, if she was lying, if she didn't actually know anything at all . . .

"I want to know who I am," she said. "I can't do that here. I can't do that locked up in a cell."

"I know who you are—it's all in my head, your file. I can give you that."

"I'm not going back," she said. "I'm never going back."

"It's dangerous," he told her, pleading, as if she didn't know. "It's unproven. We don't know where you'll come out." The hole was so deep and so jagged, and the water beginning to churn from the waves. He had seen wonders and he had seen terrible things. He had to believe that this was one more and that it was true and that it was knowable.

Her stare took the measure of him. She was done talking. She threw her gun away. She dove into the water, down deep.

He took one last look back at the world he knew. He took one huge gulp of it, every bit of it he could see, every bit of it he could remember.

"Jump," said a voice in his head.

Control jumped.

ACKNOWLEDGMENTS

Many thanks to my editor, Sean McDonald, and everyone at FSG for their expertise, passion, sense of humor, and, above all, patience. Thanks as well to everyone at the Fourth Estate, HarperCollins Canada, Blackstone Audiobooks, and my foreign-language publishers. Thanks to my agent, Sally Harding, and my wife, Ann, for helping me find the mental space to write these novels. Thanks to Black Dog Café, All Saints Café, the Fermentation Lounge, San Luis Mission Park, and Shared Worlds for giving me physical spaces to work in. Thanks to Eric Schaller, Geoffrey A. Landis, and Ashley Davis for science discussions. Finally, thanks to my first readers for their help, including Brian Evenson, Tessa Kum, Greg Bossert, Jeremy Zerfoss, Karin Tidbeck, Craig Gitney, Berit Ellingsen, and Adam Mills.

All three volumes of
Jeff VanderMeer's
Southern Reach trilogy
will be published in 2014

ANNIHILATION
February 2014

AUTHORITY
May 2014

ACCEPTANCE
September 2014

It is winter in Area X, and, out of desperate necessity,
a thirteenth expedition crosses the border. In *Acceptance*,
the final instalment of Jeff VanderMeer's extraordinary
Southern Reach trilogy, we go deep into the unknown
– and into the profoundly disquieting history of Area X,
including the story of the last lighthouse keeper and
the former director who travelled incognito on the
ill-fated twelfth expedition. Will Area X finally
reveal its terrible secrets, and will those
revelations bring any comfort?

ACCEPTANCE

The third book in the Southern Reach trilogy